THE TATTOO ARTIST

A Women of Redemption Suspense Thriller

Lori Lacefield

Cover designed by Nick Zelinger, NZ Graphics, LLC
Edited by Michelle Hope

This book is a work of fiction. Names, characters, places, and incidents either are products of the author's imagination or are used fictitiously. Any resemblance to actual persons, living or dead, events, or locales is entirely coincidental.

Lori Lacefield
Visit my website at www.lorilacefield.com

Printed in the United States of America

First Printing: December 2020
Open Book Media, LLC

ISBN: 978-1-7322890-9-3

CHAPTER 1

Reno. The Lone Horseman loved riding the streets here at night, especially this time of year. Early June, the temperature was perfect for cruising: eighty-degree days followed by evenings in the mid-sixties. The bright lights of the casinos beckoned gamblers inside, while out on the streets, music and conversation spilled from the open doors of the local bars. The glitter and flash of neon contrasted with the barred windows of the jewelry and loans on every corner, but conveyed its message clearly—pawn your items here and lose your money there. This city, known affectionately as the biggest little city in the world, prided itself on its proximity to the Sierra Nevada and the beauty of Lake Tahoe, but here on the streets, life told a different story. This city, it wanted to be Vegas, but all it had ever really amounted to was the cheap karaoke version, an Elvis impersonator. And, it seemed to him, everyone who lived here tried to hold on to that dream, preferring to believe in a superior version of him or herself.

Except for him. He didn't need to pretend. He knew exactly who and what he was— a stone-cold killer. And he had no problem with that.

He pulled his bike—a 2005 Dyna Wide Glide Hog—up next to an old Ford truck, listened to the twangy country song escape from its open windows and blend into the evening air. The sounds of the city were always present here no matter the time of day or night: the honk of a distant horn, the cry of a siren, and, always, motorcycles. This was a biker town, friendly to those on two wheels, and in the summer, they dominated the streets. His club, like others, made an annual run to Reno to visit the local chapter heads and ensure no one else was infringing on their territory. For those dealing in their trades, Reno was a prized lady, the only real jewel within four hundred miles in any direction. The motorcycle clubs came from Canada to Southern California, all wanting a piece of her.

After the light turned green, he cruised the next block, passing a pathetic-looking homeless man pushing a grocery cart. Behind him walked an equally forlorn dog, its tail tucked between its legs. He saw a lot of that look on the streets of Reno, especially

1

as the night wore on and the losers came out. The slots, the tables—the whores, conmen, and drug dealers—the hustles came in all shapes and sizes here.

At the next block, he rolled into an empty gravel lot where an old Black man wearing an orange jumpsuit reminiscent of prison garb tried to entertain the crowd with his rapping ability while a young kid showed off his break-dancing skills. A small crowd of tourists stood by, but the overturned hat that lay in front of the entertainers looked to contain very few bills. Tough night. Tough crowd.

He took out a pack of smokes, lit one up while he watched the casino door, waiting for his own payday. It had been nearly a decade since he'd taken a prize from this town, and the time felt right again. He occasionally liked to pick up something special when he went on runs—something a little sweeter and fresher than the pass-arounds that frequented the club—and there was quite an assortment to choose from here. Earlier, he'd spent five hours inside the casino observing the inventory, and he'd settled on one with an electric smile and natural red hair. She'd spent most of her evening entertaining herself on the slots with an occasional trip to the bar, stopping only to chat with a friend nearby. She wore no ring and flirted with several men, so he knew she was single and lived alone. After years of prowling, he was able to sniff them out, like a trained hunting dog.

Near midnight, his odds of a jackpot increased as she and her friend departed for the parking lot. A little drunk, they laughed as they stumbled down the sidewalk then hugged and said their goodbyes, exchanging a "better luck next time."

He chuckled. One of them would need more than luck to survive the night.

He kept the bike engine quiet as they each started up their own vehicles and went their separate ways, waited until his girl was well down Center Street before he followed. With his helmet, glasses, and neck gaiter, he didn't worry about any cameras as witnesses—no facial-recognition bullshit would ever be able to identify him.

Wisely, his drunk girl left the busier Center Street and opted for the back roads, avoiding the hot spots known to draw the attention of the police late at night. It took only minutes for her to get home, weaving through two lights and a few stop signs before slowing down outside a row of older ranch-style houses. The neighborhood she lived in rested behind a street littered with pawnshops and check-cashing stores, but the neon lure of the central city continued to brighten the night sky, providing him ample light to watch from a distance. After finding a place to park, she wheeled the late-model Toyota headfirst into the open spot instead of parallel parking, then backed up to straighten the car against the curb. She ended up at an awkward angle with one wheel pinched against the cement, but who cared? After a few rum and cokes, this wasn't her time for perfection.

Rolling to a stop two blocks down, he cut his lights and watched as she exited the car. A faint *beep, beep* broke the quiet night as she locked the door and the taillights flashed. She rounded the hood, then ambled up the sidewalk to her residence, which proved to be a small stucco number, the kind landlords always tried to beautify with flowery bushes out front to hide its cracked, ugly facade.

After she went inside, the lights came on one by one. He waited for shadows to inform him of whether others occupied the house, but only her image appeared against the backlight. When he was satisfied that she was alone, he kept the bike engine at a low volume and coasted around the block. He knew how important it was not to stay in any one spot for too long. Just as it was with club business—when he took a new trophy, it was best to vary locations and separate events by time and distance.

He removed the skull neck gaiter he wore and replaced it with a solid black sheath that covered everything but his eyes, then walked around the block to enter her house from the back entrance. With only a partial and broken fence, it was easy to gain access, but provided no protection from the prying eyes of neighbors. Luckily, most of the other houses were dark, no blue lights flashing from televisions or computers that indicated people were still awake. Unlike the student housing near the university, this neighborhood appeared to be one of those residential areas that went to bed early.

On the cement slab that acted as a patio in the backyard, he stepped over a red plastic dog bowl and several terra-cotta pots containing flowers. A single white door provided entry to the house. He glanced through the dirt-ridden panes of glass that highlighted the top half of it, could see the kitchen off to the right and his girl sitting on the couch in the next room. The flicker of the television informed him that she was eating ice cream from a carton and letting a small dog lick the spoon.

He thought of the best tactic to use to get her to come to the door. He never liked to break in and much preferred the open invitation. The police always looked to familiar suspects then, someone in her inner circle rather than a stranger. He assessed the situation. She hadn't gone to bed, and she liked animals.

He glanced around the yard, caught sight of a small branch that had broken off a tree. He gathered it along with a handful of rocks. After slipping around the corner of the house, he extended the branch out to begin scratching at the door, as if it were some stray animal. It took a couple of efforts, but soon the dog broke from the couch and began barking, digging its little paws, and sniffing beneath the door. Again, he scratched. Again, the dog barked. Soon, he heard her footsteps pound the wooden floor and her voice speak.

"What is it, boy?"

He threw a rock so it hit the neighbor's fence in back. The dog barked.

Remaining out of sight, he couldn't see her, but could imagine her face peering through the dirty glass, trying to see what was outside. A few seconds later, he heard the door pull ajar. He stuck his head around the corner just enough to see her poke her head outside. Seeing nothing menacing, she opened the door wider to let her dog out to have a pee and sniff. He didn't want the dog to pick up his scent, so he threw another rock, which landed with a loud *thwack* in thick brush. This time, a neighbor dog joined in the barking, and her dog—a terrier of some kind—went tearing across the yard.

The woman called for him in a hushed tone. "Sparky, no, bad dog. Come here."

When bad Sparky didn't return right away, his girl decided to step outside. She crossed the cement slab and the yard beyond in bare feet, and left the door open behind her.

Smiling, the Lone Horseman slipped around the corner and into the house.

A minute later, she returned with Sparky in her arms, and shut and locked the door behind her. "Nothing out there, buddy. Maybe the neighbor's cat or something. It's all good." She ruffled the fur on his head.

She put him down on the floor to get a drink, and he circled and sniffed. He started for the corner of the kitchen, and abruptly halted and growled.

The Lone Horseman wasted no time. He rushed in to cover the woman's mouth, pinned her against the kitchen table, and commanded her to freeze. Surprised, she initially did as he instructed, but upon realizing what was happening, bit his hand. Feeling the searing pain, he quickly pulled it back, only to see that the crazy bitch had chomped right through his glove. Pissed, he slapped her, then quickly moved to secure a bandana around her mouth and tie her hands behind her back. There would be no more biting, and no scratching either. In all his years of taking trophies, there were but a few times he'd left his DNA at the scene, and now, this could be one of them.

He cursed her. He would make her pay for that.

The dog returned to nip at his feet, and he kicked it to the corner, where it whined, cowered, and licked its mouth. That fueled the girl's anger and she fought with the only weapons she had left—her legs—and a knee quickly reached his groin. He winced, but made it known her efforts were futile by yanking her to her feet and pushing her through the living room. She fought him all the way, knocking over a table, a lamp, and several pictures from a decorative stand—but he finally got her where he wanted her: the bedroom.

The fight only served to arouse him.

He secured her to the bed, ripped her clothes off, and taunted her for fifteen minutes before he began to have his way with her. Throughout most of the ordeal, she screamed beneath the bandana and wrestled against him, but the fight eventually fled. When he finished, he wrapped his hands around her neck and put her out of her misery.

Afterward, he sifted through the items in her apartment—jewelry, clothes, and other trinkets—seeking something that would remind him of her. He noticed this one was partial to animal prints: leopard, zebra, and...tiger. He picked up a black-and-orange-striped scarf, threaded it through his gloved fingers. Given the color of her hair and fiery spirit, he thought it would be a perfect representation of her—the tiger.

The tiger he'd tamed.

CHAPTER 2

Zoë Cruse prepped the back of a young university student—applying another layer of petroleum jelly over the stencil she'd transferred there—before sliding the single-use needle into the machine that would create the tattoo he wanted: a large griffin, that mythological creature with a lion's body, eagle's head, and wings said to represent strength and wisdom. He'd approved the design weeks ago and told Zoë it would take some time for him to save up the money to get it done, but as he nervously shook on her table, she thought it might've been more than money that had caused his delay.

This was his first tattoo, and he was scared shitless.

"You're going to feel a prickling sensation and then burning," she said. "It will be intense at first, but it won't last long. Just remember, when the whole area starts to go numb, you're home free."

She started the machine, the constant hum invading the air, but he flinched before the needle ever contacted his skin. She pulled it back. "I didn't touch you yet. Relax."

"That thing, it sounds like a super charged stun gun. It won't shock me, right?"

"No. It's a needle, not an electrode."

He took a deep breath, stretched out his arms in front of him, cracked his knuckles. "Okay, I can do this. I can, I can," he said, repeating the words like a mantra. He returned to a flat, facedown position. "Begin."

She started the tool again, let it whir. She laid a gloved hand on this back and moved the needle closer, but hesitated as she felt his muscles tense. "Come on, relax. If you move or jump, the needle can go off target or dig too deep into the underlying dermis. So, unless you want your griffin to look more like a flying rat than an eagle, I suggest you hold still."

From across the room, she heard Screech, her skinny Vietnamese business partner, chuckle. She wanted to believe he was laughing with her, but since he was currently working on a man who'd requested a tattoo of Mickey and Minnie Mouse kissing—

across the crack of his ass, no less—she wasn't certain if he was laughing with her or at the ridiculous image coming to life before him.

After outlining the head, she started on the wings, marking the feathers that spread out across his back. With each etching, he grunted and groaned, acting as if she was killing him. "Dude, I hate to be the bearer of bad news, but I'm only on the first wing. It's a tattoo, not a balloon party."

"No, no, I get it," he said, wriggling on the table like a worm. "Don't you just, like, have some softer needles or something?"

She pinched the bridge of her nose. She wanted to jab that needle right into his neck. This single tattoo would likely take eight hours, and already this guy was whinier than the air-conditioning unit in the shop's front window that worked overtime just to keep the temperature inside under eighty degrees. She didn't know how much more of this she could take. All of these university kids, they listened to rap, pierced their eyebrows, and tatted up, all to project how street they were; yet, the only street most of them had ever spent time on was outside the McMansion where they'd grown up. Unlike Zoë and Screech, who'd met as homeless teens, they hadn't a clue to what living on the streets was really like.

Screech glanced over at her and rubbed the tips of his fingers together, reminding her of why they put up with the struggle. And, of course, he was right. The university students could be a pain in the ass, but they were also easy money. At least one-third of their business income came courtesy of the University of Nevada-Reno.

"C'mon, dude, quit being a baby," his UNR comrade said.

The friend her client had come in with was clearly not new to tattoos, as both of his arms displayed sleeves featuring gaming icons. With his black-dyed mop top, plastic glasses, and matching flesh tunnels in each stretched ear, he gave off a uniquely urban-nerd-gamer vibe, which, she supposed, was exactly the point.

"Here," he said, grabbing one of the stress balls they kept on hand in a plastic bin. "Squeeze this, take a deep inhale, and let out a breath of air each time you feel pain."

To Zoë's relief, her client followed his friend's instruction, and for the next two hours, she made good headway on the design. She constantly dabbed numbing cream as she extended each line, and gave him breaks when needed. After she completed the larger outline, she added the predatory eyes and a sharp, slightly parted beak to the eagle head, then continued with some detailed feathers on the wings. To the lionlike body that extended down his spine, she added claws with talons in front and thick paws in back. She ended by whipping out a tail with a diamond at its tip.

He'd been very specific about that, the diamond.

She sat up to take in the bigger view, liked what she saw so far. At least he wanted an image that truly meant something to him. She had to give him that. So many clients came in asking for designs that hadn't a clue about their actual meaning. They'd see cool ink on some television show or movie character and come in wanting the same thing, completely unaware that the image they were requesting designated one as a member of the Russian mafia or a Mexican gang member. Just the prior week, she'd had a kid come in who wanted his initials—AB—inked across his upper back until she'd asked him about his time with the Aryan Brotherhood. When he'd looked at her—dumbfounded and confused—she went on to explain that AB was the white nationalist organization's moniker and maybe he ought to rethink putting his initials anywhere on his body. That, or change his name. Because of such implications, it was her policy that as she worked with a client on a tattoo's design, she asked every one of them about the image's intended meaning for them. She considered it her duty to educate the ill-advised.

Her client's friend, holding a copy of this month's *Tattoo* magazine on his lap, examined her work in between flipping pages. But, every once in a while, she could sense him checking out her own tatts as well.

"See something you like?" she asked him.

"Your tatts are highly detailed, and the color, it's incredible. Vibrant. I really dig the woman warrior and dragon down your right arm."

"Screech does good work." She nodded toward the man hovered over his client's left butt cheek. She wondered if he was charging hazard pay. She would.

"You have drops on your hands. Tears?" he asked.

She shook her head. "Blood."

A pause. His right eyebrow shot up. "Can I ask why?"

She could hear the trepidation in his voice, as if he was certain she'd murdered someone. To many, blood drops on the hands meant that a person had taken another's life—that they literally had blood on their hands—and in her mind, she did. To Zoë, she was as guilty for her mother's murder nine years ago as the unknown assailant who'd raped and stabbed her to death. She felt as responsible.

But she didn't tell him that.

"Well, as you know, tattoos are very personal. For some, blood drops may mean they've taken a physical life, but for others, they can represent sin and symbolize a quest for forgiveness."

She offered a faint smile as if that was her reason, although it was far from it.

Forgiveness—especially for herself—wasn't in her vocabulary.

The front bell chimed, and her husband, Max, came in, along with their six-year-old son, Oliver. "We got lunch," Oliver announced with big brown eyes, holding up two white bags with grease spots.

"Gyros for everyone, vegans included," Max said.

Screech gave a thumbs-up.

Oliver ran over to give Zoë a hug and a kiss. "Dad got you a vegan one, too, because he knows you don't like to eat the lambs." He started to run back but stopped cold when he saw Screech's latest work. "Whoa, is that Mickey and Minnie? What are they doing on that man's butt?"

Zoë turned aside and silently laughed. Max cleared his throat, covered his son's eyes, and shuffled him away. "Come on. Let's wait for Mommy in the break room." He raised an eyebrow and threw a kiss her way.

She heard them settle in back, Max setting out plates and turning on the midday news. As she returned to the griffin, she could hear the local television anchor report on the top story, a woman found murdered in a Reno neighborhood just north of downtown.

"The woman, just twenty-seven years old, was found raped and strangled in her home Thursday after coworkers said she failed to arrive at her job. Police are investigating, but admit they have no suspects at this time. Neighbors are shocked and grieving, saying the young woman often helped the elderly in the neighborhood with groceries and errands."

Zoë huffed. The neighbors were shocked. Weren't they always? One minute sleeping in their little abodes, and the next, finding out the girl next door was dead or the husband across the street was a cold-blooded killer. She flashed back briefly to her memories of the media conducting interviews with her own neighbors: the reporter standing in front of the little cream-colored house with black shutters surrounded by strings of crime scene tape; the police walking in and out; paramedics loading her mother's body into an ambulance.

She shivered, trying to force the images away.

She turned off the tattoo machine. "Mind if we take a break? It will be good to let the outline dry a bit before I begin to apply the color."

Her client grunted, what she assumed was a yes. His friend tossed him a magazine for reading. It slid across the floor, where he opened it, unable to get up from the table.

Zoë joined Max and Oliver in the back, unwrapped her gyro, and took a bite. It was loaded with vegetables, peppers, and olives tossed in oil. "Delicious," she said, wiping a drop of oil from the corner of her mouth. "You have to go back to the office this afternoon, or are you free for the rest of the day?"

"Free," Max said between chews. Her husband was a counselor for a local teen shelter, the one where he and Zoë had met after she'd come in looking for a bed one winter night. Before becoming certified and working at the center, Max had also been homeless, so he knew of what he spoke.

"Thought I'd take little man here to the arcade so he can do some target practice."

"Bang, bang, bang," Oliver exclaimed, pretending to shoot the toy rifle they had at the shooting gallery with various moving targets in the background. Zoë didn't care much for her son's current fascination with shooting things but trusted Max to explain the differences between reality and sport to him.

As if the news anchor was listening to Zoë's thoughts, the woman switched to reporting on the next deadly incident, a shootout in a Carson City casino. "Police say one man is dead and another wounded in what appears to be retaliation for the murder of a rival motorcycle gang member in Riverside, California, last year."

Zoë grunted. "Great. Just what we need at the start of biker season. A gang war."

"Ah, but the bikers are good for business," Max said. "Sometimes I think your clients make up half of the daily court logs. Why don't you partner up with the bail bondsmen and defense attorneys and get some referral fees?" He laughed, cleaning tzatziki sauce off his fingers with a napkin.

"Funny." She winked at Oliver. "Your daddy is a funny man."

He grinned. "Funny looking," he said, pulling on Max's long beard.

Max growled at him like a bear. Zoë started to add to the conversation but was interrupted by a loud roar, a throng of motorcycles coming down the street that sounded like an approaching train. She slid her chair back to see forty or fifty riders passing outside, lined up in succession, patches on full display.

The kid on the table and his friend glanced up, curious.

"Which ones?" the guy on the table asked.

"Devils," his friend said. "A whole army."

And just like that, hell had arrived.

CHAPTER 3

oë was in the back workstation putting the finishing touches on a sleeve of roses and a face with abstract eyes when the front door chimed. She heard Screech speak to whoever came in followed by the mention of her name. "She's in the back. Hang on."

He popped between the beaded curtains. "Guy wants to know if you have time to look at a design, possibly work it in today? He says it's small, maybe an hour?"

"Ten minutes," she said. She finished coloring the roses a vibrant hue of red. Next, she tended to the tiny leaves of green so that next to the blues and oranges in the face, they really popped. She held up a mirror and ran it down the length of her client's arm so she could see the full detail in the new design. The girl was beside herself, damn near giddy.

"Awesome. Oh, it looks so good."

"Glad you like it." Zoë applied a liberal amount of petroleum jelly and bandaged her arm, then gave her the rundown on care for the next two weeks. "Let me know immediately if you see any signs of infection."

After taking the girl up front and getting payment, her gaze finally turned to the man who'd asked for her. He appeared to be a biker, wearing a black leather jacket and boots, but the jacket was plain, no patch or affiliation listed. He wasn't oversized, maybe five foot ten and 180 pounds, but she could tell that 180 packed a punch. His neck and arms were a sinewy mass of muscle. Not bodybuilder kind of muscle, just kick-your-ass kind of muscle. As a tattoo artist, she'd become accustomed to assessing a person's body type and fat percentage right away, and his was minimal.

"You Zoë?" he asked.

For some reason, the edge in his voice gave her a chill. "Who wants to know?"

"I do. Friend recommended you. Fossil. You know him?"

She wiped off the front counter. "Large laughing ogre on his back with crushed skulls in both of its hands? Yeah, sure." She gave a wry smile. "You a friend of his?"

"When he needs me to be." His lips parted to show an odd mouthful of teeth, some chipped, one capped in silver. "I got a custom I need. Like to get it done while I'm in town." He handed her a slip of paper. "I'm not much of an artist. Hope you can do it justice."

She took the drawing from the man's hand and studied it. From what she could tell, it was a cat of some sort with a collar around its neck and its eyeballs exploding. "Choking a cat?"

He chuckled. "See? Told you I wasn't much of an artist. It's supposed to be a tiger. Taming a tiger."

More like killing it, she thought, but knew better than to comment. Sometimes ink truly represented a deed done, and she'd worked on enough gang members and bikers to know to keep her mouth shut. She didn't always like what she was asked to draw, but couldn't deny the money. And this one looked simple enough—a fighting tiger, chain pulled tight, eyes popping. Two hours work at most.

"I want a series of numbers on the collar. Two-eight-six-zero-four-one-four."

Letters and numbers often held significance, but usually only to the person wearing the tattoo. Often it was a tribute to the person's age, birthday, or date of death. In this case, Zoë didn't know, and again, she didn't ask.

She took out her sketchbook, started with a simple drawing of the tiger while she asked questions. Did he want teeth showing or not? Claws in or out? What did he want reflected in its eyes? Anger, fear, or something else?

"Who's the tiger in this representation?" she asked. "A man? Addiction? An event?"

"It's a woman," he said. "A lover until she's backed into a corner. Then, she's nothing but fight. I want her rising on her haunches. Show some teeth and claws."

She cleared her throat. "Who's taming her—you?"

Silence, then: "The devil."

She held his gaze. His eyes danced, laughing.

Her blood chilled.

She erased some of the straighter lines on the body and made them more rounded, curvaceous, like a woman. She reduced the size of the head but increased the paws and extended the claws, like nails. On the collar, she added the numbers as requested.

She showed him, and he nodded, liking what he saw.

"Okay. What size are we looking at?" she asked.

"Three inches." He removed his jacket and the T-shirt he wore beneath it, revealing a torso full of tatts and scars. Across his chest was the word *Devils* inscribed above a strange Chupacabra-looking creature right below. Pitchforks adorned both shoulders and various other ink covered his stomach, but none of that compared to his back.

Her eyes widened as he turned to reveal a mural that easily could've been the cover of a storybook. A horror or fantasy, most likely, but still a book. In the middle was a large, pale horse reared back with a robed, hooded figure as its rider, dressed in black and possessing no face. In his left hand, he held a Bible, and in his right, a red pitchfork raised into the air. The horse's haunch was branded with Rev. 6:8. It didn't take a rocket scientist to figure out what the image meant—Revelations 6:8 spoke of a pale horse whose rider was Death, with Hades following close behind.

Many a person would be stunned seeing the images etched upon his skin, but Zoë wasn't shocked. She'd been making a living as a tattoo artist for five years now, and after seeing constant images of devils, demons, witches, and warlocks—death no longer fazed her. For many, death and the afterlife were a preoccupation, one that often defined their existence, and she no longer tried to read into its meaning for them. So maybe this guy preached the end of the world, or looked forward to its coming, or maybe he truly considered himself to be exactly who the image represented—the grim reaper.

It wasn't her job to interpret, just to provide.

"Find an opening around the horse," he said.

She scanned the other images that surrounded the horse, looking for a good place to draw the tiger. Each of the tattoos wasn't particularly large, about the size of her palm, but together appeared to tell a story. Animals at first glance that seemed to be exactly what they represented but, upon closer inspection, were hurt or damaged in some manner. A fox trapped. A dog without teeth. A wild horse broken. And...she caught her breath. A hummingbird with no wings.

It hit her with the force of a bullet to the chest. Zoë stared at it, heart racing.

Her mother had loved hummingbirds. Zoë had painted dozens of them for her as a kid—in watercolor, chalk, and oils—and she'd hung them all over the house. The day Zoë had returned home after learning about her mother's death, she'd stepped inside to see them spattered with blood, like the walls around them.

She closed her eyes and forced the images away.

Of all the things for this man to have tattooed on his back.

She took a deep breath, forced herself to go to that inner place where a year of therapy had taught her to retreat when anxiety overwhelmed her. Still, she felt that familiar buzzing in her chest and the shortness of her breath.

Silently, she repeated her safe words, reminding herself that in this very moment of time, she was okay, and this moment was all that mattered.

Calm. Stay calm. Just breathe.

She reopened her eyes, told herself to focus only on the empty spaces. "There's room here," she said, pointing to a space between a giraffe with a broken neck and a netted dolphin. "It shouldn't take long. Two hours max."

"That'll be fine," he said.

She averted her gaze back to the other tattoos. She noticed each of the images had just a hint of color in one of the finer details. A pink saddle on the horse. A red bandana on a coyote. And on the hummingbird—a purple blindfold.

Purple, like the silk scarf her mother had worn on the evening she went searching for her runaway daughter. The daughter that had been so stubborn and cruel to tell her mother that she hated her and never wanted to see her again. That daughter, Zoë. *You got your wish.*

"The color on this one?" she asked. Her voice wavered.

"Orange on the collar. Fiery, just like she was."

Was? Zoë held her breath, felt her brow arch. The images called to her, pulled her in. She wanted to move closer to read the numbers etched on each animal—especially the hummingbird—but they were tiny.

Stop. You're just imagining things. You know how you get.

"Come on back," she said. She turned on a heel and walked to the next room, where she prepared a stencil of the design. Screech was now sitting in a chair on the opposite side of the shop eating a noodle bowl and watching some courtroom television show on his tablet. "You can sit here," she said, tapping on the back of a chair. "And hang your shirt and jacket on the hook there if you want."

He did as she instructed, then hiked his leg over the chair and sat with his back facing her. Zoë began with a quick shave of the area followed by an alcohol cleanse of his entire back. As her fingers glided across his skin, she couldn't help but analyze some of the other images, all those suffering animals circling the pale horse—surrounding Death. She saw what appeared to be a sick dove with a green ribbon, its inscription 3770105. Checked out the broken bucking horse, 1270512 etched on the saddle. Examined a flattened gecko, 4390302 above the orange spots on its tail.

She took a glance at the hummingbird's blindfold, 2891703, sucked in air.

Her hand stopped rubbing as she froze, a deep darkness settling in her core. There it was, right there in the middle, nine-one-seven. Could that mean September 17? Her mother had been murdered on September 17.

But what of the year, 2010? And what were these other numbers, the two, eight, zero, and three? Zoë's mind went wild. Were they dates, or ages, or some strange representation of the event? Her mother had been stabbed twelve times, so that didn't match, and two-eight or twenty-eight couldn't be an age—her mother had been thirty-three.

"Hey, you still there?" the devil-man asked over his shoulder.

She caught her breath.

Stop it. You're losing it. Being completely paranoid. These numbers could be anything. The hummingbird too. You are reading too much into things...just like before.

Still...she stared at the back of the man before her and couldn't help but wonder what his story was. Most people displayed tattoos of images that represented their character, like their love of family and friends, or qualities they admired, like strength and courage. Yet, if she didn't know better, this guy was a genuine walking, talking book of death.

She shuddered.

She transferred the stencil and started the tattoo. Outlined the head and the body, rounded and feminine, but only partially included the neck. On the feet, she extended the claws out, as if the tiger was coming for him, then opened the mouth in a ferocious roar, all gnarling teeth. She added several black stripes across the entire design, then, at last, drew the neck, squeezed closed, and overlaid the collar tight around the center. The chain extended outward to invisible hands where, presumably, he—or the devil— pulled it tight.

She added the spot of orange coloring to the collar as requested, then inscribed the number—2860414. As she marked the numbers, she could sense darkness descending upon her again. She looked at the middle numbers: six-zero-four. Today was June 7. Could those three numbers represent June 4?

She thought back to the prior day when the newscaster had announced the grim discovery of a local woman found raped and strangled in her own home. She was discovered Thursday when she didn't show up for work. Thursday, June 5.

Zoë slipped, and the needle went astray. Gasping, she quickly pulled up. "Sorry."

He didn't even flinch.

Screech glanced up and took note of her shaking hands. He cocked his head, as if asking if she was okay. She slightly shook her head and wiped her forehead. She didn't know why, but the images on this man's back had unnerved her.

Zoë, your mind is creating monsters.

She could almost hear the words out of her husband's mouth, how he would tell her she was letting her imagination run away with her again. For three years, she'd driven herself crazy by investigating even the slightest sign or rumor about her mother's death. She'd followed her mother's suspected coworkers, spied on her ex-boyfriends, infiltrated a local cult, even once knocked on the door of an old man simply because he had hummingbird feeders in his front yard. Thankfully, Max's counseling prevented her from being dragged off to the funny farm, but on occasion, the urge to find the truth struck again.

"I need to let this dry for five or ten minutes," she said.

She got up to go to the back and get some air. Screech watched her as she went.

She paced, wondered what to do. Part of her wanted to ask him questions, but she'd learned long ago, with the gangs, ex-cons, and bikers—especially those that belonged to the one-percenter clubs—you didn't do that. Asking questions could earn you a trip to the desert. The rule was, if you didn't ask, you couldn't tell. And although this guy hadn't come in wearing a patch on his leather, Zoë was certain the Devils moniker and strange Chupacabra-like logo inked on his chest matched those of the outlaw motorcycle club. Yet, those numbers and images, she needed to know what they represented.

Suddenly, she desperately wanted a photograph of this man's back. She wanted to take the images home with her to view and analyze them, spend some time with them and her computer.

She chewed a nail. She knew this guy would pay in cash and would never come back, so if he slipped out before she got a picture, those images would be lost. Yes, she could be imagining things again, but if she didn't at least get a photo and investigate, it would haunt her forever.

As she walked back out, she noticed the man's eyes were closed while he rested in the chair. His shoulders were curled forward so you couldn't see his chest, but his back was right there for the taking.

Again, Screech eyed her, visibly noticing her restlessness.

As soon as she got reseated, she slid her phone from her purse and held up the camera to his back. If he objected, she'd just claim it was for her portfolio, a little something to show others what kind of work she did. Most people didn't mind a photo—even of something suspect—as long as you didn't associate it with them.

But that didn't work for him. The minute she held up the camera, he wheeled and slapped it from her hand, sending it flying across the room.

"No pictures," he said.

Screech jumped from his chair. "What the...?"

Zoë glanced at the red mark on her hand and rubbed it. "I just wanted a shot for my portfolio."

The man with the pale horse stood over her. He walked over and retrieved the phone from the floor, dusted it off. He started to hand it to her, but before he did, checked the camera for any rogue photographs she'd happened to get. When he was satisfied none existed, he handed it back.

Screech stood behind him, his mouth agape.

Zoë didn't bother looking at it, just plopped it on her workstation. "I think we're done here. I'd give you the rundown on care, but I'm sure you know the drill." She applied a layer of petroleum jelly and slapped a bandage over it.

Then she walked to the front to check him out.

He sauntered back over to the chair, gathered his T-shirt and jacket. She wrote him a receipt and, as expected, he paid in cash. After getting redressed, he pulled out an extra one-hundred-dollar bill and laid it on the countertop.

He stood in front of her, staring. "You have beautiful eyes. Anyone ever tell you that?" His voice was like a lover trying to lure her in and beg for her forgiveness.

She didn't answer, just shook her head.

"Mom or Dad?"

She knew damn well they were her mom's eyes, but she sure as hell wasn't going to tell him that. Not with him wearing that tattoo—that hummingbird with the broken wings. "I don't know. I'm adopted," she lied.

He grunted. "That's too bad." He started out, turned. "Sorry about the phone. But my ladies, they're just for me." He slid a skull gaiter over his lower face, put his sunglasses on, and headed out the door.

Zoë watched him outside as he put on his helmet and straddled his bike, a polished black number with lots of chrome—and rolled it back from the curb. Just before he pulled out into the street, he acknowledged Zoë staring through the glass with a singular nod.

Zoë stepped back, noticed she was shivering.

Screech joined her. "You really wanted that one, I could tell."

"Yeah, I did," she said, watching him drive off. She felt Screech studying her.

"No worries. I got your back. Or rather...his." He took out his phone and laid it on the counter. "Front too, in case you're interested."

She grabbed his phone, enlarged his photos, and smiled. While her client had risen to confront her and retrieve the phone, Screech had taken his own shots. He not only had the tiger but the man's entire back. The pale rider and his broken animals.

She hugged him. "You're a damn good friend, Screech."

CHAPTER 4

J*ust like she was.* Those words haunted Zoë, especially the word *was.* In her five
years as a tattoo artist, she had designed thousands of images, many of them
macabre, so why did those simple words coupled with the image of a choking
tiger bother her so much? Because of the man, because of the message, or because he
carried another image that reminded her of her mother? A hummingbird, wings
clipped.

A hummingbird tagged with *2891703.* Could it be this man was connected to her
mother's murder in some way or had even killed her? Or was Zoë letting her
imagination get the best of her again, seeing a message in the image and numbers
that she wanted to see? There were so many questions she wanted to ask of the man
that had visited, but he was gone now, presumably forever.

What did those broken animals and numbers mean?

She pulled out her phone, brought up the images Screech had captured. They were
a bit blurry, having been taken quickly and at a distance, but she could make out the
animals—the coyote, the horse, the dove—and the rest. Fourteen images total. She
wanted to show them to Max, but in her year of counseling with him before they'd
gotten involved, he'd repeatedly emphasized how she needed to let go of her obsession
with her mother's murder and forgive herself. What would he think if she told him
about her current thoughts, and showed her the pictures?

She sat on the porch steps of the little white house she and Max rented and lit up
a cigarette. She'd been trying to quit for years now, and although she'd made great
strides—often smoking no more than a few per day—nicotine was a habit she had yet
to totally conquer. When she did smoke, she always made sure to go outside and away
from Oliver, who hated the "stinky."

Max also continued to indulge in an occasional cigarette, especially after a
particularly rough day, and apparently, today was one of those days. He joined her on
the porch wearing only jeans, feet bare, hoping to get a dose of the cool night air. The

little house they rented didn't have air-conditioning, so they relied on open windows and fans in the summer. A lot of fans. He tapped the pack of smokes against his palm, removed one, and lit it.

"Where's Oliver?" she asked.

"Asleep," he said, taking a seat next to her on the top porch step and draping an arm across her knee. He sucked on the cigarette, examined it before exhaling a wad of smoke.

"Rough day?" she asked.

He nodded. Like her, Max had been quiet at dinner, leading Oliver to bounce his gaze between the two of them and initiate a conversation of his own. "How was your day?" he asked himself, then answered his own question. "It was great. Jules took us swimming, and I dove in the deep end. She said I did great and bought me a Snickers. Which I ate. Thanks for asking." The solo conversation had snapped them from their dazes, and they'd laughed.

Max had ruffled Oliver's hair. "Point taken, buddy."

Zoë had called Jules, their babysitter, to thank her.

"You want to talk about it?" Zoë asked Max. At first, it had seemed odd in their relationship to ask her husband such questions, given that they'd met while he was her counselor, but eventually, they'd become each other's sounding board. A therapist needed to talk to someone about their day as much as anyone else.

"This kid, Stevie, came in today. Skin and bones. I assumed, like most the others who come through our doors, he had to be an addict, but turns out, he hasn't eaten in weeks. A month ago, he turned eighteen, and, just like that, his foster parents cut him loose. Needed to make room for a new kid, one they could still get money for."

He grunted, disgusted. "What's even sadder, this kid, he might be eighteen physically, but mentally, he's fourteen at best. He's scared. Doesn't have a clue what to do."

Zoë took a deep breath. She thought back to herself at fifteen, after her mother's murder, when she was suddenly faced with the choice between cohabitating with strangers or a life on the streets. Given the stories of rampant abuse in the foster care system, she'd chosen the streets, but most adults, let alone kids, couldn't have handled what she went through the next three years. Knowing what was ahead for kids like Stevie, it was often difficult to hear about Max's cases.

"Any shelters open?"

"No. Beds are full. I've got him on the lists, but you know how it goes...it could take months before something opens. I just wish..."

She sighed. "I know, babe. I do too. I wish we had room here or we had enough money to open a shelter of our own. Someday. So, what did you do?"

He took another drag, stroked his beard, which was now about six inches long. "The only thing I could. I took him on a tour of the streets and gave him an education.

Showed him the best places to get food and find shelter. Some of my old haunts, like that bakery on Fifth Street."

"Stale bagels never tasted so damn good," Zoë said. "You tell him about old man Latchey's grocery?"

"Oh yeah. Told him to visit the dumpster every Tuesday at eleven p.m. Get all the cans of Vienna sausage and soups he could. They might be out of date, but they're easy cooking over an open fire."

"Yeah, if someone else doesn't get a whiff of what you're cooking and come for you." She thought back to her first experience finding an outdated pack of hot dogs tossed in a trash can. She'd poked them with sticks, and started a small fire with dried brush and a lighter. Within five minutes, she had a hungry pack surrounding her, and none of them were friendly. "I hope he makes some friends," she said.

Max nodded, understanding exactly what she meant. Whether it was in detention, or prison, or life on the streets, security necessitated you join with others for safety. "I should tell you that I bought him a small tent and a backpack, loaded him up with what supplies I could."

Zoë rubbed his back. "Don't ever apologize for helping someone out."

They shared a moment, kissed.

"How about you?" he asked. "What had you so distracted at dinner, as our son so cleverly pointed out? You barely said a word."

She crushed the cigarette out on the step, dropped it in an empty soda can. She'd thought all evening about the devil and his pale horse but didn't know how much she should reveal to Max, if anything at all. Maybe she could tell him just enough to see if it had merit or if she really was imagining things.

She sighed. "I don't know. You'll probably think I'm crazy, but...this guy came in today, and he had these tattoos." She told him about the pale horse, the animals that surrounded it, and the tiger she'd added. "They were all trapped or hurt in some manner. It was disturbing. And one of them...one of them was a hummingbird with its wings torn off and a blindfold wrapped around its eyes."

He raised his eyebrows. Inhaled deeply before he blew out the smoke. "Well, I guess I don't have to ask what you thought of that. It reminded you of your mother."

She gathered her long brunette hair and wrapped it around one shoulder. It was sticky outside and hot upon her back. "Yes. It wasn't just the bird, though. He had an inscription on the blindfold. Two-eight-nine-one-seven-zero-three."

She stared at him, waiting to see if he picked up on it or if she would need to elaborate. When he looked blankly at her, she explained. "Nine-one-seven. Like maybe for September 17? The day she was killed?"

He frowned, took another drag, seemed to think on it. "It's odd, I'll give you that, but...I'm sure there's nothing to it. A guy who likes to torture animals or display his dominance over women perhaps. Maybe in their rejection of him, he fantasizes about getting even. A lot of women like hummingbirds, and that inscription? It could be anything. Maybe her age or her name coded in the numbers. What did he have you put on the tiger?"

She told him. "Like maybe June 4? Like that woman who died last week?" That might've been too much to reveal, as she saw a slight shift in Max's mood.

He thought again, shook his head. "I don't know." He snuffed out his cigarette, squeezed her knee. "I'm sure it's nothing. Don't let your mind run away with you." He leaned over and kissed her forehead.

She briefly thought about going deeper into her thoughts and musings, but she could see the concern now etched on Max's face. If she revealed more, he'd see how much time she'd already devoted to dwelling on the man, and he'd worry. He had enough on his plate caring for all the kids at the center. She didn't need to burden him with any more of her delusions, especially since they were probably just that—fantasy. Tomorrow would be a new day with new clients and she'd forget all about the man who likened himself to the grim reaper.

She snuggled beneath Max's arm. "I'm sure you're right."

But in the distance, she could hear the roar of the bikes chugging down the interstate, echoing off the hills nearby, and wondered if he was among them.

CHAPTER 5

etective Brady Sloane of the Reno Police Department started the day with a request for money from his wife and a one-fingered salute from his teenage daughter. The drive into work wasn't much better as he came upon an accident involving an SUV and a tow truck and, after stopping to help, found himself in the middle of a fight worthy of the WWF. Maybe it was the searing early heat wave that had gripped Reno this June, but it seemed in the last few days, everybody in the city had lost their mind. In the past week, every division at the police department had seen a rise in cases, from sex crimes to robbery/homicide. Normally, he would blame it on the motorcycle clubs that infiltrated their city this time of year, but since everyone the police had dragged in so far seemed to be a local, he had to blame it on something else: the heat, the moon, or something in the water.

After he broke the two men up and was able to settle them down, he handed the scene over to the two patrol officers who'd finally arrived. As a thank-you for helping, one of the men he'd saved from getting assaulted spit on his shoe. Sloane looked down at it and sighed. Appreciation was damn hard to come by these days.

In his car, he wiped his hands and face of sweat, and glanced in the rearview mirror. Already, he had stains beneath his armpits and his blond hair lay flat. He hated how badly it had thinned the past year. He looked damn old.

Maybe he should just forego the day and head straight to a bar.

If only I hadn't given up drinking seven years ago.

He started his car and pulled back onto the interstate. Five years ago, his wife had insisted they move out to the suburbs from the heart of the city, so his drive in took twenty minutes longer than it used to. He started to turn on the radio when the roar of a dozen motorcycles reverberated the air behind him. Even though he was in his personal car, it was as if the riders knew he was a cop, and in an act of intimidation, rode along beside him until he reached his exit. This was just week three in what was certain to be two months of annual biker runs, and the entire RPD would be on call for

21

the multitude of new assaults, stabbings, and shootings that were sure to ensue during the latest territorial clashes. Last week, the Devils had made a run from the north, and this week, he expected several Southern California clubs to arrive, including Los Salvajes, none of whom shared any love with the Angels, who held the most real estate in the city. He entered the office with no solid hope that the day would get any better.

He set his coffee down only to see his partner, Manual Ramirez, shoot him a double take. "Hey, amigo. You look like shit. What'd you do? Take a swim before coming to work?"

Sloane smirked. "What did I ever do to deserve you as a partner?"

Ramirez grinned, all blazing white teeth. "You won the lottery with me."

"Keep drinking the Kool-Aid," Sloane said. He flopped down in his chair and turned toward his desk where the image of a young redhead with green eyes sat staring up at him. The girl had been raped and murdered five days ago, and already, the case was growing cold. He sipped his lukewarm coffee. "Anything new on McKinley?"

A head shake. "Nothing. Nobody saw anything. Nobody heard anything. That's their story, and they're sticking to it."

"What about the friend she was last seen with?" Sloane asked. "She still doesn't remember anybody from the casino that took an interest? Maybe followed Amber home?"

"No, bro. Girl's tore up, though, I tell you that," Ramirez said. "When I spoke to her yesterday, she cried for an hour. It was like sitting with my girlfriend through one of those rom-coms. Painful."

Sloane loosened his tie. "Well, I'm sure it was nothing compared to the pain Amanda McKinley endured." He turned to his computer, logged in. "I guess I'll look at the casino tapes again. I don't know where else to go with this one."

And he didn't. He'd spoken to every neighbor, coworker, relative, and friend he could find, and nobody had even tossed him a crumb. This girl appeared to have no stalkers, no crazy ex-boyfriends, not even an interesting one-night stand or two in her past. Yet, by all accounts, it appeared she'd invited in whoever had raped and killed her, as the police found no signs of forced entry into her residence. The house was a mess, and the signs of a struggle inside clear, but unless the perp had gotten in through an unlocked door or window, it seemed he had to be someone she knew or encountered before. To Sloane, that led back to the casino where she'd last been seen.

He booted up the tapes, began to watch again. He'd already combed over the surveillance video for two days solid, but there had to be something he was missing. A glance, a pass by, a whispered conversation. Yet, three hours later, he was exactly where he'd begun—nowhere.

He stopped the video, rubbed his tired eyes. Heard a set of familiar footsteps approach and hoped it wasn't who he thought.

"How's the case coming?" a voice asked.

It was. The voice that matched the footsteps belonged to Adam Quinn, DEA agent and man who thought he could do no wrong. The only reason he ever frequented the RPD was to squeeze others for information or complain about somebody screwing up, and Sloane feared today that could be about him.

Sloane glanced up, shook his head. "Not good. Pretty clear the perp used gloves and a condom. Not much physical evidence to go on."

Quinn planted his solid five-foot-eight frame in a nearby chair, grunted. "Sorry. You checked for similar cases?"

Sloane sighed. He hadn't yet, but that would be next on his list if they didn't get a hit on something soon. He'd enter the case history into the databases and see if anything popped up. Guy like this, it seemed reasonable to think he'd committed prior offenses, and it was possible the perp wasn't local. He could've been here on vacation, hitting up the casinos.

"Just don't let it become your next Bella," Quinn said.

Sloane grunted. Bella was Lisabella Jansen, a young mother whose case he'd caught early in his career and remained unsolved to this day. Like Amber McKinley, Bella had been raped, but instead of being strangled, she'd been stabbed twelve times. Every detective had that one case—the one he hadn't solved and couldn't forget. For him, that had been, and continued to be, Lisabella Jansen.

But Bella and Amber weren't what Quinn had really come to talk about.

"Listen, man," Quinn said, "I don't mean to rain additional shit on your head, but that information you got from your CI about the new warehouse the Angels have here? Somehow, they got word. We raided it yesterday, and it was clean. And I don't mean soap and water. I mean bleach and disinfectant."

Sloane sighed. Sloane had heard about the failed ATF raid on the club's supposed gun storage facility the day before and knew Quinn would be quick to blame Sloane's confidential informant. The RPD, DEA, and ATF had long worked together as a task force to undermine the growing presence of the outlaw motorcycle clubs and expose their illegal activities—everything from meth production and distribution to pornography, guns, and even human trafficking. Since the Angels and their illegal activities crossed several agencies and jurisdictions, it was in the government's best interest to keep each other informed. But there was always a battle of stepping on egos, and every organization—including the clubs themselves—was highly territorial.

He held up his hands. "I don't know what to say. The info was good."

Quinn twisted his lips around each other, scratched at his struggling goatee while he glanced around the place. He leaned forward in the chair, tapped Sloane's desk. "I'm telling you, you got moles in this place," he whispered. "The RPD is crawling with club informants."

There were always rumors of the sort, that the outlaw clubs had friendlies working for the Reno Police Department, just as the ATF and DEA had agents infiltrating the clubs. Undercovers often reported MC members bragging about their police informants, telling them of planned raids or investigations into certain activities days before they happened. The goal was infiltration no matter whose side you were on. The trick was figuring out who was working for whom, and why.

"What do you want me to do?" Sloane said. "Talk to the chief. It's not my job to shake down every employee here. You've got undercovers in the clubs; they've got citizens here too. It's a game between us all, don't you know?"

Quinn huffed, cracked his knuckles. "Yeah, well, that game just moved a hundred AR 15s and handguns into the hands of who-the-hell-knows, so you and your partners here in homicide better be ready for some new deliveries. In case you haven't been paying attention, there's a turf war going on. My UC says Los Salvajes have had the NorCal Devils in their target since that incident in Modesto a few years back, and my guess is, Nevada might be next. The casino shooting in Carson City was just the beginning. The Devils are pushing hard for territory here, and neither the Angels or Los Salvajes are going to go down without a fight."

Sloane nodded. He'd heard the same, but he didn't want to acknowledge it. "Look, I'll reach out to my CI and see what he knows. And next time we get something, we'll alter the channels of communication. But you contact your undercover in the Devils and find out what he knows too. I've already got a dead woman on my plate. The last damn thing I need is a morgue full of dead bikers, and worse, dead citizens caught in the cross fire."

Quinn rapped on his desk, stood. "You got it. I'll be in touch."

Sloane groaned. He could hardly wait.

CHAPTER 6

On a rare early afternoon off, Zoë's curiosity got the better of her. She knew she should just leave it alone, but for a week now, she'd been unable to sleep, eat, or work without thinking of the images on the devil's back. She transferred the photos Screech took from his phone to the computer and enlarged them so she could zoom in and note the image's details. After documenting each one with its animal and color, she put them in order based upon the last two numbers, which were the only digits that appeared to be in sequence.

First was a strangled cat with a lavender ribbon, number 4772901.

Second was a squashed gecko with orange spots, number 4390302.

Third was the hummingbird, wings clipped and purple blindfold, number 2891703.

Fourth was a dolphin caught in a dark-blue net, number 0552104.

Fifth was a sick green dove, number 3770105.

Sixth was an eagle pierced by a yellow arrow, number 4762206.

Seventh was a lion tamed with a ruby-red whip, number 0571207.

Eight was a giraffe, neck broken and orange scarf, number 2681508.

Ninth was a dog with no teeth and brown collar, number 4340609.

Tenth was a squealing pig cut with a green knife, number 4181210.

Eleventh was a coyote full of holes with a red bandana, number 0321311.

Twelfth was a bucking horse with a pink saddle, number 1270512.

Thirteenth was a fox caught in a pale-blue leg trap, number 0531013.

And last was the choking tiger with orange collar, number 2860414.

Fourteen representations, the third possibly being her mother. Were all his "ladies" victims, like her mother, or simply women he'd come across in his lifetime and had some sort of relationship with? If she was right about the middle three numbers representing dates, then it appeared the man was most active in the summer months, which, as a biker, would make sense. But what of the first two numbers, then? What did they mean?

She analyzed just the first two numbers. Four-seven appeared twice, on the cat and the eagle, as did four-three on the dog and the gecko. Zero-five appeared on three of the images, the fox, lion, and dolphin. And two-eight, the first two numbers listed on the hummingbird, also started the latest addition of the choking tiger. All the rest appeared to be singular, listed just one time.

She stared at the hummingbird and tiger, considered the numbers two and eight. If the hummingbird did represent her mom, who died on September 17 and was his third victim, and the tiger possibly the woman killed a week ago on June 4 as his fourteenth victim, then it seemed the two-eight represented Reno or the larger area in some way.

Zoë chewed a nail and thought. She pulled up a map of the United States and clicked on Nevada. Nevada was seventh in land size, thirty-second in population, forty-first in population density, and the thirty-eighth state admitted to the Union. Reno was the fourth-largest city in the state. None of those numbers equated or represented two-eight in any way.

She pondered some more. *Two and eight. Or maybe, twenty-eight.*

Feeling her brow arch, she searched for an alphabetical list of states. A list pulled up, but it wasn't numbered, so she counted from the top. The list contained some non-states—Guam, American Samoa, Puerto Rico—so she excluded those from the count.

Her heart began to race when she got halfway. Twenty-five, twenty-six, twenty-seven...and there it was. Excluding the American territories, Nevada, alphabetically, was number twenty-eight.

She counted again just to make sure she was right.

She looked at the other numbers. Zero-three was Arizona. Zero-five California. Twelve, Idaho. Twenty-six, Montana. Thirty-seven, Oregon. Forty-one, South Dakota. Forty-three, Texas. And last but not least, forty-seven, Washington.

She redid the list with the state and dates added to key items.

First, strangled cat, lavender ribbon, Washington, July 29.

Second, squashed gecko, orange spots, Texas, September 3.

Third, hummingbird, purple blindfold, Nevada, September 17.

Fourth, dolphin, dark-blue net, California, May 21.

Fifth, green dove, Oregon, July 1.

Sixth, eagle, yellow arrow, Washington, June 22.

Seventh, lion, ruby-red whip, California, July 12.

Eighth, giraffe, orange scarf, Montana, August 15.

Ninth, toothless dog, brown collar, Texas, April 6.

Tenth, squealing pig, green knife, South Dakota, August 12.

Eleventh, coyote with holes, red bandana, Arizona, February 13.

Twelfth, bucking horse, pink saddle, Idaho, July 5.

Thirteenth, fox, pale-blue trap, California, March 10.

And lastly, choking tiger, orange collar, Nevada, June 4.

Zoë sat back and stared at the list, her hand shaking even as she held it. Was she seeing things in numbers and images simply because her mind wanted to? Or was it possible that, this time, she had unearthed the truth? Max would tell her she was obsessing over her mother's death again, but this numerical code, it seemed to fit.

She didn't really know whether the orange tiger represented the latest woman in Reno to die, and she knew of no others who might represent the other victims, but...what if she was to search? The internet was a vast tool that ran on keywords. If she entered a state, date, and the word *murder*, would she get any hits?

After glancing over her shoulder to make sure Oliver was still good in the other room playing video games and Max hadn't yet arrived home, she nervously typed in the date from the first image along with *Washington* and *murder*. Several news items came up, but without a year or city to narrow the search, they were too vast to comb through.

She continued down the list, seeing if anything surfaced. It wasn't until she got to number six on the list that something hit. On the keywords of *Washington*, *June 22*, *murder*, an article popped up about a woman who was found dead six years ago off a wooded trail near her home in Olympia, Washington. The dead woman was an avid archer, and often practiced her sport in a forested area near there. Zoë shook as she looked at the woman's photo in her obituary, her hair that color that she and her friends as kids had called banana blond. A tinge of yellow, just like the yellow arrow on the man's tattoo. There was no mention of anything about an eagle, but the resemblance to the image was obvious.

Zoë sat staring at the article, her breaths as shallow as her fluttering heartbeat. She wondered if she should continue. Her skin itched and tingled with trepidation, as if she'd fallen into a batch of poison oak. A warning, perhaps, that if she kept on, this rash would only spread and get worse.

But how could she not?

The next to produce a hit was number ten. She typed in *South Dakota, August 12,* and the more specific word *stabbing* instead of murder. Given that the pig was cut, she thought that might be how this victim had died. She was right. Three years ago, a woman had been raped and stabbed repeatedly during the annual Sturgis Motorcycle Rally in South Dakota. But what made it relevant was the woman was the wife of a Los Salvajes MC member, which made the wild pig, similar to their boar logo, pertinent.

The last to provide a connection was number twelve on her list. *Idaho, July 5, murder* brought news of a local rodeo queen known for her barrel racing and roping, who was found murdered the day after Independence Day in her home outside Caldwell. The local paper had a photo of her on the front page standing next to her favorite horse, Princess. The saddle on its back was pink, just like the saddle in the tattoo.

Zoë started to shake. She folded her laptop shut, afraid to look anymore. Her mouth was dry, so very dry, and her heart pounded inside her chest. *Is my mind playing games with me or is this for real?*

She sat in the room listening to the sounds of Oliver's video game, the *boinks*, *boops*, and *beeps* of his avatar earning points by slaying dragons and evil overlords. Killing, just like she now feared the devil in her shop had killed her mother—and possibly thirteen more.

It was true. It had to be true. This was no longer just her imagination.

But how would she prove it, and who would she tell? Would anyone believe her and a story about a bunch of tattoos on the back of a biker?

She heard a car engine outside, saw Max pull up in the drive. She wiped away the tears that had surfaced and smoothed her hair. She had to pull herself together. Max could not know what she'd been doing, or what she'd discovered. He would worry about her and her mental condition. Even if he believed her, he would tell her to stop, afraid it would lead her back to that long, dark tunnel it had taken her so long to crawl out of.

She flipped her left arm over, rubbed her thumb across the scars there, now masked by ink. She didn't want to risk returning to that dark place, but how could she let this man continue to walk free knowing he might be a murderer? It would haunt her, weighing on her psyche as much as the guilt of her mother's death. Yet, if she could figure out how to prove this man killed her mother and others as well, that darkness might cease to exist.

And wasn't that worth it? A chance to extinguish for good that which had haunted her for so long? And what about the others? How many families out there were grieving like she was and longing to know what happened to their loved ones?

Yes, it was worth it. It had to be. This was her shot at redemption. She couldn't bring her mother back, but she could damn well give her justice. Tomorrow, she'd start by seeing what she could learn about this recent woman's murder here in Reno.

CHAPTER 7

Amber McKinley's place wasn't too far from the tattoo shop, a little cream-colored stucco house with a variety of flowering bushes out front and a cracked and broken sidewalk. Zoë didn't know what exactly she expected to see that might prove helpful to her cause, but thought if she could find a neighbor or two, maybe they would recall seeing her guy in the neighborhood that night, or at least remember his motorcycle. She wished now that Screech had gotten shots of the man's face in addition to his torso, as it was going to be hard for anyone to identify him.

Earlier in the day, she'd read all about Amber's murder to learn what she could about the woman and what had happened to her. Amber was originally from Elko, Nevada, and had originally come to Reno to attend UNR, but dropped out after two years. She loved adventure and dreamed of being a travel writer. She hadn't yet married or had kids, but she was optimistic her future would contain both. One of Amber's friends who'd been interviewed called Amber a dreamer. "She always had her head in the clouds, imagining herself flying off to some exotic destination. Her wish was to go to Africa."

Africa, like elephants, lions, and...tigers.

Zoë had grown nauseous at that.

Other than the background information, there was little news on the murder itself. Amber had been raped and strangled, but if the police knew anything else, they were keeping it quiet. A source for the RPD was quoted that they were looking into several leads, but Zoë got the feeling the police hadn't a clue, just like in her mother's murder.

She wondered what they would think of her new theory?

Probably nothing, just like all the other times. In the past, Zoë had taken countless theories and rumors to the lead detective, Brady Sloane, on her mother's case, but he'd done nothing other than pat her on the head and dismiss her tips as the imaginations of a young, depressed girl. Then he'd try to call child services and have her hauled away. No, she'd given up on law enforcement a long time ago. She no longer trusted any of them.

As Zoë sat across the street in her vehicle, a woman in a white SUV pulled up and parked off the curb. After remaining inside and speaking on the phone for a few minutes, she eventually opened the door and slid out. Zoë wondered if she was a friend or relative of Amber's, then quickly realized she had to be the woman's mother. She was tall with red hair, just like her daughter, and clutched what appeared to be the keys to the residence in her hand. She disappeared inside the house for several minutes before returning outside, carrying boxes to her SUV. The way she hunched over made it seem like the boxes were filled with concrete, but it turned out to be something even heavier—her dead daughter's belongings and the grief that went with them.

Zoë cautiously approached. "Ma'am? Are you Amber's mother?"

The woman turned as if molasses filled her neck, eyes hidden behind tortoiseshell glasses. "Yes?"

"My name is Zoë. I knew your daughter," she lied. "She was a friend."

"Oh," she said distractedly, as if that was all she could think to reply. "I'm sorry. I thought I met most of Amber's friends at the funeral. How did you know her?" Her voice was soft and distant, almost like someone else was speaking for her.

Zoë quickly thought. "We went to UNR together. Do you need some help with her things?" Not that she relished stepping inside the house where Amber had been murdered, but it would provide her a chance to see if there was anything that might indicate the devil with the pale horse had been there.

"That would be nice, thank you. The landlord, big heart that he is, told me to come clean out her stuff as soon as the police released the property so he could get the place ready to rent." She put two fingers across her lips, clearly holding back tears. "Can you believe that? What the hell is wrong with people? They don't even allow you time to grieve. They just clean up and move on, as if Amber was roadkill."

She placed the box in the back of the SUV, shut the hatch.

Zoë bowed her head. "I'm so sorry."

The woman walked back up the sidewalk in silence. Zoë followed, glancing around to see if any of the neighbors watched or lurked nearby. She felt strange going into someone else's residence, let alone one where a woman just a few years older than herself had spent her last hours. What had gone through her mind in those final minutes? Did she think she would survive? Or did she know the moment the man's hands circled her neck that he would be the last person she ever saw?

She stepped in to see a house once cutely decorated with plaques, paintings, and potted plants now smudged by fingerprint powder and infested with the odor of its prior owner. In the living room, there were packed boxes containing glasses, dishes, and other kitchen items sitting on the floor, as well as a grocery bag full of decorative towels and linens. Zoë noticed many of them had funny sayings. *It's wine o'clock somewhere. Life is short, lick the bowl. In our family, we don't hide crazy.*

Zoë picked up the boxes and began taking them out to the vehicle. On the second trip, she hoisted a box of books, noticed the one on top featured photographs from Africa. On the front was a mother elephant and her baby in the open tundra in front of a cascading sunset. As she placed it in the back seat, Zoë's heart sank, feeling all the weight of a lost and wasted life.

She tried to make conversation as she helped Amber's mother pack additional items in the kitchen. She cleaned out a junk drawer, and took note of several small, muddy paw prints on the floor, water splashed from a dog bowl in the corner.

"Amber loved animals, didn't she?" Zoë said.

Her mom nodded. "Yes. She had a little dog, Sparky. He's with my husband at the hotel right now. The poor thing. He just lays on his blanket and cries. I don't know what to do for him." She wrapped several dinner plates in Bubble Wrap, stacked them in a box. "But she liked all kinds of animals, especially the wild ones."

Zoë saw an opportunity. "She wanted to go to Africa."

Her mother tried to smile. "Yes. That was her dream. To go on safari. Half of the items she wore were animal prints. Leopard, zebra, cheetah—"

"Tiger?" Zoë asked.

"Yes." Her mom turned to her. "Which, would you mind? I haven't been able to go into her closet. Her clothes, they just remind me so much of her. And I can't..."

"It's okay," Zoë said. "I'll get them."

Zoë rounded the corner to walk down the hall to Amber's bedroom and felt an immediate sense of dread. Here, just over a week ago, a young woman had lost her life. She remembered what it was like going back into her own house after her mother was murdered, how she felt the walls close in and heard the ghosts whisper.

You should've been here. If you hadn't run away, she wouldn't have been out looking for you. She would've been right here—safe—and he never would've followed her home.

Before she pushed the door open to Amber's room, she closed her eyes and steadied herself. *You can do this. Take a deep breath.*

Zoë twisted the handle and entered. Inside, the bed had been removed, but the dresser and a small nightstand remained. Even though the devil wasn't there, she could sense his presence, the solid man with bad teeth and that crazy Chupacabra-like logo imprinted upon his chest. She found herself holding her breath, as if she was afraid to breathe in the same air he had.

She turned to the closet and slid open the door. There, just as her mother had said, were dozens of clothes in animal print. Blouses and skirts, dresses, even shoes. Zoë scooped an armful of hangers and hustled out to the car. She came back for a second load—all the while thinking about that choking tiger with its popping eyes.

"Who's taming her?" she'd asked.

"The devil."

She scurried down the hall with the clothes draped across her arm when Amber's mother stopped her. "Wait," she said. "Let me see those." She rifled through a hanger that had several scarves draping from its hooks.

"She had this scarf. It was a tiger print. It looked so great on her with her hair coloring." She continued to search, looked disappointed. "It should be here, but I don't see it."

Zoë suddenly imagined the devil selecting it out of the closet there, running it between his fingers like a prize. Had he taken it? Zoë had heard about such things on those television shows, criminals who liked to take an item belonging to their victims, like a trophy.

Her mother appeared as if she was about to cry.

Zoë laid a hand on her arm. "I'm sure it will turn up."

A knock on the front door and a man's voice caused Zoë to flinch. "Hello?"

She turned to see a middle-aged man with thinning blond hair and a former athlete's frame. Zoë hadn't seen him in quite some time but knew at once who he was—Brady Sloane.

"Detective," Amber's mother said. "Come on in. We've just about finished up."

As he stepped inside, Zoë turned her back to him, afraid of the questions that would surely come, especially if he recognized her. After her mother's murder, and his dismissals of Zoë's attempts to find her killer, Zoë had grown resentful of him. He could talk all day about how remorseful he was for not having solved her crime, but she couldn't get over how he, and the rest of the RPD, had treated her. For three long years, they'd tracked and chased her, trying to get her off the streets and back into foster care, despite her wishes. One of the female cops even tried to arrest her once for stealing food out of a dumpster. The officer claimed she'd only done it out of care for her, because an arrest would at least allow them to get her shelter.

Never mind that the shelter was a four-by-six cell.

Zoë suddenly wondered what the hell she was hoping to accomplish by sitting in a dead girl's house and discussing her life with her mother. Did she think she would walk in and instantly solve the crime? Did she think it would bring Amber back? Did she think it would relieve years of guilt grieving over her mother?

She started toward the door. "I should go. Let you two talk."

Zoë took the remaining clothes in her hand and slipped around the detective. "I'll put these last few items in. Again, sorry about Amber."

She hoped she'd gotten away cleanly, but a quick glance over her shoulder told her otherwise. Brady Sloane had his hands on his hips and a frown on his lips. He either knew exactly who she was, or was trying intently to figure it out.

CHAPTER 8

L ater that night, after she put Oliver to bed and Max was snoring by the light of the television, Zoë mustered up the courage to go back beneath the blue light of the computer. She wasn't sure of the best way to track down a man with no name and no address, so started with the only thing she could—the other tattoos on his body.

Although this man hadn't come in wearing cuts that said he was a patched member of the Devils, the ink etched on the front of his torso told her he was very much a part of the motorcycle club. Besides the Devils' moniker tattooed across his upper chest, she was certain the grossly disfigured devil-creature beneath it was the club logo. She pulled it up online just to confirm her suspicions. The tattoos on the man's chest were a perfect match with those on the computer.

She proceeded to read all she could about them, including their origins, territory, and members. The Devils were listed as an outlaw club—displaying the one-percent patches prominently on their jackets—which meant that, unlike the other ninety-nine percent of their law-abiding brothers, they didn't follow the rules. Besides their official logo, the number four was often used to represent them, usually displayed as four horns or a four-pronged pitchfork. That the man who'd walked into her tattoo shop had these inked on each of his shoulders was another indication that he was a patched member.

The Devils had started in British Columbia, Canada, in the sixties and slowly expanded their way south over the next several decades. Their main territory now consisted of Washington, Oregon, and Idaho, but they also had a number of chapters in Northern California. Nevada, it seemed, had historically belonged to the Angels, although many a news article and blog discussed the ongoing conflict between them and the Devils and Los Salvajes as the two clubs sought to expand. That included the latest shooting at a Carson City casino, when two Angels were shot after a confrontation with a group of Devils doing business in the parking lot. This rift was further complicated by a long-held rivalry between Los Salvajes and the Devils, who were suspected of gunning down one of their VPs in Modesto, California, two years prior. That had led to various other altercations in Riverside, Laughlin, Nevada, and even as far as Arizona.

She ran through various images of each of the clubs, photos of guys with wild hair and even wilder beards, all of them dressed in denim, leather, and bandanas. She blew up an image of the Devil's jacket to get a better idea of what the various patches meant. On the back, the top rocker noted the club's moniker, and the bottom one, the city or region the member belonged to. The logo of the disfigured devil-creature sat in the middle, grinning at those who rode or walked behind. On the front, the one-percent logo sat on the left shoulder, and additional patches indicated service anniversaries or club positions, things like vice president and sergeant at arms.

But what she found most interesting wasn't the information that the patches on the jackets conveyed but the marks on the body, particularly the addition of colors to certain tattoos. She'd long known that stars or marks on the shoulders often represented rank or status in gangs or clubs—reminiscent of the military's multi-starred generals—but colors were another matter. Colors apparently represented deeds or tasks completed, and the thing about them was—you didn't get them unless you earned them.

Which meant the guy who'd sat in her shop had done his time. All eight of the tips of his pitchforks were a different color: blue, green, purple, and red on one, and orange, yellow, brown, and white on the other. Eight for eight, a perfect match. All deeds completed.

Zoë took a deep breath. This guy may not have been wearing his cuts when he'd walked into her shop, but there wasn't a doubt in her mind that he was a Devil, and not just any Devil, but a high-ranking member. Maybe even what was known as their enforcer—the one who took needed action that others might find distasteful, things like beatings, or torture, or, yes, even murder.

Because now that she'd done a little research, his other tattoos spoke volumes too.

For instance, in one image inked on the left side of his torso was a king on his throne with his crown toppled and blood spouting from his head. Across the king's chest were two *l*'s followed by a one-one, or the number eleven, a notation meant as *Long Live the Kings*. But in this case, the second *l* had been made into a cross, representing death.

The death of a rival King? According to the internet, the Kings were a large Hispanic gang far more prominent in prisons and the upper Midwest than the Pacific Northwest. Yet, she imagined it was possible the two had crossed paths.

In yet another, there was an image of a sliced green pig with a prominent one-two-two-three etched on its side. Like a four for the Devils, and eleven for the Kings, twelve-twenty-three represented Los Salvajes. In addition, the wild boar was their logo and green their color. So, just like the image of the one on the Devil's back representing the woman who'd died in South Dakota and was married to a member of LS, it made sense. He'd killed a member of Los Salvajes—maybe even a high-ranking member.

Did his rivals know about the man the Devils employed to take them out when warranted? They must not, else he wouldn't be alive. He might've been brazen enough to reveal his torso in a local tattoo shop, but Zoë bet his bravado wasn't as big when he was among members of the rival clubs, those who could decipher what his tattoos meant.

No wonder he didn't want pictures. They'd mark him as a dead man.

He probably wasn't as protective of his prized ladies in public, unbelieving that they would make sense to anyone but him. Still, she bet he never imagined that one day he'd walk into a shop where the ink slinger sitting behind the needle was the daughter of one of his victims.

Yet, what exactly was she supposed to do with what she knew—or, at least, what she suspected? She wasn't sure, but at minimum needed to find out who the man was—his name and address—if he had one. Yet, within all the photos, news stories, and blogs she read and researched, she noted a distinct lack of name mentioning except for those who'd started the clubs and were long since dead. It was as if even those reporting on the clubs and publishing their photographs were wary of going any further than that. And who could blame them? With that one-percent patch so prevalent, it wasn't like the clubs promised to play nice. But that made it difficult, because without a real name or identity, how else would she be able to track this guy down?

Zoë sat in the confines of the blue light and contemplated what to do while listening to Max snore in the bedroom. Other than a few random clients, there was only one biker that Zoë had ever gotten to know, a guy by the name of Luis Nieves who'd hung out at a biker bar down the street from her house when she was just a kid. At the time, he'd been a hang-around, one of those guys who wanted to eventually become a prospect and member, but Zoë seemed to recall that he eventually patched in. Many of the parents hated having that bar in the neighborhood back then, but Zoë had never experienced any trouble with the guys there. Just the opposite. Luis would often trail behind Zoë and her friends on his bike when they left school to ensure they made it home safely, and would even let Zoë sit on it and pretend to ride. He also came over to the house on occasion to talk to her mother and check things out when she didn't feel safe. It had been no secret—even to Zoë as a young girl—that Luis had developed a crush on her mother, but for reasons her mom never mentioned, their relationship never evolved.

Zoë hadn't paid much attention to the club logos then, but if memory served, she thought the bar had belonged to Los Salvajes. She wondered if Luis was still with them, and if so, if he could he tell her more about the man she was searching for, as well as the Devils.

She typed in his name but received over seven hundred potential matches. She narrowed down the search by listing *Reno* and an *A* between his first and last name. She couldn't remember his full middle name, but was certain of the letter. Adding those two items brought the matches down to just under fifty.

She briefly filtered through them. At the time Zoë had known him, Luis had been slightly younger than her mom, so that would make him in his late thirties or early forties now. The people-finder site listed each match's known age, addresses, and possible relatives, and given those, just three seemed to be a possibility, all named Luis A. Nieves. One still lived in Reno, one was in Carson City, and the third in Yuba City, California. The man in Carson City also had an arrest record, and after ordering his full background check from the website for less than twenty bucks, Zoë had his information in minutes: full name, family members, addresses past and present, arrests, and known affiliations.

It was the available mug shot that sealed the deal.

She tapped the computer. "There you are, Luis."

Luis Agustin Nieves, age forty-one, was a family man, with a wife and two kids, and a listed occupation as a mechanic. He had two previous arrests, for larceny and possession of narcotics, but appeared to have done his time, and now lived and worked in Carson City. But most importantly, Luis's affiliations made it clear that he was no longer a hang-around with Los Salvajes but a patched member known as Blade, the vice president for the Carson City chapter. In mafia terms, she thought that pretty much earned him the rank of a made man.

She shut the laptop and sat in the darkness of the room. The television broadcast the latest *Law and Order* rerun, and Max continued to snore. She glanced at her surroundings. Was this something she really wanted to pursue? Her life was on track. She had a great husband and kid. She didn't need to do this. Didn't need to open a door she may not be able to shut again.

And yet, that wingless hummingbird called to her.

And Luis, he might be able to help. Sure, he might also tell her to get lost, but if he did, she'd be no worse off than she was now. So, it couldn't hurt to at least go talk to him. *Right?*

CHAPTER 9

It had taken a bit to find one of Los Salvajes' hangouts in Carson City, but after spending an afternoon cruising the streets in her late-model, faded blue Toyota, Zoë was able to follow a couple of patched members until they arrived at a bar on the outskirts of town. It was little more than a wooden shack, really, a structure that looked like someone had built it by gathering various slabs of wood and nailing them all together, which was probably why it was named the Treehouse. It looked like one. Except, instead of being surrounded by long, leafy branches and blue sky, it was encircled by a crowd of black, silver, and chrome.

Zoë pulled the Toyota into the lot but parked well to the side of the establishment, near an empty lot filled with weeds and litter. It had been months since she'd driven the old car, but it seemed better to drive it here than her newer SUV, which would stick out like a sore thumb. The car had been her salvation for more than a year on the streets, purchased for nine hundred dollars, which proved to be quite a deal when she considered it had provided both transportation and shelter. Max kept telling her to get rid of it, but she couldn't let it go. It was like a trophy given to her for survival, a reminder of what she could do and could get through when life dealt the heavy blows.

A reminder she needed right now.

She slid out of the car and dusted herself off. She'd dressed for the heat but made sure to select nothing revealing as to not send the wrong message, choosing ripped jeans, boots, and a sleeveless top. All her arm tatts were on full display, but not the nose ring she sometimes wore, as she didn't want somebody pulling on it if she got into a confrontation. The few piercings she had were really for show anyway; her customers liked them more than she did.

Out front, a group of guys passed a football while various women hovered around. They weren't the kind of women Zoë typically associated with bikers—all big hair and leather—but looked more like herself. From what she'd read about the clubs, some women belonged to one guy and some were shared, but nonetheless, women were considered possessions, property of the club. The women who usually frequented these places were ones who wanted to eventually become a biker's old lady, which again, was not the message she wanted to convey. She just wanted to speak with Luis without causing any commotion.

But first, she had to find him, see if he was even here. Given the age of the mug shot, she wasn't sure if she would recognize him. It was her hope that, once inside, the bartender or other club monitor could point her in the right direction. This wasn't the kind of place you wanted to stand around in sizing people up.

As she approached the entrance, the guys stopped tossing the football, the women stopped talking, and all eyes turned to her—the stranger in their midst. She didn't cower or avoid eye contact, however, as she knew that would be a mistake. She couldn't show fear, even if her insides were melting like butter.

She gave them a brief nod as she opened the door, flinched a little as it slammed behind her harder than she expected, the result of a broken spring. Inside, you wouldn't even know it was the middle of the day given how dark it was, like a cave without sunlight. Yet, the place was packed, not an empty table in sight.

Her heart rammed against her chest wall as adrenaline coursed through her body, sparking fight-or-flight syndrome. In one ear she heard her telling herself to be bold and go forward, and in the other, Max's words of warning and utter horror if he could see where his wife now stood. That he would not be happy was putting it mildly.

She quickly took a seat at the end of the bar nearest the door. She didn't want to stare at people, nor did she want to sit with her back to the crowd, which would be setting herself up for a surprise attack. One pissed-off woman with a pull of Zoë's hair and she'd be down on the floor in an instant getting her ass kicked.

The bartender, an old man with the kind of sagging arm skin that said he'd once been into bodybuilding but had since given it up, broke her silent conversation. "What can I get you, miss?" He eyed her suspiciously, threw a towel over his shoulder.

"Beer. Bottle. Domestic. Cold."

He laughed a little at her mention of domestic. Popped the top off a bottle, set it on the counter. "Domestic is all we've got here, honey. We don't care for outsiders." He wiped his hands on the towel. "You want to pay now or run a tab?"

She put a five on the counter. Told him to keep it. She took a drink, letting the cold brew help relax the muscles in her throat and calm her nerves. Then, casually, she glanced around the bar. Several haggard faces had their sights fixated upon her, but she pretended not to see them as she scanned over the crowd and tried to identify Luis. It wasn't easy. These guys, with their beards, long hair, and similar attire, all sitting in the dark space, made it difficult to discern one from another.

She focused on those who looked important. The last time she'd seen Luis, he'd been little more than a hang-around, a scrawny young man. Now, he was a VP and a vital member of the club. Getting to him would be much tougher. There would be protectors all around. Not to mention his women, his property.

As if one of them had read her thoughts, a woman wearing a halter top and jeans sidled up next to Zoë at the bar. She was probably in her thirties but looked much older, with thick skin and dry dirty-blond hair. "I think you're in the wrong place, honey," she said. "This is Los Salvajes territory."

"I know. I'm looking for someone," Zoë said. "An old friend. I heard he was here."

The woman looked unconvinced. "Yeah? And who's that?"

"I think he goes by Blade. Back then, he went by Runner. His real name is Luis— Luis Nieves."

The woman clicked her tongue, cast her gaze into a distant corner. Zoë followed and watched it land on a far table where a lone man sat with three women. Although it had been years since she'd seen him in person, and his hair and beard had grayed, Zoë knew right away it was him. His eyes still held the same fixed expression that she remembered, and down his right arm, a tattoo of a serpent slithered through a skull. She'd forgotten about it until right then.

"That's him," Zoë said. "Can you tell him I need to talk?"

The woman slid off the stool. "Tell him yourself, honey. I ain't your bitch."

Zoë turned her attention back to the bar and took a few deep breaths before she took her beer in hand and wound through the tables. Luis, and the women surrounding him, watched precariously as she approached. Those at each table grew quiet as she passed until, finally, three men stood and blocked her way. She felt, more than saw, the others come up behind her until they had her circled.

The lead man in front—long face, angled jaw, green bandana—crossed his arms. "Where do you think you're headed?"

"I need to speak to Luis."

He looked at his brothers beside him. "Don't know anyone by that name."

"No? He's your VP." Zoë tilted her head around the beef standing next to him to catch a glimpse of Luis. "You don't remember me?"

A snap of the fingers, and the men cleared a path so he could see her. He visibly checked her out, running his eyes over the length of her body. "Should I?"

"No. I was just a kid the last time you saw me. I wanted to talk to you about a matter...about Bella."

He didn't respond, but he didn't have to. The way the corners of his eyes twitched, she could see he remembered.

"In private," she added.

He seemed to give it thought, took out a cigarette and lit it. Finally, he waved the women, and his brothers, away. "Give us a moment." His voice was gravelly, like he'd spent years eating dry chalk.

Zoë waited as the women reluctantly got up and joined others at the bar. When the men also returned to their own business, she took a chair and sat.

"I'm Zoë," she said. "Bella's daughter."

"Jesus, you're *that* kid?"

"Yeah."

He looked her up and down again. "Not anymore," he said and chuckled.

She flushed and briefly glanced away. The way he'd looked at her—like a piece of meat to devour—wasn't the way he'd once looked at her mom, but she guessed he was used to viewing women as property now, objects to possess.

"Yes, we've all grown older. Except my mother, of course. She's still dead," Zoë said. Her words came out more sharply than intended, and they caught his attention.

He inhaled on the cigarette, let out a trail of smoke. "Pretty hard to change that. Unless you're Jesus Christ." He flicked his ashes. "So what's this little impromptu visit about, Zoë, kid of Bella? You come here looking to ask me if I killed your mother, like those idiot cops did back in the day?"

She sat back. The question caught her off guard. "No. Of course not." She frowned. "They interrogated you?"

He huffed. "They interrogated everyone, all the club members. They suspected a biker might be involved after they found a riding glove near the house. Nice leather. The good stuff. And, well, we were in the neighborhood."

Zoë cocked her head. That was news to her. She'd never heard about a glove. She wondered what else the police might have in evidence that she didn't know about.

"That detective had a hard-on for us. Think he was disappointed when all our alibis checked out." He finished his beer and motioned to a guy near the bar to bring him another.

"And yet," Zoë said absently, "he might've been on to something."

Blade rapped his fingers on the table. "Yeah? Why's that? Because we're bikers, we must be rapists and killers too?" His raised voice caused several members to pay renewed attention.

Zoë snapped from her daze. "No. That's not what I meant." She took a glance over her shoulder, leaned in a little closer. "I don't think my mother was killed by a member of your club. But another club? Yes. In fact, I'm certain of it."

His eyes narrowed. "What makes you think so?"

She wondered if she should tell him, or just let it be. These were untrusting people, hardened men and women who didn't take kindly to others asking questions about a man's own business. What would he think of her taking pictures of a man's body and nosing into his personal life by investigating his tattoos? "I'd rather not say, not yet."

He grunted. "What is it you want with me, then? Why are you here?"

He was already growing impatient with her. She needed to get to the point. "Because, although I know what my mother's killer looks like, I don't know his name or how I can find him. And frankly, you're the only person I know who might be able to help me. You're in a motorcycle club, a one-percenter, and you know how the clubs operate. I need to understand that too. Not because I give a shit about what you do, but because I need to understand what role he plays for his club. If I can figure that out, then maybe I can figure out how to find him, and link him, somehow, to my mother's murder."

He smoked and waited. It was clear he wanted more information.

Zoë sighed. If she wanted help, she better start talking. "He came into my shop. I own a little tattoo place up in Reno. He wanted a new design, and I did it for him, but...he paid in cash so I don't know his name. He didn't come in wearing cuts, but he had the Devils' moniker and logo tattooed on his chest. And he had pitchforks on both shoulders, with a different color on each of the four prongs."

She took a deep breath. "I was hoping maybe you could tell me what you know about the Devils and how I could find him."

At that, the corners of Luis's eyes pulled and narrowed into thin slits. He took one long last draw on the cigarette, then snuffed it out. A cloud of smoke invaded the space between them. A guitar riff from an old ZZ Top song dominated the background.

"What makes you think I would know him? And even if I did, why would I tell you? I don't know you. So you're Bella's kid. I don't know where you've been the last ten years. What you really do. For all I know, you could be a cop. Or worse, a fed."

It was her turn to huff. "I am most definitely not a cop. I have no use for cops, or for any law enforcement, for that matter."

The guy Luis had motioned at the bar—younger, unshaven, hazel eyes—brought him a new beer, popped the cap. He asked Zoë if she wanted another. She shook her head. "I'm fine."

Luis eyed her. "What happened to you after the funeral?"

"The authorities stuck me in foster care, with a sweaty old man and woman in Sparks. I ran away. I joined up with others like me, lived on the streets. I spent three years avoiding the police. Now, like I said, I'm a tattoo artist. I have a shop in Reno. I have a husband and a son."

He took a long pull on the beer, set it down. "This husband of yours...does he know you're here asking questions about the Devils?"

She swallowed the lump in her throat. Just the mention of Max made her guilt manifest, as if she was here cheating on him. She felt her cheeks grow warm.

His eyes sparked. "No? I didn't think so."

He pulled on his beard, scratched the heavy scruff on his neck. "Listen. You seem like a nice girl, Zoë, so I'm going to give you some advice. I don't think you know what you're getting yourself into. This guy? If he has the ink you say, he isn't someone you want to go around asking questions about. He's high level. Protected. And the Devils? Their name is fitting. Understand?"

Zoë closed her eyes. Of course, he would say that, and she knew he was right, yet how could she live with herself if she didn't pursue justice for her mother? To Zoë, walking away from this would feel like she was killing her mother all over again.

"But I have to. I can't let it go. I can't stop thinking..." She bit her lip.

Luis shifted in his seat. He glanced out at his fellow members, lit another cigarette, seemed to consider her plight. "Look, what reason do you have to think this guy killed Bella?" His voice scratched like an old record.

She scanned the grim faces at the other tables, all of them pretending to be in conversations of their own but very much watching the interaction occurring between her and their VP. She could imagine Luis laughing when she told him of the tattoos, then the others joining in, all at her expense, but what choice did she have? If she didn't give him something, this conversation would end.

"It's his tattoos," she said. "His entire back? It's dedicated to death." She proceeded to tell him about the pale horse and its rider, the images of the animals surrounding it, including the hummingbird.

"I know how crazy it sounds, but I've already linked three other murder victims to the images surrounding the horse and the dates inscribed. Given time, I can probably locate more. I understand this guy is connected, but Luis..."

"Blade. Call me Blade."

"Okay, Blade...this guy isn't just doing bidding for some motorcycle club. I mean, I'm sure he does that too; in fact, again, I know he does, but, this man? He's a rapist and a killer of women. And maybe I'm wrong, but I don't think this club, or any club, would be on board with that."

He again tapped on the table, cigarette burning between his fingers. She could see her story had piqued his interest, but the hardened muscles in his face gave her the sense an internal conflict was brewing. He turned to her. "Let's say you find this guy. Maybe you can prove he killed Bella, maybe you can't...but you know the truth, just the same. Then what will you do?"

Zoë stared at him, felt her heart skip, her emotions swell. She shook her head.

He nodded. "That's what I thought."

Amid the silence that followed, the sounds surrounding them took over: an old Metallica song playing in the background, the clink of a glass, a burst of laughter. Blade studied her for what seemed an eternity before he spoke.

"Listen, Zoë. I feel your pain, but what's done is done. Go home to your kid. Leave it alone. Trust me. The Devils and this guy? He's bad fucking news. The worst kind of news. You don't want to invite trouble with him. If this man killed Bella and he gets wind of you nosing around? You'll earn yourself a trip to the desert in a hurry. And not just you either...your husband and your son."

He pushed his graying shoulder-length hair away from his face, and when his eyes met hers this time, they were softer—empathetic, even. "It sounds like you have a nice life. And after what you've been through, you deserve it. I understand you wanting to get justice for Bella. I do. These guys," he said, motioning to the other tables, "they'd stop at nothing if one of our own was taken out. But we have numbers and... methods. You? You're not up to this."

She sighed, feeling a heavy weight descend. She knew he was right—Max would tell her the same—and yet, it made her so very angry. She felt just as she had after informing Detective Sloane of her theories and him verbally patting her on the head before sending her on his way. She was tired of being a woman, sick of not being taken seriously, pissed off at being dismissed.

"So, you won't help me? That's what you're saying?" she asked, her voice clipped.

"I am helping. I'm trying to save you," he said.

She abruptly pushed away from the table, causing the chair to scrape against the floor and everyone in the place to go rigid. She took three steps toward the door but couldn't make herself leave. Not yet. She turned back, unable to help herself. Couldn't stop what she was about to say.

"Just one thing," Zoë said. "What you said about your guys stopping at nothing for one of their own? You should know, this guy, he has another tattoo you might find interesting. It's of a green pig with a crown wearing the number twelve-twenty-three, and it's strange, because that pig, it looks a whole lot like your logo. Except in this one—the pig has been sliced up like a dinner ham and the devil behind him is taking a bite."

She took a step back.

Blade glanced up. He didn't say a word, but he didn't have to.

The beer bottle in his grip exploded.

CHAPTER 10

A t midnight, the Lone Horseman left the motel he was currently staying at off I-5 near Sacramento and headed out. He was due to meet Maverick, the president of the Northern California chapter of the club, in thirty minutes at their hangout just north of the city, and he was running late. On the phone, Maverick had sounded concerned, and promised to have the club cleared of other members so they could speak in private. Like the rest of the chapter boards spread throughout their territory, Mav didn't care to make the Horseman's presence known unless absolutely necessary. Members of the Devils knew of his existence, and many had seen him at club functions on occasion, but who he was and what he did for the club was best kept secret. It was why he rarely wore his cuts or joined in multi-club gatherings. As the national president's special enforcer, he, and they, preferred he remained in the shadows. It was his job to take care of things even the most ruthless of club-level enforcers couldn't stomach and keep the distance between deeds done and the club. This kept the Devils' members where they belonged—out on the streets earning. Plus, if anyone ever got pinched and the feds put the squeeze on them for information, they wouldn't have anything good to talk about. The less the members knew, the better.

You couldn't rat without the cheese.

The fog sat low across the largely silent highway as he arrived at his exit, where he headed west into densely forested terrain. The clubhouse was located where the trees climbed fifty feet tall and blocked the sunlight even at the height of day, so the drive at night was pitch black. His lone headlight wound down the road and around the curves, with only the luminescent eyes of deer and owls to see it.

The single-level ranch home that the NorCal president owned was equipped with military-level security, so Mav would know when he arrived. If any enemy—be it government or club rival—ever tried a sneak attack on NorCal, they would be in for a surprise. The place had eyes above and all around, with homemade explosives planted one hundred yards out in every direction just waiting to be triggered. To the best of their knowledge, no one in law enforcement had ever attempted to visit the place—at least not the ones dressed in their blues and grays.

The UCs, or undercovers, however, that was another matter, and what the Lone Horseman suspected Mav wanted to discuss tonight—the latest rumor that the Devils had been infiltrated by the DEA.

Three miles later, he drove up the foggy, dark drive and guided his hog around back. Maverick opened the door and stood there grinning, AK-47 in hand.

If there was a man the Horseman would call an equal, Mav was it. At six-foot-two with a bald head, slits for eyes, and a beard cut in the shape of a V, he looked every bit of the namesake on his cut. Like him, Mav was the guy people didn't so much part for as run in the opposite direction when they saw him coming. The two of them had met three decades ago while playing music in the Seattle grunge scene, and had become fast friends. They knew damn near everything about each other, right down to the whiskey they drank and the women they screwed. The Lone Horseman even suspected that Maverick knew of his outside activities with his prized ladies—although he'd never mentioned it.

"Brother, good to see you," Mav said.

They slapped each other on the back and went inside. Although it had been a few months since the Horseman had been here, the place smelled like it always did, somewhere between a bar, brothel, and garage, with beer, urine, and oil-soaked rags blending into one aroma. Cases of booze pilfered from the latest grab-n-go filled the back room, and enough guns and ammo to supply a small army occupied a large closet. The club was an add-on to the main house that, like the living and dining room inside, was covered in seventies-style dark paneling. Neon signs and club memorabilia decorated the walls.

"Quiet night," he said, examining the cue sticks lying silent across the pool table nearby and no music playing from the speakers.

"We held church earlier. Sent everybody home afterward."

That explained the pile of pizza boxes in the trash ready to be discarded.

"Come on. Let's go in the house," Mav said.

Inside, Mav's old lady, Vero, short for Veronica, sat on one of the couches while smoking a cigarette and watching reruns of some reality show on her computer. The Horseman started to take a seat at the table before he noticed a change in the house. The room still contained the same furniture, but the floor had recently been replaced. "You doing a little remodeling?"

Maverick grunted. Vero raised an eyebrow. "It wasn't planned," she said. "We had a little...accident."

The Horseman nodded. In other words, somebody got their ass kicked with a finality that required the evidence to be disposed of. "Shit happens."

He followed Mav to the kitchen, where the president offered him a beer.

"So how was church? Good sermon?"

"Mostly. Things are running smoothly north of the border, and we're making headway in Reno. Up twenty grand just in the last week. Sparks alone could double our profits."

The Horseman grunted. "Angels and Los Salvajes won't be happy us infringing on their territory and taking their cut. You expecting retaliation?"

His friend showed a wicked mouthful of capped teeth and smiled. "I sure hope so."

They shared a laugh. The truth was, any chance of spilling blood made both of them happy. Maverick didn't feel alive any more than he did unless he was fighting and killing.

"We're planning to head down again next week."

"Back to Reno?" the Horseman asked, a little surprised.

"Yep. You game?"

He thought for a moment, taking a pull on the beer. He didn't usually circle back to a city for a time after he'd taken one of his prized ladies, but all indications said his case was as cold as a six-pack. And if it meant the chance at more blood... "Sure. I'm in. We running protection?"

"That and..." Mav's face darkened. He took a seat at the table, lit a cigarette. "We got that other thing."

The Horseman joined him, nodded. "So, it's true? Been verified?"

"Unfortunately. UC and DEA puppet."

The Horseman checked out Vero, who was engrossed in her television show and now smoking a joint instead of a cigarette. He didn't normally discuss such business in front of anyone except the chapter board, but Vero kept the club's activity logs for national as well as NorCal, so there wasn't much that got by her. She had the entire history of the club documented for the last twenty-five years. "We know who it is?"

Maverick popped a beer for himself, then brought out a large manila envelope. He took a couple of photographs out, slid them across the table toward the Horseman. "I got friends back East, near Richmond, Virginia. A month ago, they tell me one of our recent patch-ins looks a whole lot like a guy who used to be affiliated with the Outlaws there. Word was he took a slide one night and died. They held a funeral, then two weeks later? The arrests began. So, what we're thinking is, this guy? It looks like he's very much alive."

He tapped one of the photographs, then the other. "This is him then, and now."

The Horseman picked up both photographs, studied the features in the man's face absent of facial and other hair. He had a high forehead, wide-set eyes, and an angular nose that crooked to one side, like it'd been broken a time or two. The long hair and full beard he wore previously with the Outlaws worked well to hide his true features, but he couldn't hide his body. He had a long torso with arms like a swimmer, and large hands, the kind that could palm a basketball with no trouble.

"Yeah. Same guy," the Horseman said. "Raised from the dead. Hallelujah." He fixed the man's face to memory. "Who sponsored him?"

"Sergeant at arms in Yuba City. Guy played himself up as an enforcer and proved to be well connected in the trade. He negotiated several deals in the area."

The Horseman huffed. "That should've raised a red flag. DEA can get their hands on all the merch they need and the names to go with it. If a deal goes down too easy, they should always suspect a trap."

Mav sighed. "I know. And the sergeant and chapter prez feel like shit. They saw an opportunity for big gains and took it. But both said they conducted a full proctology on this guy and put him through hell as a prospect, and the guy passed."

The Horseman slapped the photographs on the bar. "DEA is getting better and better with the backgrounds. Full IDs, work history, even adding felonies and prison time to the records. Scumbags."

"Yeah, they are."

"Will he be in Reno next week?"

"Unless he gets word that we know something, he should be there. Word is his handler is out of Reno too, so they might try to meet up. If you can find out who's running the op, that would be good knowledge to have."

He lit up a new cigarette, exhaled smoke toward the ceiling already stained a deep yellow. "You should know, the sergeant begged me to do the deed himself, but I said no. It would be too obvious for the DEA to look at him, so, like always, we'll need a solid story in place for him and Yuba City. Also, I don't know how much the feds have gathered, but I need you to get what you can out of the UC before you take care of the matter."

The Horseman matched Mav's smoke with his own. "Anything specific?"

"Main concern is that they took him to Vacaville a few times. I'm working to move the lab but it could take time. As you know, we've got one hell of an op there. Also, I suspect our routes and distribution methods may've been comprised."

The Horseman nodded. The Devils' main income came from meth, which was why the DEA was always trying to get their foot in the door. He'd delight in finding this guy and giving him his just due. "Consider it done."

Vero started laughing as two women on the show she was watching started fighting. "Damn crazy bitches," she said. "You should see this. It's funny."

Maverick and the Horseman weren't sure if it was the show making her laugh or the weed, but joined her watching the crazy white women scratch, claw, and pull each other's hair. The rest of the night, they drank, smoked, and it seemed like old times, when the Horseman used to hang out with Maverick and A.J.—now the Devils' national president—back in the day. It was crazy to think how far the three of them had come with the Devils in thirty years. Tonight, he'd reminisce with them, then tomorrow, he'd ride back to Reno, the scene of his last, and apparently, future crime.

CHAPTER 11

O ne of Zoë's clients was nice enough to offer her his ex-wife's motorcycle—a silver-and-black V Star custom that was known to be popular with women for its low center of gravity and seat height—to practice learning to ride. Those familiar with the motorcycle clubs told her it wasn't necessary for a woman to ride, but Zoë wasn't going to take a chance on being labeled a pass-around if she decided to infiltrate the Devils and seek out the man who'd come in her shop on her own. When trying to make inroads with the members of an outlaw club, she wanted to appear as an experienced biker. Her hope was to pose as a member of one of the women-only clubs looking to partner with the Devils on some new action. She also just wanted to understand the allure of riding a motorcycle.

Her client, a suburban school teacher and father, had volunteered to take the bike out for her and teach her to ride, but Zoë lied and told him she used to ride and thought she'd be able to get back up to speed once she got back on the proverbial horse. She didn't know why, but she preferred to learn new things on her own. Still, she promised to take the bike out to the country roads where it, and she, wouldn't get run over if she took a spill. So, nice guy he was, he helped her load the bike in the back of Max's truck, which Zoë had borrowed under the guise of helping a friend move some furniture, and waved her off as she backed out of the drive.

She drove out of the city to a place where the roads were flat and ran in straight lines between farm fields and pastures. Here, only a few houses dotted the landscape— the cows and horses more prevalent than people—so if she made a fool of herself, only they would see. After she parked the truck, she propped a wooden ramp against the bed and rolled the bike off. She was careful to lean its weight toward her, as her friend had instructed to keep it under control, yet even as it moved, she could feel the weight and wondered if it was going to be too much for her to handle.

Once she got it out to the middle of the road, she straddled it and rocked it back and forth. When it felt comfortable, she made sure it was in neutral and started the engine. The bike hummed, ready to go. She revved it a few times, liked the sound it made. She put on the helmet after pulling up the bandana she wore around her neck to cover her nose and mouth. The roads here were dry and dusty, and she didn't care to eat a mouthful of dirt.

Settled in, she took inventory, tried to remind herself of the function of each of the bike's features. Left foot gear shift, left hand clutch, right foot brake, right hand throttle. Oh, and don't forget the lights, turn signals, and front brake. The thought of controlling all these parts while also paying attention to the road, signals, and traffic around her seemed overwhelming, but she'd driven cars with manual transmissions before, and thousands of people rode motorcycles, so how hard could it be?

She revved it a few times, then let go of the throttle, pushed down for first gear, and released the clutch slowly until the bike began to roll. She didn't want to gain any speed initially, or even bring her feet up to the foot pegs, just wanted to let it roll and basically walk with it down the street.

She made it a few feet until she popped the clutch and the bike stalled. She set it back to neutral, started the engine, tried again. Popped it again. On the third try, though, she found the sweet spot and let it roll all the way down the country road. The few cows she passed glanced up, chewing their cud. At the end of the lane, she stopped and turned it around, then came back the same way, passing the same cows. But this time, she put her feet on the pegs and handled the bike at a slow pace, getting a feel for it.

Now feeling more confident, she decided to add a little throttle and see if she could kick it up into second gear. She started down the road and had it rolling well before she turned the throttle, but made the mistake of adding too much. The bike lurched forward, and suddenly, it felt like she was riding a horse trying to kick her off its back. A little yelp escaped her mouth, but she held on as she wobbled down the road like a kid riding a bike without training wheels for the first time.

At the other end of the lane, she braked and tried turning in the width of an intersection without stopping. It was harder than expected, and she found herself going across part of a man's lawn before she maneuvered it back to the street. That's when she noticed an old man sitting on the porch, rocking in his chair, and chuckling through the few teeth he had left.

She waved and muttered her apologies as she headed down the lane once again. At the other end, she attempted another U-turn. This one turned out better, but she still swung too wide, taking out a few cornstalks. It seemed, at slower speeds, the handlebars moved the front wheel effortlessly, but as the speed increased, the handlebar didn't require so much a turn as it did a push.

As she increased the speed and the bike felt more manageable in first gear, she let the speed increase until she could hear it want to change gears. She squeezed the clutch, pushed her left foot, heard it click into second, but found herself pressing on the right hand brake as well. This whole coordination of left hand, right hand, left foot was proving most difficult. Every time she wanted to move one hand or foot, she wanted to repeat the same action on the other side, which caused the bike to start and stop in fits, not knowing what the hell she wanted it to do. She stopped and let the engine idle to give it a rest.

She took off the helmet, pulled down the bandana, and took in air.

Jesus, I suck at this.

At the other end of the road where she'd parked Max's truck, she saw a bike pull up next to it, chrome glinting in the Reno sun. At first, she thought maybe it was her client, but the motorcycle was far too slick to be his, a custom Harley of some kind. She couldn't tell who it was, but as she started the bike and inched closer, he began to clap, a slow measure meant not exactly to praise but at least give credit for trying. The long graying hair and Los Salvajes cuts gave him away. It was Blade.

She took off the dark sunglasses she wore, squinted. "The man I borrowed it from swore it was a chick's bike," she said.

He sized it up. "It is that."

"Then why does it feel like work? My muscles are already shaking. Riding two, three hundred, miles on this? Excuse my language, but I won't feel my vagina for weeks."

She cringed as she slid her leg over the seat and parked the helmet on the back.

He laughed, that same odd growl she'd heard in the Treehouse.

She took off her gloves, laid them on the seat. "Surprised to see you out here in the middle of nowhere. Just happen to be passing through?"

He checked out the surrounding fields. "Something like that."

She noticed off in the distance, a second rider acting as sentry near the turnoff. "Is there a purpose to this visit?" she asked. "Maybe you have some information for me?"

He slid his sunglasses on top of his head so she could see his eyes. He took out a pack of cigarettes, offered her one. She shook her head. He put them back in his pocket. Lit one. "Not so much information as, say, a proposition. Your little revelation the other day caused a bit of a stir within the club, although I'm guessing that's what you intended."

She kicked the dirt with her boot. "I may have overstepped."

He grunted. "No, honey, you didn't overstep. You marched right in and took a dump in the middle of the floor."

She took a deep breath, glanced away. *Well, that was one way of putting it.* "So that tattoo of his, it's what I think? One of yours?"

"Yeah. Modesto, two years ago. The vice president. You don't want to hear the details. Suffice to say the ink you described does it justice. And the pig on his back, that belongs to the Riverside president's former old lady. I don't have to tell you he's putting pressure on me for your name. He wants information."

"But I don't have it," Zoë said. "That's the point. That's why I came to you."

"Well...you got our attention." He inhaled deeply, let the smoke trail out slow and smooth. "Seems your problem is our problem. Thing is, you know what this guy looks like. We don't."

She squinted, confused. "How can that be? I thought all you club members crossed paths from time to time? When I told you about his ink, the pitchforks and the colors, you reacted like you knew who he was. You must know something about him. I can't be the only one who's encountered him."

"Just because I know *of* him doesn't mean I *know* him. What I do know is this— they call him the Lone Horseman, which explains the tattoo on his back that you described, and because he's just that—a loner. Quiet, he works in the shadows, like a ghost. The Devils, they get involved in shit that make us and the Angels look like Boy Scouts. They need someone to clean up their messes. Word is, he's the guy. But he keeps his distance from the club. Rarely wears his cuts, especially when he's doing business, and only makes appearances when necessary. Make no mistake though, he's a Devil, and a high-ranking one."

Zoë walked around the bike, the heat suddenly getting to her. Without a breeze, and with the sun beating down and Blade's news, it felt like one hundred degrees. She rubbed the back of her neck where the sweat pooled. "Great. So basically, he's an assassin. How am I supposed to go up against that?"

Blade snuffed his cigarette beneath his boot, then removed a small tin can, stuffed an ounce of chew between his gums. The guy had a serious nicotine addiction. "You don't."

She stopped circling. "What are you proposing?"

"A trade. You want to see justice for your mother. We want justice for Modesto and Riverside. You help us find him, we'll help you deliver."

The way he said *deliver* left her cold, even in the searing heat. "How so?"

He cocked his head as if she was crazy for asking such a question. "That's not for you to worry about. First we have to find him, then we have to see if there's enough evidence for the club to issue a ruling. If what you say is true, that this guy has killed as many as you say, there's going to be a whole lot of people who want a piece of him, including law enforcement far and wide. But you have to know, a bunch of tattoos and some made-up stories aren't going to be the evidence they need to pull this guy from the streets and convict him."

"I didn't make them up. The victims are real," she snapped.

"I believe you. But will the cops? The DAs? More importantly, who will watch your back while they're working to gather evidence? This guy has connections—whether he's in a prison cell or out of one. He hasn't survived not getting caught this long because he's careless."

"So you're just going to, what? Cut him up and bury him in the desert?"

"Let's not get ahead of ourselves." He spit a wad of chew on the ground, scraped it under his boot like it was a cockroach. "Look, I've thought of a way to help you get close to the Devils. Given who he is, the only way you'll have a chance of seeing him again is to go straight to the top, and that ain't easy. But you might have a way in, because the president of NorCal is also the national VP, and his old lady, Vero, she's an ink slinger. A tattoo artist just like yourself. She's also the club's historian. Keeps track of the ancestry, the runs, the routes—you get my drift? You get in, you make friends..." He shrugged. "What you do from there is up to you."

Zoë studied him. Despite what he did for a living—which she imagined involved drugs, guns, and other things best not known—there was something trustworthy about Blade that she didn't always get from other people. It was a genuineness that told you, even if you didn't like what he was saying, you could at least take it as the truth.

She paced, kicked at the dirt, thought. Keeping in line with her real occupation seemed a far better option than pretending to be a part of some chick biker club, which they would probably see through in an instant. "How do I get in?"

"I have a prospect no one in the Devils has ever met. He's never been on runs where we've crossed paths, never been to multi-club gatherings. He's an unknown. Next weekend, there's a music festival outside of Vegas that many of the clubs will attend. We'll be there too, but he can go as a citizen, with you as his girlfriend. You look over the crowd, find your targets, start a conversation."

Zoë stared. "Dude, I can't be someone's girlfriend. I've got a husband, a kid."

He held up his hand. "I know. I'm saying, you'll pretend. My prospect will know why you're there, and he'll help you make contact. But...can't rule out some kissing and touching. I mean, you got to make it look real. Otherwise, these guys will smell a rat, and believe me, you don't want to see what they do to rats."

She glanced across the landscape of crops and pastures, wondered what the hell she was getting herself into. Bikers, boyfriends, undercover work. Plus, she'd have to find an excuse to go to the concert and spend a weekend away from Max and Oliver, and she already felt terrible lying to him about needing to borrow his truck to move furniture. This wouldn't just be her putting her ass out there, she could be putting her marriage on the line.

She glanced at Blade, bit her lip. "I don't know."

"You wanted a way in. This is what I can offer." The wind blew his hair and the sun burned his already baked skin. "That and...I can help you with this girly bike. He knelt and looked over the chain, touched it to see how much slack was in it. "Jesus, how long has it been since somebody has ridden this thing? It's pathetic."

Zoë laughed. She wasn't sure what she was agreeing to, but if it would get her inside the Devils, closer to the president and a chance to find the Lone Horseman, then she had to do it. "Okay, it's a deal."

He smiled, brought his sunglasses back down to cover his eyes. "Good girl." He started the bike, told her to hop on. "Now, about this lack of coordination you have. You ever play drums? No, I didn't think so. Okay, so this, this is a throttle..."

CHAPTER 12

That weekend, after Max decided to take Oliver fishing for the day, Zoë drove over to her client's house to switch out her SUV for the motorcycle, then took a ride down to Carson City. Blade had contacted her and asked her to come to the Treehouse to meet his prospect and talk over plans for the following week. Zoë couldn't believe she was actually considering trying to infiltrate the Devils, but the more she thought about it, the more she thought it might be possible. Because of her job, she was good at making chitchat, and unless this Vero was one cold fish, Zoë should easily be able to start a conversation with her. The woman would have no reason to think Zoë, as a fellow ink slinger, held any hidden agenda. She'd just consider Zoë some random girl at the concert, one of thousands. And for whatever reason, people had always inherently trusted her. Maybe because, as Max had once said, she always met people wherever they were at in life, and expected no more or no less of them.

Blade's lessons on the bike had proved immensely helpful, and Zoë felt fairly confident riding it now, but she still kept her speed at sixty on the highway. Yet, even at that, she had to admit that riding it was exhilarating. Unlike driving a car, which felt like a separation from nature, being on the bike made her feel like she was a part of it. The open air and views without restrictions made her forget everything and just enjoy the ride.

At least until she got to the bar, when reality came rushing back.

Like she'd done before, she parked off to the side and cut the engine. There weren't as many people hanging out in the parking lot this time, but there were dozens of additional motorcycles, many with California plates. It looked like some of the other clubs had come up for the week.

Once again, heads turned and stares persisted as the patrons watched this unknown girl enter their domain. The place was packed even more than before and, as she'd surmised, was filled with members from other chapters, including Riverside,

Chino, Fresno, and Bakersfield. They surrounded the bar and a table in back, where it appeared an arm-wrestling tournament was underway. Prospects popped beers and restocked as fast as they could while bets were made and won or lost.

After searching the crowd, Zoë saw Blade sitting with a woman at a corner table. Noticing her, he motioned her over. Zoë joined them, but not before the woman, who turned out to be his old lady, issued Zoë a glance that stated she didn't appreciate the interruption. Still, after a whispered urging from her husband, she slid from her chair so he and Zoë could discuss their business. As Zoë sat, Blade whistled to the same guy he'd commanded during their previous visit. He was about six feet tall with sandy-brown hair and hazel eyes, and when Blade spoke, he ceased everything he was doing and focused on his leader.

"Get us a round and join us."

"Are you sure? It's damn busy—"

"I need you to sit in on this. It's important."

Asking no more questions, he retrieved the beers, notified his fellow bartenders of his new orders, and sat. Blade made the introductions. "This here is Riot, my latest prospect. Riot, this is Zoë. She's the girl I told you about."

Riot gave her a once-over. "The tattoo artist?"

She nodded, returned the examination. With his permanent five-o'clock shadow and firm build, he was a decent-looking guy for being among such a tough crowd— not yet worn and leathered like his patched comrades—but Zoë guessed that would come with time and deeds served.

"Blade said you're looking for somebody? You think he killed your mother?"

She wasn't sure how much Blade had told his prospect about her situation or the man they were hunting, and didn't want to say more than she should, so simply answered, "That's right."

"What do you know about him?" Riot asked.

Blade answered. "In reality, not a damn thing, but I can tell you what I've heard. He goes by the name of the Lone Horseman. Rides alone and is rarely seen, although he's a fully patched, high-ranking member of the Devils. Word is he's their top enforcer, and I don't mean bar bouncer and fist-fighter. Nobody I know knew what he looked like..." He motioned at Zoë. "Until now."

Riot took a drink, licked a spot of missed effort from his upper lip. "No offense, but he's not one of ours. Why do we care?"

Blade's dark eyes flickered like a match struck. "Because I say we care." He lit a cigarette and stared at Riot to make sure he got the message—he was a prospect and wasn't to question, only obey. "Although, in this case, we may also have our own interest in this guy—that little problem in Modesto we had a couple years back."

Riot straightened. "No shit?"

Several men shouted around the arm-wrestling tournament as two guys were sweating it out. Biceps popped, veins bulged, and teeth gritted as the locked hands teetered one way, then another.

"If that's so, that mean-ass chihuahua over there would be damn interested to hear that," Riot said.

Zoë glanced over to the brown-skinned man whose solid black hair jutted out beneath a hat. His gaze was set firmly upon her, as if she held a secret. A label on the front of his jacket said *President*, his back rocker, *Modesto*.

"He would, but he's not to know," Blade said. "Not yet. Word of this...situation gets out before we have our facts in hand, we'll have a war on our hands. Understand, what we talk about today, it stays right here—for now."

"What about Spike and Lizard?" Riot asked.

"Spike knows. The president knows everything. He also knows how delicate this matter could be. It has to be handled correctly, got it?" Blade said this more toward Riot than Zoë, but she got the intended message: if word got out, unnecessary blood could spill, including possibly her own.

She took a long, cold drink of the beer. She could feel the sweat pool against her neck.

Riot looked at her. "Why do you think this guy killed your mother?"

Zoë glanced from him to Blade, silently asking if it was okay to share, as it hadn't taken long for her to understand she needed to run everything she said or did by him first. She was in a culture with rules she didn't understand, and navigating outside them could have consequences. Better to be safe and all that.

Blade nodded once.

She proceeded to inform him about the Lone Horseman and his tattoos. The more she told him, the more he drank, and the more he drank, the more slack his skin became.

She took out her phone, went through the photographs. "The hummingbird, horse, and eagle? I've identified those victims. And, of course, the tiger, the image he had me add in Reno. As far as the numbers, the middle three represent the date they died, the first two indicate the state, and the last two, the order in which they were killed. The tiger was number fourteen."

Riot stared with his mouth agape, looking like she'd just hit him with a cast-iron skillet, or maybe a brick. "Jesus Christ," he said. He sat back, rubbed his face, appeared uncertain. "Is this shit for real?"

"The tattoos don't lie, man," Blade said.

"You're saying this guy is a serial killer? Dude, this should go to the cops. Why should we keep this?"

He nodded at the phone. "Show him the pig."

Zoë took a deep breath, pulled up the image of the slaughtered animal, the devil behind it gloriously smiling with a forkful of meat headed into his mouth. Knowing where, and who, she sat among, her hands shook as she showed it to him.

He leaned over to see it better in the light, wiped his mouth as he issued a string of words that even made Blade sit up and take notice. When he turned away, he lowered his head and pulled at fistfuls of his hair, as if he was mentally trying to work it out. Finally, he came to.

"Guess you weren't kidding. Okay, what's the plan? What do you need me to do?"

"You take Zoë with you to the festival in Vegas next week. You can ride with us, but when we get there, you go out on your own, no cuts. You hang out, find the Devils, help Zoë get in. Act interested in becoming a hang-around for them, maybe talk to some of the members. Let Zoë get a look and see if she sees our guy."

"Hey, if he ain't wearing a shirt, I'll find him myself."

Blade took a long drink of his latest beer. "My guess is, he'll be hard to find. He has to be careful where's he seen—with, and certainly without—his shirt. No way he goes exposed when multiple clubs are present unless he has a death wish."

He took out his phone, pulled up a photograph, and set it between them. "This is the Devils' NorCal president and his old lady. He's known as Maverick. Veronica is her name, but she goes by Vero. "I know you'll want to get information, but I think it's best you go slow with her," he said, his attention now focused on Zoë. "Don't push. The minute you think she's suspicious, back off. She's not going to give you info without first establishing trust."

He put the phone back in his pocket. "You two won't hang out at our camp at the festival, but we'll be there looking out. Anything goes wrong, I'll be a phone call or text away. Got it?"

"What will you tell the club about why I'm not in camp?" Riot asked. He looked disappointed that he wouldn't be able to prominently display his loyalty to the club.

"I'll tell them you're on a mission for us. A little undercover action."

Riot turned to Zoë. "That's it, then. I'm Tom Cruise on a mission impossible with my main sidekick, Zoë. Do we get any of those great gadgets they have? Exploding devices? Lipreading technology? X-ray vision?" He raised his eyebrows up and down. "Make sure the ladies aren't hiding any weapons?"

Blade shook his head, slapped the man on the back. He looked at Zoë. "That's why we call him Riot, because he's so damn funny." He turned to the members and shouted out: "Who wants to hear a joke from Riot?"

"Tell us a joke, Riot."

He flushed a little, realizing he'd walked right into that.

He stood up. "Knock, knock," he yelled.

"Who's there?" they shouted.

"Mustache."

"Mustache who?"

"Mustache you a question, but I'll shave it for later."

The crowd groaned and threw their cigarettes and beer bottles at him. Zoë couldn't help but laugh. Well, at least if she had to ride with someone, it would be someone with a sense of humor.

CHAPTER 13

Detective Brady Sloane was halfway through a breakfast of steak and eggs at his favorite diner when his peaceful morning was interrupted by the most annoying of voices, Special Agent Quinn of the DEA. The stocky, hyper man saddled up on a stool next to him and ordered a coffee, black, and something called avocado toast. Sloane gave him a sideways glance. "Avocado toast? I thought that was for yoga instructors and hippies."

"I turn fifty this year. Got to keep fit, watch what I eat," Quinn said, tapping his abs. He hooked a thumb at Sloane's plate. "I see you still prefer the heart-attack special."

Sloane grunted. "You sound like my wife, all quinoa and granola. Since she's gone vegetarian, the only time I get a decent meal anymore is when I eat out." He wiped his mouth with a napkin, pushed the rest of the plate away. "What's on your mind, Quinn? Couldn't wait for the office to open?"

"No. I don't trust discussing sensitive matters in there anymore." He rubbed his hands as if he was washing them without soap and water. The energy bouncing off him was palpable, like hail on a windshield, and equally destructive. "I've got a bad feeling, and I don't know what to do about it."

Sloane frowned. "What's going on?"

"My UC in NorCal is missing. We were supposed to meet up this week, but he didn't show. Hasn't called or checked in either. Last time I heard from him was over a week ago, and the Devils, they rode down this week and stopped here, so he should've been with them. But no one has seen him, and I'm damn nervous."

Sloane felt a darkness crawl over him. Quinn had a solid operation running in California and spoke highly of his UC's work within the Devils' motorcycle club. Sloane had met the man twice, and he seemed like a pro, detailed and reliable. Still, it wasn't unheard of for a UC to go quiet. "Maybe he's keeping a low profile, worried someone is tracking him. You said yourself, he's got great instincts."

"He does, but he normally at least sends a text." He sipped his coffee and Sloane noted the shake in his hand. "You don't have any John Doe's in your morgue, do you?"

"No. Damn. Don't think like that."

More hand wringing. "Sorry. I hope he's just being careful, but even if that's the case, it isn't good news. Better than the alternative, but it still means he thinks someone might've made him, and that isn't good. The Devils find out he's a UC, they will kill him. So, if he is naked and out in the desert, I have to find him and pull him out. It will mean two years of work busted all to hell, but he's too valuable to risk."

"Do you have enough to go at the Devils now?" Sloane asked. "Make some arrests, cause some disruption in the ranks? Wouldn't hurt to try if that's your only option. Someone might talk."

"Yeah, yeah, yeah," Quinn mumbled as he chewed his toast. A smattering of avocado stained his lip. He nodded at the waitress as she held up the coffeepot. She refilled his cup.

Sloane studied his friend. Quinn was always paranoid, but he was definitely more strung out than usual. "I tell you what. You say the Devils are in town? That means they're probably headed down to that big club-sponsored metal fest outside Vegas. I'll put my feelers out there with my CIs, tell them to keep their eyes and ears open."

Quinn slapped him on the back. "I appreciate it." He finished off his toast, chased it with coffee. "Oh, one other thing I wanted to bring your attention. One of our other undercovers reports that a new girl has been hanging around Los Salvajes' clubhouse of late down in Carson City. Says she always talks to Blade, the VP there. His real name is Luis Nieves. You remember him? He was a member of the Reno chapter before moving south."

Sloane glanced up. "Nieves? Yeah, we had a few run-ins with him but nothing serious, as I recall."

"He was a suspect in your Bella case, though, wasn't he?"

Sloane thought, nodded. "I had him in my sights for a time, but it was a longshot."

"Well, what proved interesting was...the girl at the bar? UC said her name was Zoë. So, of course, I had to look into her. She's a tattoo artist here in Reno, runs a little shop near the university. Her name is Zoë Cruse now, but you probably remember her as Zoë Jansen?" He took out a roughly printed picture his UC had taken at the bar and slid it over to Sloane.

The name made Sloane do a double take, and a pain pierced his gut. "Jansen? As in Bella Jansen?" He examined the grainy picture. "This is Bella's daughter?"

Quinn cocked his head. "Don't know for sure, but how many can there be?"

Sloane stared at the image, the oblong face, the long brunette hair, the dark-brown eyes with lashes like feathers. It wasn't a great picture, but those eyes left no doubt. "You think she's working with LS? Doing what, running meth?"

"Again, I don't know. Los Salvajes like their guns more than their drugs, but with the Devils cutting in on their territory, they could be looking for new outlets."

"Right. Like a tattoo shop." He sighed, couldn't stop looking at the photo. It was like opening the door into one of the darkest times in his past—finding a young mother raped and stabbed—and that was before learning of the fifteen-year-old daughter she'd left behind. Zoë had often come to him in those subsequent years with new theories about her mother's killer—a homeless man, a drug dealer, a crazy ex-coworker with a grudge—but like his own leads, they never amounted to anything. He knew she blamed him for never having solved the case, but held on to plenty of guilt for herself too. If her mother hadn't been out searching for her runaway daughter, she never would've encountered the man who'd followed her back home and surprised her later that night.

"You think the two—Luis and Zoë—kept in contact all this time?" Quinn asked.

"It's possible, I guess," Sloane responded. "He was a friend of her mother's."

He rubbed his upper lip, sensed Quinn observing him. "Case still haunts you bad, doesn't it?" he said.

Sloane sighed. "Yeah, it does."

"Whatever happened to this Zoë afterward? Relatives? Foster care?"

Sloane shook his head. "No. Social Services tried to place her with a family in Sparks, but she wasn't having it. Kept running away. Said she'd heard all the horror stories she needed about abuse in foster care. She'd rather take her chances on the streets. To be honest, I can't say I blame her. There's no true safe place for kids when they don't have other relatives to take them in."

He tapped on the diner counter, a gold-and-white speckled laminate top that hadn't changed since the place had opened in the seventies. There was something else eating at him about her photograph, about that long dark hair and ripped jeans.

"I'll be damned," he said aloud.

"What?" Quinn asked.

Sloane squinted. "This is the same girl I saw at Amber McKinley's place, helping her mother move her daughter's belongings out of the house."

It was Quinn's turn to raise an eyebrow. "What the hell was she doing there? Don't tell me she knew McKinley?"

"I don't know," Sloane said. "But now I understand why she turned tail and ran the second I walked in. I sensed she looked familiar but couldn't put my finger on who she was, but she sure as hell did me."

He clicked his tongue. "Amber's mother told me her name was Zoë, but I just never imagined... What the hell would she be doing at Amber McKinley's house and visiting an outlaw biker bar in the same week?"

Sloane finally set down the photograph and motioned for the waitress.

"You need something, sugar?"

"I'm going to need another cup of that strong coffee after all."

CHAPTER 14

Zoë spent the next three days trying to come up with a plan that would have Max be fine with his wife trekking off for an entire long weekend alone. The concert was a two-day event, and although she would insist that they leave early enough Sunday for her to return home that day, it was a seven-hour ride to Vegas, so they would have to leave Reno Friday in order to have all day Saturday at the festival. Finally, she'd had the idea to check into conferences that weekend, and was surprised to find a tattoo event scheduled to take place. It was in Laughlin and not Las Vegas, but it was far enough away that it would require an overnight stay. She'd tell Max that she was going down with her good friend Katrina, and ask Kat to cover for her.

She heard him drive up and Oliver run out the door to greet him. She stared at her image long and hard in the mirror and asked herself if she was doing the right thing. Lying to her husband, infiltrating an outlaw biker club, and posing as another man's girlfriend—what would Max think if he learned the truth?

She gave herself one last look, wiped the palms of her hands on her jeans, and told herself she could do this. All day, she'd been trying to muster up the courage, and now it was time.

Zoë greeted her husband at the door, gave him a brief kiss, and asked about his day. The spring in his step said it'd been good. "Remember that kid I told you about?" he asked. "I found him a shared rental today. Basement with a bedroom and living area, shared kitchen upstairs, six hundred per month. And he got a job working at the home improvement store."

Zoë squeezed his arm. "Aw, that's the best news."

"It is. Days like today are why I do what I do." He undid a couple of buttons near the collar on his shirt, grabbed a beer from the refrigerator.

For the next half hour, they continued their conversation while Zoë made dinner and Oliver ran off to play. He'd eaten a bowl of macaroni and cheese earlier and wasn't interested in the healthy salmon and brussels sprouts the adults would be having.

When they were finally seated and enjoying the meal, Zoë turned the conversation toward the tattoo shop. "Screech is bugging me to bring in a third partner again," she said.

Max flaked off a piece of salmon, stuck it in his mouth. "The same guy? The friend from his church he keeps talking about?"

Zoë nodded. "Except, if you ask me, they're a little more than friends. He doesn't come right out and say it, but I hear him whispering into the phone a whole lot these days, and the guy spends hours in the shop when I'm not there."

"You think Screech is gay? I never really picked up on that vibe from him."

"I think Screech is...whatever he wants to be." She ate a roasted brussels sprout, took a sip of the one glass of red wine she allowed herself every night. "That Universalist church where they met is well attended by the LGBTQ community."

They both glanced at each other, then said simultaneously: "Not that there's anything wrong with that." They laughed. They'd always been able to sync their thoughts and often spoke the same things aloud or finished each other's sentences without trying.

"What's your concern?" Max asked. "That adding a third person will spread the work too thin, or you just don't like the guy's work?"

"No, his work is solid. He's got an impressive portfolio. And Screech keeps emphasizing that he'll bring in another layer of business with his specialty in realism. I mean, his images look exactly like the photographs his clients bring in—of celebrities, family, their dog—it's crazy. And his knowledge of realism will complement the shop with me as more of the traditionalist and Screech as an animator. Plus, we'll split expenses three ways. What I really worry about is what happens when he and Screech have a falling-out. You know, he comes on board, things go well for a few months or years, then, boom...they split up and now the business is at risk. I don't want to be in the middle of that. Doing business with friends is tricky enough. Family or lovers...just bad news."

"Then I think you just have to be straight with him. Tell him you're not trying to meddle in his personal business but you have to know the truth about their relationship to make a good decision. Nobody likes being lied to," Max said.

Zoë glanced at him over the top of her wine glass. *No. No, they don't.*

She took a long swallow. She needed to ask him about the weekend or she was going to lose her nerve. She got up to rinse her plate as she spoke.

"Speaking of specialties, I know it's last minute, but how would you feel having Max solo this weekend? There's a conference in Laughlin that's featuring an optical illusion artist I really admire, and I'd like to attend. It's just the two days, but I'd need to leave on Friday to drive down. I should be home Sunday night."

When Max didn't answer right away, she turned toward him to find him staring at his plate. "What?" she said.

"I don't know, it just seems like we haven't been spending much time together lately as a family. And even when you are here, you're distracted."

She walked over, sat back down with the dish towel in hand. "I'm sorry. I didn't realize. It's probably all this business with Screech. You're right, I just need to talk to him. I promise to do that as soon as I get back from the conference."

He kissed her forehead, nodded. "All right. Father-and-son weekend, it is." He stood, leaving the empty plate behind. "I'm going to go lift for a few and take a shower. And then maybe—he raised his eyebrows up and down quickly—"I'll have dessert."

Zoë laughed as she backed away, slapped him playfully with the towel.

She turned back to the dishes. Getting the weekend away hadn't been as hard as she'd thought, yet, after this, she would really need to watch how much time she spent away and make sure Max felt attended to. Blade had said she would need to befriend Vero over time, but she may not have that luxury. How could she do that without being away and making Max suspicious?

When the dishes were done and she could hear Max lifting weights upstairs, she took out the burner phone Blade had given her and texted him and Riot. *It's a go.* She snapped the phone shut.

In the next room, Zoë opened up the laptop and began to do research on the music festival so she would know what she was getting into. As she suspected, it largely featured metal bands, headbangers and industrial rock artists that, frankly, she didn't listen to because that sort of music gave her a pounding headache. She would have to act as if she knew some of the acts, however, so she read up on them while she could.

Twenty minutes later, she got a text from Blade, a simple thumbs-up. That one was followed by Riot, with an address of where to meet. *Ten a.m. sharp. You can leave your car at my house.*

She took a deep breath. So this was it. She was going to ride to Vegas with a man she didn't know to search for an outlaw she also didn't know, but who she suspected of killing at least fourteen women, including her mother. Max wouldn't say she was crazy. He would say she was certifiable.

A clearing of the throat behind her and a brief knock interrupted her thoughts. Max poked his head around the side of the door, fresh from a shower. "Hey, baby, got a minute?"

She closed her laptop. "Sure. What's up?"

Max turned his head to whisper behind the wall. Zoë couldn't see who he was speaking to, but it had to be Oliver. "Come on, it's okay." He turned to Zoë. "Oliver has something he would like to show you."

She could tell by Max's words that something was amiss, but she could only imagine what it was. Maybe Oliver had played in the mud, or smeared peanut butter all over the cat, as he had once before, but whatever it was, she could tell by her husband's reaction—somewhere between angry and laughing his ass off—that she should be prepared.

Oliver slid around the side of the wall and straightened his arms out to show her what he'd done. "Look, Mommy, I look just like your clients."

She glanced at his arms, felt her heart do a deep dive. Not a bare patch of skin existed there; they were completely covered in ink. Drawings of cats and dogs, hearts and diamonds, planes and rockets, even the name of his hamster covered every inch of his arms and face.

Behind him, Max waved the pack of markers, pointed to the notation on the package—permanent ink.

Zoë covered her eyes and groaned. She didn't know whether to laugh or cry.

"Are you mad at me?" Oliver asked.

She looked up to see him staring intently at her, through a face of pink, purple, and green butterflies. "No, baby. I love that you're so talented, but...we're going to have to take some of these off." She scooped him up in her arms, glanced at Max. "Might have to take a rain check on dessert. This could take a while."

He turned away, his shoulders rising and falling. Of course, he thought Oliver's actions were hilarious. Zoë wanted to punch him.

Using a combination of a specialty scrub and alcohol, Zoë sat Oliver in the tub and rubbed down his face and arms. His skin turned raw and red, yet he didn't complain, just kept jabbering and asking one hundred questions. Why do dogs bark? How do butterflies get their colors? Seriously, why *do* chickens cross the road? She started to clean a design on his arm that displayed three stick people inside a heart—what she supposed represented Max, her, and Oliver—but he stopped her. "No, not that one. Please?"

"Okay." She stared at it, felt a tear grace her cheek, quickly wiped it away. *Damn. What a softie I'm becoming.* What was it about your kids that did that to you?

An hour later, she wrapped him in a towel and dried him off, all the while thinking about just how much she loved Max and Oliver and what she was supposed to do the next three days. If Max or Oliver ever got hurt because of her actions, she would never forgive herself, so she had to ask herself again, why take the chance? She could almost hear her mother's voice warning her, telling her not to do it. She had a great husband and son—why undergo something so dangerous to prove an action happened that couldn't be undone?

Because, she silently answered her, all those other families, and especially the women who'd died, would never have moments like this one, holding their son after a bath and putting him to bed. And Zoë was the only one who could identify the man who'd taken it all away from them—and worse, would keep on taking future victims if she didn't stop him.

Like the woman warrior on her arm, she needed to slay the dragon.

CHAPTER 15

O n Friday morning, Zoë kissed Max and Oliver goodbye and promised to be home as early as possible Sunday afternoon. As she got into her SUV, her chest ached, and she prayed to the god she was so often at odds with that she, and they, would be okay as she undertook this mission. At the time Riot had described it as such, it had seemed funny, but now, that's what it felt like—a mission. Zoë was on a quest to hunt down a serial killer and bring him in. It sounded crazy, and it was, but it was also accurate.

She drove to the address Riot had given her, which ended up being a small brown-and-white framed ranch house tucked at the end of a country road with large weeping willows shading it. He stood in the driveway waiting beside his bike with the garage door open. Without his cuts on, he looked more like an everyman, a construction or oil-field worker. She wondered if life was like that for the majority of club members, one life lived among the neighbors and coworkers, another life lived among the club. He directed her to park in the garage where her SUV would be safe and out of sight from any prying eyes.

He came up to the side of the vehicle and opened the door for her. "Knock, knock."

Uh-oh. Here we go. She laughed. "Who's there?"

"Hawaii."

"Hawaii who?"

"I'm fine. Hawaii you?"

She slid from the car, smiling wryly. She opened the back hatch to grab a small duffel. "I wasn't sure what to bring, or how to bring it. Is there a place for this on the bike?"

"That's fine," he said. "Anything that we can't make fit, we can add to the RV."

"The RV?"

"Yeah, the club has an RV that they bring along to big events. That way, if people need a place to crash or just get out of the heat, they can go get some rest. Plus, if someone breaks down, we've got parts and a tow if need be. He took her duffel. "Hey, knock, knock."

She glanced over her shoulder. She didn't want to play, but the grin on his face was equal to one Oliver would make. "Okay. Who's there?"

"Alpaca."

"Alpaca who?"

He shook the duffel. "Alpaca the bike and you pack the food." He motioned to a small cooler sitting on a nearby bench. "I grabbed a few power bars, cheese, salami, and crackers. There's an ice pack in the freezer inside, if you don't mind grabbing it. Oh, and if you need to pee, this would be the time to do it."

Zoë chuckled. "Thanks, Dad."

She went up the garage steps to the kitchen to grab the ice pack and decided to take his advice about the pit stop. On the way, she couldn't help but notice how sparse his house was, the only furniture in it a well-used couch, television, and an oak kitchen table with a laptop sitting on it. In the bedroom, a mattress lay on the floor next to a pile of clothes, and in the bath, even an extra roll of toilet paper was hard to come by. After doing her business and washing her hands, she went back to the kitchen and couldn't resist checking the cupboards. Nothing but a few glasses and paper plates adorned the dusty shelves, and the refrigerator offered just a few beers and a jar of hot sauce.

She shook her head. Either Riot had just moved into the place or he truly didn't spend much time here. Zoë had known her share of bachelors, but even the most minimalist among them kept more stuff at home than this guy.

She went back out and packed the cooler.

When they were ready, Riot handed her a camouflage bandana for her face and neck. "You'll want to wear it over your nose and mouth when we get on the highway. Unless you want to eat a bug bowl, that is, and load up on some protein."

"No, thanks." She took the mask and tied it behind her head, then put on the helmet he offered. He slid into his cuts and hopped on the bike. She sat on the bitch seat behind him, hanging on to his waist for support. "Will we meet up with the others first?"

He nodded as he started the bike, revved it a few times. "Headed there now."

Ten minutes later, they joined the rows of silver and black lined up in an empty parking lot like soldiers ready to do battle. The engines roared, and the riders whooped and hollered, pumping themselves up for the long ride. As Zoë and Riot rode up, they took position in the back of the pack where prospects, like Riot, belonged. It was the worst of positions to ride, the location where you breathed the exhaust of all those bikes ahead of you, but dropping back—either because you wanted to breathe or maintain a safer speed—wasn't an option. Dropping back meant you were a pussy and couldn't keep up with the ride, which, Riot warned, could push ninety to one hundred miles per hour at times.

"Sounds like a party," Zoë muttered.

Blade came up from behind and slowly rode past, checking to see if his prospect and spy were present. Seeing them, he nodded before he took his position in the ranks, just to the back and left of the president. Next to him was the club's sergeant at arms, positioned just to the back and right of the road captain, and the rest lined up in rank behind.

Zoë took a deep breath, feeling her nerves rattle right along the revs of the pipes. So, this was it. She was going on a run, and as Riot's old lady, no less. For the next seven hours, she would sit in the bitch seat and endure wind, spit, and exhaust, and when they finally arrived, her legs would be concrete and her face numb. But it would all be worth it, because the next day, she would have a shot at meeting the NorCal president—and more importantly, his wife, Vero—who could become her link to locating the Lone Horseman.

She reminded herself why she was doing this: to find her mother's killer.

As she took a last stretch, she thought back to the girl she was at fifteen. At one time in her life, she'd been spontaneous, the girl who thought she had the whole world in front of her. The one who said F-school, F-home, and F-society. Freedom was where life was lived. When she'd run away the year her mom was murdered, she'd had dreams of hitting the open road and never looking back. In that respect, she imagined she wasn't so different than the men and women who surrounded her right now. Who knew? If her life hadn't been altered forever by her mother's murder, and the next three years spent on the streets using up the rest of the attitude and adrenaline she'd once possessed, who was to say she wouldn't have ended up right here? Life had a strange way of circling you back to wherever it decided you needed to be.

From the front, the road captain raised a fist, and suddenly they were off.

They rumbled through the streets of Carson City, forty strong, flags and colors flying. Horns honked and fists pumped, and those on the street stopped what they were doing—hosing down the sidewalk, pumping gas—to gawk at the contingent riding by. Before they turned on the exit to merge onto the highway, the truckers at the corner café all blew their horns and waved.

Zoë thought how odd it was, that even though the men riding were self-described outlaws, they were accepted and even revered by factions of the community, a genuine piece of Americana.

For the next three hours, they rode south with nary a waiver from their formation. No one broke down. No one stopped. They were eighty wheels rolling across the pavement, the heat cascading an endless mirage upon the horizon.

Zoë was thankful when, halfway into the ride, they stopped at a roadside diner for lunch and a break. Zoë stood over the bike and rubbed her thighs to get the blood flowing before she swung her leg over. "Not going to lie, I can't feel anything between my legs."

Riot started to comment when Zoë shut him down. "No knock-knock jokes."

He took off his helmet, grinning the whole time. Blade approached. "Good to see you two getting along. How is it in the rear?"

"Oh, you know, like putting your mouth over a tailpipe and inhaling," Riot answered. "Especially Rocky. Man, that guy needs to get over his love for that old beast of his."

"Well, he bought that beast in 1974, and as he'll tell you, it's paid for." He looked at Zoë, who had pulled her camouflage mask down and was washing her face with what remained in a water bottle. "How's the ride?"

"She can't feel her..."

Zoë shot him a look.

Blade laughed. "Go grab yourself some sandwiches."

After she went in the diner to order lunch and line up for a turn in the bathroom, Zoë returned to find Riot and Blade seated at an outdoor table sharing a smoke. Blade seemed to be instructing his prospect on an important matter, something about runs and proper etiquette. Zoë started to join them when she heard it—a roar that sounded more like a jet approaching from the highway—and then they were upon them, a sea of chrome flying the red-and-black colors.

Zoë's stomach twisted and turned. With all those grinning Devils buzzing by with their faces covered in skull caps and knuckles clad in rings that glinted off the intense Nevada sun, she couldn't help but feel the pass by was either a warning or a precursor of things to come. She wondered if he was among them—the Lone Horseman.

As soon as they saw the sea of green by the roadside, the one-fingered salutes came out. Riot, Blade, and the others fired it right back.

"No love lost between your clubs, is there?" Zoë said, sitting. "How long has it been this way? Since Modesto?"

"No. That was just the latest. It goes way back. Twenty years, at least," Blade said.

"What started it?" Zoë asked.

"The usual, territory and women." Blade exhaled a cloud of smoke into a stark blue sky. "They came south from Canada. We went north from the Inland Empire. We were bound to meet at some point. By the late nineties, we were fighting each other all over California. But the killing didn't start until a few years ago. It's been going on ever since. A constant quest for justice."

Zoë took a bite of her sandwich, although she had little appetite. "So, tit for tat. When does it end?"

Blade lit a new smoke. "When someone comes out the winner."

Zoë nodded. Although she'd never belonged to a gang, and the MCs preferred to be referenced as a club, it seemed to her that both possessed the same mentality:

territories and property. You kill mine, I'll kill yours. She didn't understand it, but knew once you bought into the mindset, it was difficult to change.

Blade seemed to read her thoughts. "What are you doing going after the Lone Horseman, if not seeking justice and revenge for your own?"

He stared her down. Riot raised an eyebrow.

She swallowed. "I see your point. I'd best come out the winner, then."

"Good girl."

After another four hours riding and a night spent by the campfire hearing war stories, she and Riot slipped off to learn what they could about each other before posing as a couple. Although he was selective in sharing information about his past, she learned he had an ex-wife and a son in Redding, California, and traveled there once a month to be with his kid. With them both having sons around the same age, they bonded over parenting stories, including the one Zoë shared of Oliver recently coloring his arms with brightly colored—and permanent—tattoos. Like Max, Riot thought that was damn funny and gave Oliver kudos for being creative. He told her how his son had once taken green paint to his wife's prized bichon frise and his wife had nearly killed Riot for allowing it to happen. By the end of the night, she'd decided Riot was a pretty decent guy and not at all what she expected. She wanted to ask him what appealed to him so much about Los Salvajes to want to join them and live the life of an outlaw biker, but thought it better saved for a later time.

He pitched her tent, and she said her good nights. It had been a long day, and the next promised to be even longer.

That night, she went to sleep and dreamed of grinning devils.

CHAPTER 16

The next morning, Riot took off his cuts and left them with Blade, then Zoë and Riot separated from the club. As expected, they got some strange looks from the other members, but Blade assured Riot they would soon understand that Riot was doing them a good deed. From now until the end of the festival tomorrow, there would be no interaction between them or the other members. Zoë and Riot were on their own.

The festival featured multiple stages and covered acres of open fields. The grass was sparse at best, so revelers brought in blankets and chairs to sit on along with beach-size umbrellas and canopies to keep the intense Nevada sun from baking them to a crisp. Still, the first items people shed were any unnecessary clothing, and it didn't take long until a wet T-shirt contest was underway. Zoë noticed that the red, white, and blue star-spangled bikinis were especially popular with the women—and men.

As with such events, concession stands lined the perimeters and offered plenty of food and drink at highly inflated prices. Drinking in such high heat would only add to the numbers expected to seek medical care during the event, which was likely why the organizers had ambulances and fire trucks at the ready, to treat those with heat stroke as well as the cuts and scrapes bound to occur. The firemen also had a second obligation, however, which was to periodically hose down the crowd between sets, which everyone looked forward to with great enthusiasm.

With the multiple stages and big-screen broadcasts, there wasn't really a bad spot in the place, except, in Zoë's opinion, the northeast and southwest sides, where port a-potties lined up a half mile deep. Zoë didn't care how far away the organizers tried to place them, or what kind of chemicals they tried to use to cover the odor, there was only so much one could do to mask the smell of a thousand people after two days of partying in the Nevada sun.

Just the thought made her gag.

They stared out over the expanse. "Let's take a walk and find our new friends," Riot shouted over the music. "Hopefully, we can get a spot nearby." Together, they maneuvered through the crowd, stepping between bodies on blankets and in circles of chairs. Coolers abounded in every color and design, as did flags designating certain camps.

"I see a whole lot of red and black about a hundred yards north," Zoë said.

As soon as she said it, their flag was raised, and a large grinning devil began flapping in the wind. They exchanged a glance. Zoë's heart pounded.

They were really doing this.

Once they were close to the Devils' camp, she looked at her and Riot's seating options. "What do you think? Stay to the back so we can observe or stick to the side where it might be easier to make contact?"

"Observe," Riot said. "I want to see who gets along and, more importantly, who doesn't. With the sunglasses and distractions, there couldn't be a better event to sit and watch people. In fact, I bet there are dozens of feds and johnny laws here this weekend observing the clubs and taking notes."

Zoë winced, glanced around. "Great," she said.

She hoped she didn't end up on their radar.

After walking around a few times, they claimed a spot not twenty feet from the Devils' site, which sprawled over a large swath of land and grew even bigger as many of those previously seated nearby decided to go elsewhere once the club moved in. If their ranks continued to swell, they would soon be cuddled up next to Zoë and Riot.

A new band took the stage, and for the next ninety minutes, they observed the Devils and pretended to be into the music. Or, at least, Zoë did. By the third song, Riot was headbanging and slamming beers. "Hey, take it easy there, cowboy. You get drunk and take a header, I'm leaving you wherever you pass out," she shouted over the screeching guitars, which rattled her core.

He crushed an empty can against his forehead, stumbled, and practically fell into her lap. "Knock, knock," he said, laughing.

She shook her head. "No."

He stuck out his lip. "C'mon. Knock, knock."

She rolled her eyes. "Who's there?"

"Yacht."

"Yacht who?"

"Yacht to know by now I can handle my booze," he said, moving in close to her ear. "Watch. I'll have these guys wanting to party with us in no time." He kissed her cheek, then jumped back and made a series of dance moves that made her want to crawl under the blanket. Yet, sure enough, his crazy antics had the Devils' attention— and they were laughing.

She scanned the group—all long beards and bandanas, denim and dirt—feeling safe to analyze them behind her dark glasses. Their ages ran from a few young women that looked barely legal to old men on oxygen. The women also seemed to slightly outnumber the men, as if the club had brought extra just in case they ran out. They weren't exactly the fittest group or the best looking, but there was no doubt where their devotion lay—nearly all had tattoos of devils in various poses, complete with pitchforks and split tongues.

Zoë took a deep breath, her insides rattling with the same electricity as the music on the stage. These weren't the kind of people you sought out. They were more like the ones you avoided at all costs—changed direction, went down a new street, or just turned around and went back where you came from—the minute you ran into them. They weren't the kind of people you walked up to and started a conversation with, and they sure as shit weren't the kind of people you infiltrated, lied to, and later betrayed.

So once again, she had to ask herself—why was she doing this?

In her head, she heard her mother's voice tell her to turn away. It was too dangerous, and nothing—not even exposing the Lone Horseman as her killer—could undo the past. She needed to go home and take care of her family and be grateful for all she had, before she lost it all.

And yet, that other side spoke as well, the one that couldn't let go of the rage at what this man had taken away from her. It infuriated her that her mom hadn't seen her get married, or ever had a chance to find a true love of her own. She certainly hadn't experienced that with Zoë's father, who thought her mother no more worthy than a punching bag and a sex toy. And it angered her that her mother hadn't gotten to see the birth of her grandchild, and that Oliver would never know her beyond a photograph and a few handed-down stories.

The Lone Horseman had taken everything from them.

As Riot continued to dance, Zoë observed a woman who appeared from beneath a large red canopy to stretch her legs. She was thin, with long, dark braided hair and careful features, and when she navigated through the crowd, several members gave her a respectful nod. Zoë didn't have the picture Blade had shown them previously, but she was positive the woman was Vero, the NorCal president's wife.

She punched Riot in the arm to get his attention. Seeing Vero, as well as Maverick, who appeared from beneath the canopy shortly afterward, Riot took out the binoculars he'd brought and acted as if he was watching the show. "Damn, this guy really gets into his role," he said. "He looks like a real devil with that pointy beard and slit eyes."

He moved the glasses away from the members so as not to cause a stir and observed the crowd behind them. "Wonder where our other mates are," he said. "I think that's them on the east side." Riot started laughing. "Yeah, there's Blade. He's got the glasses out too. Motherfucker is looking right at me, giving me the finger."

Riot returned the favor, making a great display of his middle digit.

Zoë stepped back as two men glared at Riot's gesture and walked in his line of vision. "Is that for us, son?" one of them challenged.

Riot lowered the binoculars to see two bare-chested, heavily tatted Devils standing in his path. He jumped back, quickly lowered his hands. "Whoa. Damn, man. No, not at all. This asshole in the crowd was looking right back at me with his own goggles, and he flipped me off, so I returned the favor."

Zoë feared the interaction would turn bad, but Riot clearly saw it as a moment of opportunity. Within five minutes, he'd struck up a friendly conversation and was telling jokes. It shouldn't have surprised her; he knew how to handle these guys, and without them knowing he was already affiliated, was able to play up to their egos by asking them questions about their patches and rank.

He turned back to Zoë. "These guys are the real deal. I've told my old lady here I'm going to prospect one day. You know, if someone will have me."

"He does. Talks about it all the time," Zoë said.

The two guys smirked. "That so? Well, why don't you two join us so we can get acquainted. Always looking for new talent, brother." They winked.

Zoë didn't know what to make of that, but Riot didn't seem to have a problem with it, and the two guys hauled their things to their camp. Her unease began to lessen when, an hour later, Riot had half the Devils in a stitch, telling stories about his travels and time spent filming porn stars up the California coast. She didn't know how much, if any, of it was true, but given his raunchy humor, she now understood the knock-knock jokes were the light side of his comedy routine.

As the next set got underway, Zoë sipped warm beer and kept her eye on Vero. The woman didn't appear to talk much, but she smoked like a chimney and appeared to favor flavored vodka. Every once in a while, Zoë would see her take one of those tiny little bottles out of her backpack and add it to her cup.

When the woman got up, threw a T-shirt on over her bikini top, and whispered in her husband's ear, Zoë knew, like Riot earlier, her opportunity was nigh—Vero was headed to the line of port a-potties. *This is it. Time to ride.*

Zoë approached her. "Hey, you mind if I tag along? I don't really want to walk through this crowd by myself."

Vero checked her out, seemed to decide she was harmless. "Sure."

Vero maintained her silence until they joined the lines, which were enormous. "Shit, look at this, would you? All of this to take a piss." She lit up a new cigarette, offered Zoë one. This time, Zoë took it. When in Rome and all that.

"Boyfriend's a funny guy," Vero said.

"I guess. Jokes about tits and ass. He keeps the entertainment coming, so to speak," Zoë said and smirked.

Vero offered a little smile. "You don't like it?"

Zoë shrugged. "I don't mind. He's into people, likes to make them laugh. The more, the merrier. Me, not so much. I need my space. I like to stick with a few friends and let others do their thing while I watch."

From what Zoë had observed so far, she was certain Vero was the same. Now she would find out if she was right.

"Yeah, I noticed you checking the club out," Vero said, "even before they brought you in." It was direct, and told Zoë that she was correct—Vero was very much the protective observer, the club matriarch.

Zoë didn't buckle. "I was, yeah—kind of hard not to with such a cast of characters—but mainly I was looking at your ink. Yours and the guys'. It's damn well done. I'm an artist. You get yours done local, here in Vegas?" She dropped a few well-known names of artists she admired, work that inspired and looked similar in style to those inked on Vero's body.

Vero raised an eyebrow. "Ink slinger, huh? Should've known. Me too. But no, I don't get mine done here. I get mine done by a friend in Sacramento. That's where we live. My old man, he's president of the NorCal chapter of this club. I do the majority of ink for the members and moonlight at my friend's shop."

Zoë tried to look impressed. "All of them? Wow."

Blade had been right. Vero was her in. One simple trip to the bathroom and a revelation of a common interest, and the next thing Zoë knew, she was sitting next to Vero beneath the canopy, sipping on blackberry vodka and sharing adventures in ink. The club's queen and her court had an elaborate setup too: comfortable chairs, coolers filled with drinks and ice, even a battery-operated fan. The VP's old lady occasionally sprayed water into the wind so it would cover all of them with a cooling mist.

While Riot worked his angle, she worked hers, all the while keeping Blade's advice in mind—to go slow and keep the questions about the art and not the club. There would be future opportunities to talk, and Vero had already proved to be hawkish. She would immediately pick up on anything Zoë said to sway the conversation toward a member of the club. So she stayed focused on the industry and where she saw it going, discussed trends and styles, and what she liked and disliked. And over drinks and stories about bad clients and even worse tattoos, Zoë found out that she liked her. Vero was real and genuine, and nice. Which was not at all what Zoë imagined her husband, Maverick, to be, who looked like he could stick a spike through the top of your head and laugh while doing it.

He ducked beneath the canopy, kissed his wife on the cheek. "You ladies enjoying yourselves?" He was at least six feet tall and built like a brick. He puffed a cigar, and smoke filled the area.

"We're good, baby."

He pointed the cigar at Zoë, his eyes narrowing. "Who's this?"

"Zoë. She's an artist. We got to talking shop on the way to the can." Vero motioned outside to where Riot and the others were gathered. "That's her boyfriend out there."

He looked out to see Riot doing push-ups while the guys threw down bets. "That guy? He's crazy as shit." Maverick puffed some more, smiled, revealing capped teeth. "I like him."

Zoë exhaled, realized she'd been holding her breath since he'd walked in. "Yeah, he's a riot," she said, privately laughing at her own pun.

"He affiliated?" Maverick asked.

The question caught her off guard. "You mean like with a club? No. He talks about patching in, but we're near Reno where the Angels and Los Salvajes seem to rule, and he hates them both."

The president grunted. "He's right. They're pussies."

"Truth is, he's enamored with you, the Devils," she said, hoping to gain favor.

Vero cocked her head, looked at her old man. "Hey, you said we needed more talent around there. Who knows? Maybe he's your guy. Maybe he knows others to recruit."

Maverick took several more puffs of his cigar. "We've been advancing in Reno, but prospecting is not for the weak. Neither is being a Devil." He checked Riot out again, now beating his chest and screaming like Tarzan. "You want, you bring him around the camp tonight. There will be some...initiations. We'll see how badly your boyfriend really wants to be a Devil."

Zoë listened to him chuckle as he departed, and it left her cold. She would give Riot the information, but it would have to be up to him whether he wanted to go or not. Intel or not, it could be dangerous. She was pretty sure their initiations didn't involve making s'mores and telling campfire stories.

CHAPTER 17

O f course, Riot wanted to go. They were on a mission to gain the Devils' trust, and refusing an invitation would end it all. But Zoë feared exposure, as outside the concert venue, the Devils' outdoor camp was but a tree line away from Los Salvajes, and already the tension between the two the clubs was ratcheting up. Twice, she'd seen Blade ride by with the sergeant at arms, eyeing the growing presence in their rival camp.

"Who's that?" Zoë asked, pretending not to know.

"The enemy," Vero said.

Maverick spit on the ground. "Scum," he replied.

A light flickered in Riot's eye. Zoë put her hand on his arm.

The campfire raged and sent flames ten feet high, licking at the sky. Seated around the warmth, the members and their old ladies continued to do what they'd done all day—drink, smoke, and tell stories. Once in a while, a couple would slip off to get naked in a nearby tent, and everyone would rouse them when they came back.

"That was a quick one. Did your old lady even get her pants off before you finished?"

The taunts and cheers followed.

Zoë sat there looking out on all their faces, wondering what real tales these men and women had to tell. She recalled Blade's description of the Devils, how their deeds done made Los Salvajes look like Boy Scouts. What crimes had these guys committed, and what was the women's understanding of them? Did they participate right alongside them or turn and look the other way?

And Vero, how much did she know and routinely cover up? Probably more than the others. Probably everything.

Zoë turned to find her, saw her talking to a man just outside their RV. At first, Zoë gasped, thinking the man was the Lone Horseman, until he wheeled to speak to

Maverick, who came up behind him and rested a hand on his shoulder. The nose was too angular. The face too gaunt.

"What is it?" Riot whispered in her ear.

She was sitting on his lap, playing the part of his girlfriend. It wasn't comfortable. "Nothing. I thought it was him for a moment, but no." She sighed. "Damn it, I really thought he'd be here."

All day long, she'd watched for him, and all day long, she'd been disappointed. Riot emphasized the positive—how easily they'd made inroads—but she was impatient. It wasn't so much that she wanted to see him again, and she definitely didn't want him to see her, but she did want to prove to Riot and Blade that she was telling the truth about him and his tattoos. Otherwise, how long would they help her pursue a man they couldn't prove existed?

With a no-show by the Lone Horseman, she wondered if there was any purpose to her and Riot staying here any longer. Maybe it was time to pack it in so they could get a head start home the next day. Earlier, she'd snuck away from the crowd to call Max and Oliver and wish them a good night, and she missed them like crazy.

On the road behind their camp, a pack of Los Salvajes once again rode by, green colors flying. And just like the prior day when passing the roadside diner, they flipped their rivals off. The gesture earned shouts and invitations to engage, and several Devils jumped up to grab nearby weapons, causing Zoë to react. She wasn't used to seeing so many guns.

Vero stepped to her side. "Want a break? I've got my machine in the RV, and one of our guys wants a new tatt. I could use the company."

Zoë nodded, happy for the distraction and thankful to get off Riot's lap.

The Devils' RV was a nice unit, a thirty-foot-long Winnebago that had to have cost them good money. Unlike the interior in the one Los Salvajes owned—which was dried, cracked, and yellowed by years of use—the leather seats in the Devils' rig still looked and smelled new. Sitting at the dining table, which had been flipped out to provide more space, a shirtless and already heavily tatted man awaited new ink.

After pulling the front curtains closed, Vero plugged in her tattoo machine, slid in a needle, and got to work. She didn't use a stencil. Obviously didn't need one given her experience.

Outside, someone threw high-octane booze on the fire, and shouts and yells ensued as the flames grew higher. Los Salvajes' drive-by had riled the Devils up, and they didn't appear to plan on backing down.

"Is it always like this?" Zoë asked Vero with a furrowed brow. "Rivals going at each other?" She acted as if her concern was for Riot, but her real worry was getting caught between flying bullets if a war broke out between the two clubs.

"It goes in cycles, but lately, it's heated up again. Don't worry. We'll be fine here. There's nothing short of a small arsenal in the bowels of this rig."

Zoë raised an eyebrow, imagined piles of AK-47s and AR 15s in the storage bins. *Great.*

Zoë watched Vero adeptly outline a skull, as if she could do it in her sleep. Given how long she'd been an artist, she probably could. Zoë thought about what she could ask that might lead to a conversation about the Lone Horseman, and the only thing she could think of was the ink.

"What other kind of images do the guys in the club like, besides devils, that is? That other club, what is that on their jacket, a wild pig or something? Do the Devils have any animal representation?"

"Not really. I've done a few wolves, and some eagles, but those mostly represent a club member's wishes."

Zoë nodded. "I do a ton of animals—lions and tigers—and a whole lot of horses for some reason, mostly raised on their haunches." She waited for a reaction, but when none came, continued. "Gods and symbols too. The college students like their Greek mythology."

Vero inked a snake slithering through the skull's open sockets.

Zoë fidgeted. Vero hadn't given even the slightest reaction to the mention of the horse. Maybe she didn't know the Lone Horseman? But no, she had to. As the club's historian, how could she not?

She didn't want to press it, though, so changed the conversation. "What can you tell me about what women do for the club? I confess I really don't know. Do they have roles like the men do?"

Vero cocked her head. "Your status is largely dependent on the role your husband plays. If he's a prospect, like your boyfriend would be if someone chose to sponsor him, he, and you, would primarily be here to serve others. He would be at the mercy of the patched members to do whatever they commanded of him. You would assist the women. Get them coffee or drinks, help with various functions being planned, and keep the club clean." She glanced up. "Honestly, that's the worst. If you can imagine what thirty or forty teenage boys can do in a weekend when they're all together, just multiple that by one hundred."

Zoë groaned. The guy on the table laughed.

Outside, a new round of shouts, a few gunshots, and the fire intensified.

"Once your guy moves up," Vero said, "then it's your turn to get served and help with events. Organize the charitable rides, help plan any weddings, and, of course, the funerals."

Zoë glanced up, wide-eyed.

Vero met her gaze, shrugged. "Fact of life, honey. These guys live hard and play harder. If they aren't taken out by the road, our rivals or bad living gets them. Last three years, we've lost five members: two from motorcycle crashes, two from liver disease, and one shot in the head in a drive-by. And that's just our chapter."

Zoë stared as if she was afraid for Riot's well-being. And in a way, she was. Why would a guy who seemed to have his whole life in front of him want to shorten it?

"You have to be prepared for that," Vero said. "The life isn't for everyone."

She turned off her tool, applied the petroleum jelly and an antibacterial to the man's new ink, and protected it with a bandage. "Ready to roll," she pronounced.

He slid off the table and thanked her. As he opened the RV door, Zoë could see the crowd outside had gathered in a circle away from the campfire and were throwing down money on some contest happening in the middle. "What are they betting on?" she asked.

Vero peeked around the corner. "Fights probably. They enjoy beating the shit out of each other. Bragging rights and all that."

Vero sat in the RV's front passenger seat and closed the curtain to the front window for privacy. She lit a new cigarette with the window down. Zoë stayed where she was, on a side bench in the middle of the rig. "Are there other jobs to be done in the club? Like bookkeeping or secretary?" Maybe if she could get her talking about the history, Zoë would learn something important.

"The guys elected for those positions keep track of the finances and meeting notes, but yes, there are some different roles. Like our VP's wife, the one you met today, she heads up all our charitable events, and me, I'm the club's historian. I document our members' ancestry and events, post pictures. You know, basically keep a history of the club. For me, it's kind of like scrapbooking."

"That's cool. Yeah, that would be a good job. And doing the ink."

Vero smiled and chuckled. "Geez, you're like my little sister or something."

Zoë started to reply when a heavy rap on the passenger door startled both of them. A face appeared in the darkness outside the window, and he spoke. "Got a minute?"

Zoë caught her breath. The minute she heard that voice, she knew who it belonged to—the Lone Horseman.

She quickly slid down the bench toward the back of the RV and away from his prying eyes. Brain scrambling, she stood and pointed silently at the partition that divided the main living area from the bedroom in back and mouthed the word *bathroom* to inform Vero where she was going.

Vero nodded.

On the other side, Zoë quickly slid the partition shut and hid behind the bathroom door. From inside the tiny, cramped space, she listened as the Horseman entered and spoke to Vero. "I just told Mav. Our little problem? It's been taken care of."

"That's good. Any damage control?"

"Nothing we can't handle."

"Chance of discovery?"

"No. Big Red has been there for a hundred-fifty years. It'll be there a hundred more. Not even the most dedicated hikers go in once they see all those warning signs."

A pause, some shuffling of feet.

"What's this?" she asked.

"I took a pretty landscape."

"A close-up of a bush?"

"Fiery red blooms. Like a burning bush. It's a message. Get it?" He laughed. Zoë shivered.

Vero didn't join in, just responded with, "I'll make a note of it."

Again, silence took over. Zoë couldn't see what was happening, and worried that Vero might be tipping him off to someone else being in the RV. But then she heard additional shuffling and confrontation, and Vero issue him a command to stop. "Get your hands off me."

He laughed again. "Can't blame a man for trying, sweetheart."

"You do that again, I'll tell Mav—"

He cut her off. "You'll tell him what?"

Zoë listened intently, heard Vero make a strange sound.

What the hell was he doing to her?

Zoë stepped around the bathroom door, peered through a thin crack between the partition and the wall. The Horseman was standing in front and pressing himself against her, and she looked downright uncomfortable. It was only then Zoë realized he had his hand shoved between her legs.

She pushed him away. "Just, get out."

He backed away and laughed, enjoying her fear. He smelled his hand, licked it. "Mmm. That's some good pussy," he whispered. Then with another cackle, he charged out the door, back into the night.

Vero turned to face the wall and adjusted herself, embarrassed. Zoë slipped back in the bathroom and flushed the toilet so Vero would know she was about to come back out and would have time to gather herself.

When she undid the partition, Vero was back in the front seat, smoking a new cigarette. "If you don't mind me asking, who the hell was that?" Zoë said.

"Nobody you'd ever want to know," Vero said. "Believe me." Her hand shook. She was unnerved. "Listen, I think it's best you should go now."

Zoë nodded. She wanted to ask if Vero was okay—even more, wanted to ask additional questions about the Horseman—but knew better. Like Blade had warned, it was better not to push it. Zoë stepped around her and down the three steps to the door, but before she did, took a quick glance at the photograph the Horseman had taken, a bush with fiery red blooms. In the background was a tall dilapidated structure with a red tin roof backing into the hill.

What was the importance of that bush, she wondered? What problem had the Lone Horseman taken care of?

And did she really want to know?

Afraid the Horseman might still be lingering near the RV, Zoë inched the door open only far enough to slide through and immediately slipped off into the darkness down the length of the rig. Once near the back, she crossed the lot between parked bikes and trucks so she could stand near the road and assess what was going on—and where the Lone Horseman might be now.

Straight ahead about fifty yards, a crowd circled around two men, both dancing around each other like men in a boxing ring. As Vera suspected, the fights were on, and if Zoë didn't know any better, one of the men was Riot.

She silently muttered. *Shit. What the hell has he gotten himself into?*

Zoë turned in a circle, unknowing what to do. Would they harm him? Would they harm her? Or was this a part of their so-called initiation? It would seem like something they would do, test his ability to fend for himself.

She scanned the crowd surrounding them. She didn't see the Horseman, but that didn't mean he wasn't there. She needed to get up there and signal to Riot that they needed to leave. Maybe he could take a purposeful dive and they could make a quick exit.

Too late. As she cautiously approached, she saw Riot deliver a knockout blow, and the next thing she knew, he was parading around the ring with his arms raised in the air declaring himself the victor. His cheek was swollen and lip bleeding, but he seemed little worse for the wear. After receiving several slaps on the back, she joined him to the side. "What the hell are you doing?" she whispered.

He wiped his face with the shirt he'd removed and laid over the back of a chair. "Proving my worth. It's okay. We do this all the time. Why, what's the problem?"

"He's here, that's what." As the fire continued to flicker nearby, she stepped back, wanting to remain in the shadows. She nervously scanned the faces nearby, hoping he wasn't close. Yet, she needed to find him so Riot would know who he was and could identify him for the club in the future.

He grabbed her by the waist and pulled her to him. "Give me a little congratulatory kiss and a hug, then look for him over my shoulder."

Zoë did as he instructed and, while mostly hidden by his mass, searched the crowd until she found him—just to the front of several tents next to a line of trees, huddled with Maverick and Lizard, the sergeant at arms. "Okay, I see him." She pulled away, told Riot where he stood.

Riot nodded and brushed her hair back from her face, looking as ever the caring boyfriend, but she could sense the change in his demeanor, the increased tension in his jaw and neck. He took a swallow of beer and turned to glance across the fire to the dark corner beyond where the trio gathered. Riot stared, as if memorizing his face.

Suddenly, he stepped away from her and raised his fists in the air. "Come on. Who's next? Give me your biggest, your best. Bring out your enforcers."

He screamed and beat his chest, riling up the crowd. They laughed and cheered, started pounding on whatever they could find, and chanted, "Enforcer, enforcer."

Zoë backed into the shadows, her heart pounding like crazy. *What the hell is he doing? Is he fucking crazy?* She tried to grab his arm to no avail.

A man stepped forth, a solid mass of muscle and grit. A tattoo of boxing gloves inked his left upper arm, and a firing gun dominated the other. It wasn't who Riot had hoped to lure, but Zoë noticed, he'd caught the Horseman's attention just the same.

Someone shouted, "Lay your bets," the crowd cheered, and the money started to flow. As they did, Riot and his opponent danced around the inside of the circle, sizing each other up. The Horseman gestured toward the impending fight, and he and Maverick started toward the crowd, wanting to see this unknown take on who was sure to be one of their top muscles. Zoë slipped to the far back of the crowd where no one could see her, kept her arms crossed and her head down.

She was afraid to watch what was about to unfold.

As the bets ceased and the crowd closed in, she wondered if she should run down the road and inform Blade of what was happening. He wouldn't take kindly to his prospect getting his ass kicked and might want to come to his rescue. She remembered the phone he'd given her and nervously dug it out of her back pocket. But just as she started to text, Riot caught her attention. He shook his head. *No.*

That's when the first punch landed to his jaw.

His head spun, and he wheeled, stumbled, and landed on his knees. For a moment, the crowd quieted, thinking the fight was over before it started, but then Riot got up and laughed wildly, blood running from the edge of his mouth. The cheers erupted as he charged forward.

The next minutes felt like hours as the two did battle. Zoë flinched and ducked, feeling the pain of the jabs right along with him, yet Riot hung with the guy, returning the favor time and again. But the more it went on, the more Riot fatigued, until he found himself back on his knees staring up at the crowd.

The taunts started. "Come on, get up, pussy. I got my money on you."

"Yeah, show us what you're worth."

"Finish him off," others yelled to his opponent.

The opponent stepped forward to do just that when another man reached out and tapped on his shoulder. Zoë couldn't see who it was, but maybe she didn't want to. She squeezed in with a few sweaty bodies to get a better glance.

Then she watched in horror as the Lone Horseman stepped forward.

The guys went nuts as he took off his shirt, spit on both hands, and began to circle Riot. Hearing the chants, Riot glanced up to see his new challenger and smiled through a mouthful of bloody teeth. He cast a gaze at Zoë from a swollen and bruised eye.

She held her breath.

The fight didn't last long. Riot barely got to his feet before two solid punches to the face sent him reeling and a few jabs to the ribs finished him off. And when Riot went down, he didn't get back up.

The Lone Horseman raised his arms and declared victory.

CHAPTER 18

The following week, standing outside the shop ready for a day's work and a much-needed distraction, Zoë called to check in on Riot. "How is he?"

"He's not dead," Blade said. "So that's something."

Zoë hung her head, saw her reflection in the shop window, felt the intense sun of the day beat down on the back of her neck. "I should've texted. I'm sorry."

Blade grunted. "Would've turned into a bloodbath. He'll live. Don't sweat it."

She hung up the little flip phone, slipped it into her pocket. Back in the reflection of the shop window, she saw a man approach. She couldn't see his face, but instinctively sensed he was a cop, as the little hairs on the back of her neck stood at attention. The three years she'd spent on the streets running from the police still initiated the same reaction. "Can I help you with something?" she said, standing steadfast in her spot.

"Zoë Cruse?"

The minute he spoke, she knew who it was—Brady Sloane. How could she forget the voice who'd once informed her that her mother was dead?

"I'm Detective Sloane. You don't remember me. That's okay."

"No, I do," she said. She offered a cursory glance over her shoulder but didn't turn around. "You're the detective that never solved my mother's murder."

His head lowered. "I guess that's not something you would forget."

"No, it isn't."

He sighed. "Look, I don't want to get off on the wrong foot here, but I need to ask you some questions, about your shop and some of your recent...associations."

Zoë swallowed. *Perfect.* "You don't like who I hang out with?"

"Not my preferred cast of characters, but your friends are your choice. I'd like to alert you to some recent events, however, of which you may not be aware. I'd hate to see you put yourself, or your family, in danger."

It sounded like more of a threat than an offer of assistance.

She glanced down the street at the neighborhood businesses offering everything from massage and hemp clothing to the best breakfast burrito in Reno. Blade had been adamant about not speaking to the police, but if Sloane had knowledge that could help, or threaten, her mission to expose the Lone Horseman, she needed to hear it.

"I can't be seen talking to the police. I don't know who could be watching."

"Can you come down to the station, then? Say four o'clock? We can meet in an office, out of the way of prying eyes. No interrogation rooms."

Zoë nodded. Funny he'd remembered how she'd hated those rooms.

After he departed, she stepped inside, said hello to Screech, then casually observed the street outside for several minutes. She prayed no one had seen her and Sloane speak. That would be all she needed, caught in the middle of the Reno PD and two rival motorcycle clubs.

She went about her day, then begged off early and arrived at the station just after four. She parked a few blocks away and walked the distance, wearing sunglasses and long sleeves, just to ensure nobody was following, or, if they were, at least make it more difficult to identify her. As she took the gray cement stairs to the second floor, the memories of the Reno PD and those halls came flooding back: the Crime Stoppers posters, the age-enhanced fliers of missing children, the cracked and aging tile that popped beneath her feet. It didn't seem much had changed.

When she entered the division, Sloane was standing by a desk, speaking to another officer. The moment he saw her, he motioned her his way and led her into a nearby office. "Thanks for coming. Cap's out today, so we can meet in here. Have a seat."

She opted for the chair nearest the door to keep the exit at the ready, another old habit that wouldn't die. She removed her glasses and took stock of her surroundings, noted a shelf filled with police procedurals and legal manuals, a framed certificate of some kind, and a photo of their captain shaking hands with some political bigwig. She observed him as he sat, ever wary.

"You still don't trust me after all these years." It wasn't a question. He knew the answer. He folded his hands on top of the desk, stared at his thumbs.

Zoë got a good look at his face and realized just how much he'd aged since the last time she'd seen him. The former tiny lines that once feathered his blue eyes now formed deep ridges, and his previously firm jawline was now a bit slack, as if he'd lost muscle there but not the skin. And his gaze—although it continued to carry that dagger of determination—had also relaxed, perhaps proof that he did possess empathy, that his concern wasn't just an act.

"Before we discuss current matters, Zoë," he said, "I feel like I owe you an apology. Your mom's case...I'm sorry it's dragged on so long. I know you don't believe me, but I haven't given up. Her death, it haunts me."

She felt an unexpected sting zap her eyes, blinked it away. "Is that so?"

"Yes, it is."

She frowned. "I never felt like you ever took any of my suggestions seriously. Every time I came here, you looked like you'd rather eat dirt than have to talk with me."

He cringed. "I didn't mean to dismiss your ideas. It was just that, most of the time, the evidence we had didn't fit with your suspects. It's not that I didn't look. I want you to know that. I did." He took a deep breath. "I wasn't very good at relating to teen girls then."

He glanced at a framed picture of his boss's wife and daughter, huffed, as if he was thinking about his own family. "Hell, maybe I'm still not."

Zoë followed his gaze, examined the photo that showed a thin, petite blond woman hugging a dour girl of about fourteen with mussy brown hair. "Teenagers," Zoë said. "They can be tough on parents—killer, even."

He cocked his head. "It's not your fault your mother died, Zoë. I know you blame yourself—you always have—but your mother didn't die because you ran away."

She felt a strange blend of emotion boil within her—anger, sorrow, guilt, and embarrassment—all mixed into some toxic brew. "How can you say that? She never would've been out looking for me that night if I'd been home. All those people in the park, they said a man who'd been hanging out nearby left the area right after she did. He followed her home and raped her."

But Sloane was shaking his head. "We don't know that. It's only speculation. Whoever her killer was, he could've been watching her for weeks, or even months, waiting for the perfect time to attack her."

"Right. And because I was gone, it was the perfect time."

He started to open his mouth to say more but shut it just as quickly. He had that look that said he knew fighting about it wasn't going to accomplish anything—something he'd probably learned after many an attempt trying to win arguments with his own wife or daughter over the years.

She rubbed the legs of her jeans. "Look, is this why you asked me to come down here? To try and make amends for my mother's murder? Because it sounded like maybe you had something else on your mind."

He wasn't the only one who wanted to change the subject.

"You're right," he said. He grabbed a folder on his desk and opened it. "Let's start with Amber McKinley and what you were doing at her house that day I stopped by. Her mother said you told her that you and Amber were friends, but I didn't find any indication of that being true."

Damn. She was hoping he hadn't recognized her there. She should've known better.

"Okay, fine. Yes, I was there. And no, we weren't friends. It's just that...her murder, it reminded me of my mom's. The no forced entry, the rape. I realize she was strangled and not stabbed, but..." She shook her head. "Something felt connected."

What exactly that *something* was, she had no intention of telling him. He'd think she was crazy, maybe even more than all the times he had before.

"Connected? How so?" he asked.

"I don't know. That's why I wanted to go inside her house, to see if something would trigger. But nothing did." She fiddled with the fabric of her shirt. "I'm sure I was just being crazy, like before."

She noted him checking out her fidgeting hands and stopped. He was probably trained in lie detection, and she didn't need to spell out her dishonesty for him in her body language.

"I never thought your ideas were crazy. Just...misguided," he said.

"Misguided? You mean like suspecting Luis Nieves?" She leaned forward. "How come you never told me that you once suspected my mother's murderer might be a biker?"

He slowly sat back in his chair and studied her. "Well, I didn't, not really. I just used that glove I found outside on the street as bait to see if I could get anyone in the club to talk. But I do find it interesting that you should bring up Luis Nieves. Is that why you've recently reconnected with him?"

"I find it more interesting to know that you know I have reconnected," she said.

"And I find it more interesting to know why. Do you know something that I don't? Something that connects him or the club to the death of your mother?"

They sat there, staring each other down, waiting for the other to flinch.

"No," she finally said. "Actually, I don't suspect him at all."

He tipped his chin up, narrowed his eyes. "So, what, then? Why work with him?" He sat back up. "Look, I'll be honest with you. We've had some intel come forth about your association with Luis and Los Salvajes outlaw motorcycle club."

She felt her back straighten. "We? Who's we?"

Just then, the door opened and a squat guy with fat fingers and no neck entered and stopped beside her chair. "Special Agent Quinn, DEA."

She glanced at his outstretched hand, didn't bother shaking it. The man grabbed a chair and moved it next to hers with nary an inch between them. Already she didn't like him. He was violating her personal space.

"DEA? As in Drug Enforcement Agency? What the hell is this about?" she asked.

Sloane got up to shut the door that Quinn had left open, probably afraid Zoë would bolt through it. Truth was, she was about to. She didn't have any involvement in drugs, so whatever kind of trap they were laying or trying to pin on her was pure bullshit. She told them as much.

"You sure about that?" Quinn asked. "We've heard you've been hanging around Los Salvajes' clubhouse. Talking to a guy they call Blade? You want to tell us what that's about?" His mustache hair twitched. She wanted to reach out and slap it to make it stop.

"No, I don't. Especially to you. But I can tell you it has nothing to do with drugs."

"What, then?"

Sloane joined their proximity and conversation by leaning against the front of his captain's desk instead of returning to his chair. Zoë made sure to give him her best evil eye for inviting this little man with the big ego in. "It's really none of your business. But if you must know, I asked for his advice on how to deal with a little problem I'm having, that's all."

Quinn nodded with every word she uttered, like one of those annoying bobbleheads. "This problem, does it in any way relate to the Devils?"

She threw up her hands, glared. "Jesus. What, am I under surveillance?" She thought about Riot's words at the festival, how there were probably a dozen different law enforcement agencies present, all taking notes.

Apparently, he'd been correct.

"We have eyes on all the outlaw clubs," Sloane said. "Joint task force between federal and local agencies. We've got people inside and out. They get us information."

"Yeah, particularly when someone new comes in and stirs things up," Quinn said. "Like a few weeks ago, when you entered the picture. Luis Nieves, aka Blade, has been hopping around like the goddamn Easter Bunny ever since. Why don't you tell us what that's about?"

Zoë issued him the kind of look that said she'd rather kiss the ass of a mule than answer his question. After three years on the streets, and ten in the tattoo business, she'd developed pretty good instincts about people, and she had to say, this guy was in her top echelon of assholes. "How about I don't? I'm not one of your CIs."

"No, you're just Blade's new side girl. What's he got you doing? Making deals through the tattoo shop? He sends in his clients so you can pass along a message and deliver an eight ball or a wiped .45 in your spare time?"

She felt her jaw drop. "What? Are you kidding me?" She turned to Sloane. "Is that what you think I'm doing? Dealing drugs and guns?"

She laughed, but didn't know if it was because it was so ridiculous or because she was afraid that they really believed it.

"No," Sloane said, "at least, I don't want to." He gripped the edge of the desk, bit his bottom lip, as if he was carefully selecting his next words. "Look, we know that last weekend you went to Vegas with a prospect for Los Salvajes. He wasn't wearing his cuts, and the two of you purposefully infiltrated the Devils' camp. I saw it myself on the video our undercover recorded, of you hanging out with the NorCal president's old lady. The question is, why? What possible reason would you have for doing such a thing?"

Shit. That fast. The authorities already knew what she and Riot had done, and if they knew, she had to wonder—who else knew? Blade had warned her that all the MCs, as well as various law enforcement agencies, had undercovers and confidential informants everywhere, including citizens inside government. But that quick? If information could change hands that rapidly, how could she and Riot ever feel confident about meeting up with Vero and the Devils again? No wonder Blade had been adamant about keeping their knowledge just among the three of them and the club president.

"Who are you working for?" Quinn asked, impatient. "One of our agencies? ATF? Homeland? Or are you working directly for the clubs?"

She looked at him, shook her head. No way in hell she was saying shit to either of these guys, especially this bozo. "I don't know what you're talking about. I'm not working for anyone."

Quinn chortled. "You just like hanging out with gangsters." He leaned closer, so close she could smell his sour breath. "What, you got a thing for them? Long to be a pass-around so they can have their way with you?"

She felt a fire rise in her chest, but bit her tongue.

"Does your husband know you're having an affair with this prospect for Los Salvajes? Does he know about your little penchant for bikers? We could certainly give him a heads-up."

Zoë started to come out of her chair and grab the little twerp's throat, but Sloane stopped her by blocking her way and laying his hand on the chest of Agent Quinn and pushing him back. Although she agreed assaulting a DEA agent would not be a good first entry on her arrest record, it would certainly be deserving. The guy was an ass with a capital *A*.

"That's enough," he said. "Back off, Quinn. Zoë is not the enemy here. She's not on trial, and she doesn't deserve your accusations." He loomed over the man until he scooted his chair a fair distance away. He kept the snarl on his face, however.

Sloane leaned back on the desk. "Zoë, there's a war going on here that you may not know about, and it's not one you want to be caught in the middle of. These two clubs—Los Salvajes and the Devils—they have disagreements that go back decades. I don't know what your dealings are with them, but I would highly advise you to get out now, while you can. Tell us what you know, and we can help you. You get in any deeper, there won't be any guarantees."

Again, her nervous laugh surfaced. "You want me to rat on the MCs? Are you crazy? You know what they do to those who talk? You've got UCs and CIs, let them take their chances with those guys."

Out of the blue, Quinn slammed a fist into the wall.

Zoë sprung to her feet, ready to exit stage right.

Sloane grabbed her arm. "Wait."

Reluctantly, she stopped, but not before giving Quinn a sideways glance.

Sloane took a deep breath. "You'll have to forgive my friend's reaction. Until recently, the DEA had an undercover in the Devils organization. He was making inroads, moving up the ranks, and now..." He shook his head. "He's gone dark. No one has seen or heard from him in days."

Zoë felt the color drain from her face and a chill sweep through her, like a brisk winter wind. She rubbed her arms. "What do you mean?"

"I mean he's disappeared."

Her mouth went dry. She thought back to the Lone Horseman's words to Vero in the RV the previous weekend, how he'd taken care of their latest problem. Then the photo, of that fiery red bush. Burning, he'd said, like a message.

Her chest hurt. She couldn't breathe. Is that what the Lone Horseman had been referring to when he'd mentioned he'd taken care of their latest issue? An undercover? A DEA agent?

Jesus.

Sloane sensed her discomfort. "What is it?" he asked.

Zoë turned away. "Nothing. I don't know anything. I mean, it sounds like you have a problem, but it doesn't involve me." She grabbed her small backpack from the floor and strapped it on. "I have to go." She headed toward the exit.

Sloane attempted to reach her one last time as he stepped in front of her and put an outstretched hand on the door. "Zoë, you showing up at Amber McKinley's and hanging around Blade—are you sure this doesn't have anything to do with your mother's murder? You'd tell me if it did, right? I would listen. I would help."

She stared at him, thought about speaking, noticed Quinn balancing precariously on the edge of his chair in the corner, hanging on her every word.

She tightened her lips. "Have a good evening, gentlemen."

CHAPTER 19

With the festivities of the last weekend over and their informant problem taken care of, the Lone Horseman returned to tending to business as usual. Tonight, he was back in Reno, searching for a lowlife known to frequent the casinos late into the night. A gambler and meth dealer, the guy had spent too much time the past few months consuming what he should've been selling, and it had started to interfere with business. Previous warnings from local enforcers had been sent, including a beat down that had left him bloody in a motel bathroom, but this guy didn't seem to be getting the message. His behavior hadn't changed, and he was in serious trouble. He kept trying to win back the money he'd lost on product and profit, and the dangerous downward spiral had begun. One more play. One more round. One more pull of the lever. Now, the money he'd gambled was gone as well as the meth, and he owed the club more than he would ever be able to repay.

Which meant time was up. Currency could no longer help him.

Reno was keeping the Lone Horseman busy of late.

He rode through the parking lots seeking his target's ride. The old Indian he rode was easily identifiable by the paint job on the tank, a red rose with the inscription *Lady Luck*. At a lot near the Eldorado, he found it squeezed in a space between two enormous Ford trucks. It wasn't where you'd expect a motorcycle to be parked but informed the Horseman of one thing—the meth might've cooked this guy's brain to the point it couldn't prevent him from committing certain actions, but it hadn't yet relieved him of the knowledge that those actions had consequences.

He knew he was a dead man.

Inside the casino, where the flashing lights and sounds continued their false promises of future riches and glory, the Horseman walked the aisles searching for his target. Most people, especially the ones who had any sense, made a wide berth for him as he passed, but others, too drunk or stupid to get out of his way, ended up forcibly pushed aside. Yes, cameras were everywhere, but he knew those watching behind the lens were far more interested in seeking out card counters and slot cheats than paying attention to a heavy-handed citizen biker.

Especially when the visibly affiliated bikers were six deep at the blackjack tables and eight deep at the bar, their green rockers and wild boar logo dominating the room. Los Salvajes claimed this casino as their territory and didn't much care for other club members to join them, which was probably why his pussy target had chosen to roll the dice here and not elsewhere. He didn't expect any of the Angels, Devils, or whoever else was in town to come waltzing in. But the Lone Horseman, who wasn't wearing his cuts and wasn't known by his appearance, outside a chosen few, to be a Devil, felt comfortable to move freely among them. Maybe he would even join them later for a drink, see what they had to say about his friends up north before he finished his business this evening.

He roamed by the poker and blackjack areas the casino had cordoned off, tucked in remote corners where people could focus on the cards without the distraction of the slots. The cards were his target's favorite, followed by roulette and craps. Almost immediately, he saw the man sitting at one of the blackjack tables watching hopefully as the dealer turned a card over, then slumping when he realized he'd busted.

The Horseman caught his eye as he passed and gave him a wink.

The target, scrawny, with arms full of freshly picked scabs and a mouthful of rotting teeth, began nervously tapping his foot against the leg of the stool. He didn't know who the Horseman was, but as the tweaker's gaze followed him with wide-eyed paranoia, he seemed to figure it out. The Horseman was there for him. The target already knew.

As the guy scratched at his wayward blond hair and looked uncertain of what to do, the Horseman leaned against an empty wall where he could keep an eye on his friend and ordered a drink from a passing waitress. Soon, the target began to hyperventilate and, much to the chagrin of the other players at his table, broke out in an enormous sweat. The Horseman smiled as two of them picked up their chips and moved to a different table, laughed as the dealer took a step back and sniffed in the target's direction.

Scrambling, the man scooped up what few chips he had left and shuffled off. As he did so, he glanced back over his shoulder several times, waiting for the Horseman's response.

The Horseman figured he might try to make a run for the door, so he followed along, watching him stumble and bumble his way between the crowd of gamblers. Several people turned and issued the tweaker a disgusting look as he physically ran into them, while others fanned the air, trying to rid themselves of his smell. Unable to make a break for it with the Horseman blocking his path, he continued to the only place he could—down a long hallway off to the right to the men's room. The Horseman stopped at the main bar and ordered a drink.

He chuckled. He really loved fucking with these clowns. Did this tweaker actually think he would be idiot enough to kill him in the middle of a crowded casino with two hundred sets of eyes present and watching? No. He would wait until later when his target least expected it, long after the man thought he was home free and his luck was improving. The Horseman only acted when his deeds could neither be tied to him or the club.

As he sipped a new whiskey and coke, he eye-fucked Los Salvajes' members just for the fun of it, then noticed a server he recognized set a tray of dirty glasses on top of the bar. The server, a young man with spiky black hair the Horseman knew from prior visits, often exchanged information for a little cash, believing the Horseman was an undercover ATF agent. He liked to think of himself as a spy.

"Hey, I'm going to take a quick smoke break," he said to the bartender. "Be back in ten." As he headed around a corner, he slung a towel over his shoulder and shot a quick gaze the Horseman's way.

The Horseman finished his drink before heading the kid's direction, then put a twenty in a slot machine and pressed spin. Slowly, the server shuffled his way while he scrolled through his phone, until he was standing directly behind him. "Hey. I thought you might want to know—the little piggies are asking some strange questions tonight."

The piggies he referred to were Los Salvajes. "Like what?"

"They're looking for a guy they call the Lone Horseman. Say he has a pale stallion tatted on his back. Rumor is he's affiliated with the Devils."

The Horseman felt his brows furrow, was glad the server couldn't see his reaction. "What do they want with him?"

"They think he's the guy who popped their VP in Modesto a few years back."

He clenched his jaw. *What the... ?* "Is that right?"

"Yeah. They're asking the staff if they know him, or have ever seen a guy with those tattoos. They say he has another one of a pig carved up like a ham with a grinning Devil taking a bite." He huffed. "Crazy, right?"

A darkness came over the Horseman and his veins began to pulse. He couldn't believe what he was hearing. Only those in high places—the national and chapter presidents—knew of those tatts that represented deeds done for the club. Sometimes during poker games or board meetings, one of them would make a joke about eating pork, and they'd have a good laugh, but only those few knew what they were referencing. He never removed his shirt anywhere other than dark, friendly spaces—like the campfire the previous weekend—and had those tattoos that told of deeds done inked in places only those who truly got close to him could ever see. That leaned toward women he screwed and the ink slingers themselves, none of whom would be smart enough to understand their meaning, or give a shit if they did.

Who in the hell had provided them this information, and how had that individual acquired the knowledge? *When I find out, I will kill them.* "Who told Los Salvajes this?"

"Uh, that I don't know," the kid said, disappointed.

The Horseman nodded. "Well, it doesn't matter. I mean, it's damn funny, but it's bullshit. I'm afraid somebody is yanking their chain. I've investigated the MCs for years, and I've never seen a Devil with any such ink. Good information though. Thanks for passing it along. I'll leave you a little something at the bar."

The guy put out this cigarette. "Thanks. See you around."

The kid went one way, the Horseman the other. Back at the bar, he ordered another whiskey and stared at the Salvajes' members gathered at the other end. It seemed some additional brothers had joined them and they were deep in conversation. Maybe it was the information the kid had just shared with him, but the air in the casino suddenly felt tense, as if an unseen agitator was floating among them.

He suddenly saw what that agitator was: three Nevada Devils wearing their cuts and roaming the casino. The Horseman figured they were here for the same reasons he was—searching for their rogue tweaker—but wondered why: A.J., the national president, had already laid down his orders, and the dealer was now the Horseman's responsibility.

Maybe they hadn't gotten the message?

He started to approach them but thought better of it. After what he'd just learned, it could be detrimental for him to make contact in the presence of their enemy. He wasn't wearing his cuts, and as far as he knew, the Nevada boys didn't know he was one of them, so he slid to the far side of the bar and let them do their job.

They didn't make it far until four members of Los Salvajes stepped forward, with an additional four backing them. "What's your business here?" one of them asked. Most of the Los Salvajes crew appeared to be from the Carson City chapter, with a few Nomads thrown in.

"None of your concern, hamsteak. Step aside."

The guys didn't take kindly to the Devil's insult. They inched ever closer.

The bartender, realizing what was happening and knowing how quickly it could turn ugly, began to clear glasses from the bar. The other patrons, noticing his reaction, followed suit and took their drinks, and bodies, elsewhere.

The rest of the casino, however, remained oblivious, too entranced by their bells, whistles, and spins to understand what was going on. It always amazed him, how people couldn't see what was happening right under their noses until it was too late.

"This is Los Salvajes territory. You're not welcome here."

The lead Nevada Devil, a beast of a man at six five and three hundred pounds, who the Horseman knew as a local enforcer they called Buster, sniffed the air. "It smells like bacon in here. Makes me hungry."

The Horseman wanted to laugh, but gritted his teeth. Normally, he'd be fine with his guys antagonizing LS—hell, earlier in the night, he'd planned to have a little fun with them himself—but they didn't know what he did, that the Salvajes were already fired up with this news about their VP's killer, a man they believed was a patched Devil.

He wondered if he could get word to them, but he couldn't figure out how without tipping their rivals of his association. The Devils weren't going to take their eyes off the enemy in front of them, and if the Horseman walked up to them, they wouldn't know what to make of him. But he needed to do something, because the tensions were rising, and he'd seen this kind of shit go down before: Laughlin, just recently, Carson City.

And it never ended well. Never.

"Why don't you three go back to hell, where you belong?" the LS strongman said.

"Only if you join us," Buster said.

"How about we all make sure you get there?" another Salvajes asked as six other members suddenly saddled up from behind, having left the poker tables in back. They cracked their knuckles and rolled the shiny silver rings they wore around their fingers, anticipating whatever came next.

Just then, a small crowd near the front doors parted, and five more Salvajes brothers entered. One of the men sent two of his comrades to another destination, and the three remaining joined forces at the bar. Yet, even with the additional guests, the casino patrons cast no more than a few curious glances their way, even though the bartender had effectively shut the main bar down and fled the scene.

A man with scraggly salt-and-pepper hair and dark eyes stepped forward to face the lead Devil. Compared to the enormity of Buster, he appeared small and manageable, but the Horseman knew he was not. He was Carson City's VP, a highly paranoid but whip-smart dude they called Blade.

"What's this I hear about an invitation to hell?" he asked.

The Horseman watched. The odds were seventeen to three now, and it wasn't looking good for his boys. If they were wise, they'd back it down.

Buster assessed the situation, did exactly that. "Look, we're not here to engage with you—not tonight. We're just here to find a little weasel who has something that belongs to us."

Blade nodded. "Yeah, I know who that weasel is. Two of our guys are gathering him from the little boys' room right now. How about we make a trade?" He stepped forward. "See, we're looking for someone too. You help us. We'll help you."

Shit. He was going to ask about the Horseman.

Blade proceeded to describe the tattoos on his back, the large pale horse surrounded by broken animals. He also noted his height and weight, and of all damn things, his teeth. "Crooked, with a couple silver caps."

The Horseman fumed. *How the fuck did he get that information?*

Buster chuckled. "Well, that narrows it down. Sounds like damn near every biker I know, minus the ink."

"Yeah?" Blade said. "Well, they call this one the Lone Horseman."

Buster raised his chin. Clearly, he'd heard of him, but offered nothing. "Doesn't ring a bell." Good man.

But the VP didn't buy it. He stepped into Buster's space. "No? Maybe it's one of you, then. Why don't we take those cuts from you and have a look at your skin?"

The two Devils to Buster's side reached for their waistbands and many Los Salvajes followed suit. Threatening a man's cuts was serious business. If the Salvajes pushed this any further, the shit was going to fly, and he, the Horseman, would have to get involved.

But then, maybe that wasn't such a bad idea. The Horseman needed to get this VP alone and force him into a confession. *Who told him about the Lone Horseman?*

The impending altercation was delayed as the other two Los Salvajes members hauled the tweaker from the bathroom. He looked hopeful about whatever the two piggies had promised him until he arrived at the bar, when he saw the Lone Horseman and proceeded to piss himself. Blade and the other Salvajes groaned but, thankfully, didn't pay the Horseman much attention, at least, not until the tweaker did the dumbest damn thing possible. He dropped to his knees and started begging for his life.

The Lone Horseman wanted to shoot him on the spot.

When Blade and the other Salvajes wheeled to see who the man was afraid of—all hell broke loose. The guns came out, shots were fired, and retaliation followed. The noise and chaos finally woke the mesmerized zombies sitting in front of their donation machines, and panic ensued.

Some dove to the floor. Others stormed for the exits. But all began to scream, including the tweaker, who suddenly found himself abandoned in the middle of a raging battle. The Horseman grabbed him as he took out the .45 from his waistband and held it front and center in case any pig got in his path. Then he told him to keep his head down as he pushed him into the crowd and they made their way toward the exit. He thought they were making good headway until, behind him, he heard a voice call out. "Horseman!"

Fuck.

He didn't turn around, but it didn't matter. The fact that he'd stopped in his tracks at the mention of his name gave his enemy all the information he needed. The Horseman spun to see the Carson City VP, Blade, standing before him, the look in his eyes as wild as his hair. The Horseman could've shot him, but the Salvajes didn't give him the chance. The guns raised and they fired. The Horseman used the tweaker as cover and watched two bullets pierce the man's chest, courtesy of Los Salvajes, as he returned the favor and emptied his .45 toward his enemies. The remaining Salvajes ducked and dove, including Blade, who was shouting commands to his brothers in Spanish.

Seizing the opportunity, the Horseman pushed into the crowd, shoving two women out of his way and stepping on the back of an old man who'd fallen in the panic. He knew the Salvajes would not fire into a crowd of citizens, so as long as he kept himself surrounded, he could get out. He returned the gun back to his waistband and forged ahead until he made it out the front door, where officers shouted at people to run down the street and get as far away from the casino as they could.

A single look back inside, and he saw the big Devil, Buster, lying bloody on the floor and, in a far corner, a member of Los Salvajes clutching his chest. Surrounding the fallen were four others with weapons drawn, protecting him as their brothers tried to gather him up and remove him from the casino. Like the other two Devils and the Horseman, the Salvajes knew cameras abounded and SWAT would soon charge in. It didn't serve any of them any good to stick around and continue this battle.

Not here, not now.

But it would come. That was not in question.

CHAPTER 20

Zoë watched the evening news covering the casino shooting and grew ever more restless. In the bedroom, Max was packing for a conference that would take him out of town for the next four days, and the timing couldn't be worse. The shooting between the Devils and Los Salvajes had been a direct result of the information she'd given to Blade about the Lone Horseman, and now she feared for her safety more than ever. What if the Lone Horseman traced the information back to her? What if he returned to confront her or, worse, came after Max or Oliver to teach her a lesson?

"Do you really have to go?" she asked.

She stared at the television, chewed one of her few nails left.

He rolled up a tie, stuck it in the suitcase. "You've been chewing on your nails a lot lately, you know that? You used to always keep them long. What happened?"

"I don't know. Stress, I guess." She sat on the side of the bed, rubbed her face.

"It's just for a few days," he said, grabbing her shoulder. "Just like your recent conference." He offered a wry smile.

There was something about the way he said those words that she didn't like.

What was he implying? Did he know that she'd lied to him? She wondered if she should just confess her sins right now, tell him that she'd gone to an old friend to see if he could help find her mother's killer and, instead, ignited a war. Admit she spent the weekend with a bunch of bikers in the middle of the Nevada desert trying to get close to the leader's wife and nearly got a man killed. Yet, all she said was, "Yeah, I know."

He zipped the suitcase shut, and she stood to see him out. At the door, she brushed her hands down the length of his chest, smoothing the unseen wrinkles from his shirt. "You look good. Give those politicians an earful." She kissed and hugged him longer than he probably expected.

He looked her over, concern arched in his brow. "I'll be back Friday."

She nodded, blew another kiss as he walked out the door.

As he pulled out of their tree-lined gravel drive and turned onto the state road that ran beyond it, she felt the invisible shield of protection surrounding her and Oliver, and their home, disappear.

She sat at the kitchen table with a cup of coffee and tried to build her resolve. *Come on, girl, you got this.* The Lone Horseman was not going to link her to the knowledge that Los Salvajes suddenly had on him. She was not the only one who'd ever seen this guy with his shirt off. She couldn't be. Hell, fifty-plus people saw him just a week ago. The snitch could be any one of them, or dozens of others.

She repeated this over and over until she believed it, and for a time, it worked. Yet, all day long, outside the shop and Oliver's day care, she'd catch herself watching, worrying, and waiting for something bad to happen. That first night alone, she dreamed about all of them coming for her: Riot for letting him take a beating, Blade for talking to the police, the Lone Horseman for ratting him out.

At three p.m. the next day, Zoë finished work early and stopped to pick up Oliver again. Normally, she and Max rotated this duty. He'd pick up Oliver and take him back to his office on the afternoons he reserved for patient paperwork; Zoë would get him on days she scheduled clients early and ended early. Whether it was school or day care, they kept up the same routine and picked him up at the same time. They liked the consistency and the special parenting time it gave each of them.

As she pulled up just shy of the fenced-in playground, Oliver came bursting out the doors and ran across the yard. In his right hand, he carried a toy airplane and held it high above his head as if it were flying. Behind him, another little boy followed, his arms outstretched like wings. Ever since she and Max had taken him to the Reno airshow the prior year, Oliver had declared he wanted to be a pilot. He'd spend his time outside flying pretend airplanes, and Zoë would often hear him in his room talking to pretend passengers. They'd only taken him on one real flight to date, a quick jump to Southern California to see Max's parents, but it had proved enough for him to absorb the lingo. Tomorrow, his career ambitions might change, but for now, they enjoyed seeing his passion—and it was certainly preferable to his other fascination with guns and shooting.

She met him at the side of the car, helped him into his booster seat in back as the friend behind him flew off in the direction of his own mother. Oliver continued to make flight noises with his mouth, flew his plane across the seat until it crashed against the window. "Mayday, mayday, we're going into a mountain."

"Hey, buddy," Zoë said before she shut the door, "the goal is *not* to crash the plane."

Oliver giggled.

At home, she turned on the television and started fixing dinner, Oliver's favorite, spaghetti and meatballs. From her purse, she heard the slight vibration of the cell phone Blade had given her and let it ring. For two days now, he'd been calling, but she didn't want to talk to him. She'd seen his face on the casino news footage, knew the police had to be interrogating him and the entire club. She was surprised Sloane hadn't called too, but she imagined he had his hands full, and truth was, she didn't want to talk to him either. This week, she just wanted to be left alone with her son and figure out what the hell she'd gotten herself into, and whether it was time to quit before anyone else got killed.

The news said a Devil and one citizen had died in the shooting and four others were wounded. Two remained in critical condition, one Devil and one Los Salvajes, and were, ironically, being treated in the same Reno ICU. Zoë could only imagine what the nurses and doctors were enduring there, having to control rival clubs and their members as they roamed the same hospital corridors to visit their ailing brothers. She didn't envy them, not one bit.

She put the phone on silent, finished fixing dinner, then cuddled with Oliver on the couch the rest of the evening while watching his favorite Pixar movie for the hundredth time. Hearing his giggles made her relax, at least for a time. But later that night, she woke several times to the sound of motorcycles on the state road that ran outside their house, and if she didn't know better, they purposefully revved the pipes as they passed.

The sound gave her chills.

She spent the third day of Max's absence jumpier than ever. She used the workstation nearest the front window so she could keep an eye on the street and take note of anybody checking the place out. Twice, she saw a large group of bikers pass by, and she was positive she saw Brady Sloane's unmarked car make a round as well, the same one he'd driven when he'd stopped outside the shop before.

Screech, noticing her unease, asked if she was okay.

She stated repeatedly that she was fine, but she could tell he didn't believe her.

That evening—in addition to retrieving a gun Max kept locked in the closet and sticking it in her bedside drawer—she decided to make some preparations, put some extra barriers between the great outdoors and the inside of the house. Across the last step of the porch and the front door, she routed string eight inches high and stapled it to the posts and doorjamb. She also pounded a few nails in the porch itself but left them protruding an inch high so someone could easily trip on them. Inside, she blocked the windows with lamps and other heavy objects. None of these things would stop an intruder if they really wanted in, but at least it would wake her up and let her know someone was there.

Max would find her tactics silly—call them her *"Home Alone"* initiatives—but when she'd lived on the streets, similar strategies had served to notify her when someone was around and had saved her from harm on more than one occasion.

She had hoped Oliver wouldn't notice the changes, but as usual, his little observant self didn't miss a beat. "Don't worry, Mom. I'll protect you if the bad guys come." He took out one of his toy guns and fired several times. "Boom, boom, boom."

That night, she sat beside him on the couch and watched him play video games while she thought about how best to proceed with exposing the Horseman. If Blade had his way, the man would end up dead—as he nearly had already—but that's not what Zoë really wanted. To her, death was too easy. What she really wanted was to see him stand trial after trial and rot in jail. And not just for her mother, but for all the women represented by those animals tattooed on his back.

The more she thought about it, the more she thought it was the right thing to do. She had to get Blade and his trigger-happy comrades to back off. And she had to figure out a way to nail the Horseman for specific murders. Which meant she needed to get actual evidence that linked him to the crimes.

But how and what?

Outside, she heard the wind stir and a soft thump hit the porch. She frowned, looked toward the door. She wanted to get up and check outside, but Oliver was in a sword battle with a meaty one-eyed ogre, and she didn't want to disturb him with her worries.

Until it happened again. But this time, following the thump, something stirred and made a crack, then scraped across the window like the branch of a tree. Zoë gasped, and Oliver turned to stare wide-eyed at the door. "What was that?" he asked.

Zoë put a finger to her lips and asked him to quiet the game while she slipped toward the door. Oliver did as she instructed, then nestled himself on the floor between the couch and coffee table, intent on his mom's every move. Zoë was careful not to walk in front of the window, but duck beneath it, until she stood on the side between it and the front door. Breathing heavily, she pulled back the curtain ever so slightly to see out. The porch light was on, but nothing seemed amiss—until she heard shuffling, another bump, and the stairs creak.

She quickly pulled back, laid flat against the wall.

Her heart thudded in her ears. She had to get the gun.

She motioned for Oliver, told him to go into the closet. At first, he refused, shaking his little brown bangs over big brown eyes, but she put a finger to her lips and pointed at the door. "Go," she whispered. "Stay in the corner, don't make a sound. No matter what happens."

"Mommy."

"It'll be okay. If anything happens, I want you to shut your eyes and dial this button." It was her preprogrammed number to 911. "Tell them we're in trouble and to get here right away. Got it?"

He didn't like it, but he took the cell phone, rested his little finger on the button.

Zoë went to the bedroom and retrieved the gun, loaded bullets with a shaky hand. A couple spilled to the floor. She put her finger on the trigger but kept it at her side pointed toward the floor. The last thing she wanted to do was to accidentally shoot herself or, God forbid, Oliver. She killed the remaining lights on in the house absent the television, which showed a frozen image of the game Oliver had been playing, and stood near the front door. She listened intently, waiting to hear the pop of a nail, the scrape of a shoe, or crack of a branch. Five minutes, ten, the world was silent except for her breath and the thrumming of her heart. Then, suddenly, a flash of movement came from behind a tree outside and a blue shirt could be seen running down the driveway.

She yanked the door open and shouted, "Stop! I've got a gun. Show yourself."

The man, back turned, put his hands in the air. "I'm sorry, I'm sorry." His voice was high-pitched and conveyed a bit of a lisp.

"Turn around," Zoë said. Her hands shook.

He slowly spun until he faced her, revealing a scrawny kid, maybe eighteen, with thin blond hair, pale skin, and a face full of acne. He continued to hold his hands, abnormally long and misshapen for his thin frame, up in the air.

She shot a glance at the nearby trees and brush, the driveway leading to the road. "Are you alone? How did you get here? What's your name?"

He frantically nodded, staring at the gun. "Alone, yes. I walked. I just, I'm hungry, and Mr. Max said I could come by if I got hungry. My name is Jason."

Shit. Zoë took a breath and tried to slow her frantic heart. She lowered the gun, hands shaking, and placed it on the table just inside the door. She grabbed the doorjamb and tried to breathe, tried not to break out in tears. She stood erect and wiped her face. "You're one of Max's kids? From the shelter?"

The blond kid nodded repeatedly. "I'm sorry I scared you."

Zoë bent over, put a hand across her stomach. Thank God she hadn't shot the gun. She heard the closet door open behind her. "It's okay, buddy. Come on out." Oliver's little feet pitter-pattered across the floor. He grabbed Zoë's leg and looked outside.

"For God's sake, why didn't you just ring the doorbell?" she asked.

He fidgeted with his hands, his fingers dancing while the muscles in his face twitched. His eyes searched the dark night sky. "I...I tried, but I tripped on the porch. There was something on my ankle. It scared me."

Of course. The string.

His brief stutter tripped her memory. Max had mentioned this kid before and said he was mentally challenged—something about a fall from a balcony as a toddler—and suddenly, Zoë felt terrible. "Please, come inside, Jason. This is Oliver."

The man-boy seemed uncertain until Oliver poked his head farther around the corner and he smiled. Seeing a child clearly made him feel more at ease. Oliver asked if he liked video games.

Zoë noticed his clothes were wet, as if he'd been caught in a rainstorm, and he was shivering. "Come on," she said, reaching out. "Let me get you some dry clothes. Then I can make you something to eat."

She gave him some of Max's old clothes and had him shower and change in the bathroom. They were far too large and hung on him the way a bed sheet hangs on a clothesline, but he was dry and that was what mattered. She cooked a box of macaroni and cheese and green beans—*comfort food,* as her mom would've said—and he chowed down on a late dinner. Afterward, she heard Oliver chattering and Jason laughing as if he were a child himself. An hour later, she tucked Oliver in bed and put the young man on the couch. He quickly went to sleep.

She turned out the lights and rechecked all the locks. In the darkness, she couldn't help but stand there and stare at the kid a few minutes, remembering how it felt when she was homeless and got a rare night with a roof over her head and a couch or bed to sleep on. The sleep would be deep, the dreams endless. She decided that for the next few days, at least until Max's return, she would have Jason stay. He needed a place to sleep and food to eat, and she felt better having an extra person in the house. Taking care of her boys would be the distraction she needed to forget what else the world contained outside, at least for a while.

CHAPTER 21

After a happy reunion weekend with Max home, Zoë once again started thinking about the Lone Horseman. Blade had continued to call, and she knew he wouldn't be put off for long, but before she contacted him, she wanted to do a little investigating on her own. Her conversation with Sloane, coupled with the photograph of the fiery red bush the Horseman had given to Vero, had her mind working overtime. An undercover agent was missing, and the Lone Horseman had taken care of their little problem. Maybe she was crazy, but once again, she couldn't help but think the two were related—maybe the red bush was the place he'd tossed a gun or knife, or even killed and buried the man.

If he had buried something—or someone—in the desert, that could be reason for Sloane, or the DEA, to arrest him, which would put the Lone Horseman in custody and save her from having to work with Los Salvajes anymore. It would also buy her time to further investigate his other crimes, and if she wanted, continue to build on her relationship with Vero. If there was anybody who possibly knew the Lone Horseman and his deeds and could provide the needed links, it would be her. Zoë felt certain of it.

The Lone Horseman had taken the photo someplace he called Big Red. She wasn't much into nature so didn't know much about Nevada's parks and wildlife, but she remembered him saying that even the most dedicated hiker would turn back after seeing the warning signs posted in the area. To her, that sounded like a place that had been abandoned, maybe an old factory or farm.

She was close. The internet said Big Red was a nickname for an old mine about sixty miles northeast of Reno. It had produced silver as late as the early twentieth century, then, like so many others, faded into disrepair. It sat on land governed by the Bureau of Land Management, as about 90 percent of Nevada did, and was protected by various signage warning of its dangers and possible contamination. But it was a large area, acres and acres, and she wondered if there would be any possibility of finding the proverbial needle in the haystack. She hoped that, even if there were hundreds of red bushes, there wouldn't be many at the location showing the dilapidated structure in back with the bright-red roof disappearing into the side of a mountain.

After calling Screech early the next day and letting him know she wasn't feeling well, she once again borrowed the motorcycle from her client and headed to Big Red. She didn't need to keep riding the bike but thought she might be able to make better inroads into the mine on it rather than by car. Hiking wasn't her bag, so she'd rather get as close as she could to whatever she was searching for before having to hoof it.

The ride north was hot, but there wasn't much traffic heading that way on a weekday and she made good time. At the exit listed on the map she'd memorized, she turned and followed a series of ever-narrowing roads until she saw a single old white-and-black sign denoting the town of Colt, one of Nevada's many ghost towns that used to be a flourishing mining community. Here the roads became dirt, and she slowed down as she began to wind up and around the rugged terrain.

As she turned another corner, her side mirror caught movement behind her that glinted off the morning sun. She'd seen a few cars on the roads after she'd exited the highway, but she couldn't imagine there would be many—if any—coming up here for the day. Paranoia kicking in, she decided to take a few wandering laps around the area to see if it continued to stick with her. Her misgiving waned when, after a mile, it no longer appeared in any of her mirrors.

She stopped at a road where, at the top, several wooden structures jutted into the sky and that red tin roof stood out like a billboard. Her heart raced along with the bike's engine. She felt she was close to where the Horseman had taken his picture, the bush with its hidden "message."

She revved the bike and began the long climb up the mountain. As she got closer, the structures grew ever larger, along with the fences surrounding parts of the land that had several signs attached to it, warning of the dangers within. At the point she could go no farther, she parked the bike, took off her helmet, and checked out the terrain. Like the rest of the state, it was dry, with cracked earth and an abundance of rocks and boulders intertwined with sagebrush and grasses. Wild desert marigold and periwinkle phlox covered the ground, along with colored flowers of every kind, showcasing the desert in bloom. And sprinkled here and there among them were a rare bush with a rich green leaf and bright-red flowers.

She examined one up close, heart pounding.

She scanned the area with the perspective of the photograph she remembered, started hiking around the fencing until she had the red roof jutting into the mountain as she remembered. The hillside was steep in spots and the dirt and rocks small and loose, which caused her footing to slip at times and send small slides down the slope.

Finally, she came upon a flatter surface that stretched south for a good solid mile. To the north was the mountain and fence that rose twelve feet high, effectively blocking the entrance to the mine, which had also been boarded up and filled in with rock and debris.

She glanced up at the looming red roof, turned, and started walking south. The angle of the picture put the fiery red bush directly in front of the red angled roof, but it had to be located much farther out for the structure to appear so small and singular in the background. Her heart fluttered when she came upon the first bush in her path and wheeled to look back. The mine still appeared too large for the image she remembered, so she kept on, searching for the next one.

For a moment, she thought she heard the echo of an engine, another vehicle in the area, wondered if BLM trucks monitored the place and would soon catch up with her and ask her to leave. She needed to find the spot quickly before that happened.

Another hundred yards or so, she came upon a second bush that appeared to be in the right location. Circling it, she noted the ground beneath it seemed recently disturbed, the cracked and dried earth not as prevalent there. On the back side, she held up her phone camera and took in the image, realized it was the path she remembered.

The Lone Horseman had recently stood where she was right now—she was certain of it. She stared down at the bush as if it were an oracle, wondered what secrets it contained. She started to kneel and brush away the earth when she suddenly heard the approach of footsteps from behind her, boots crunching across the desert terrain.

She wheeled.

"Nice day to take a hike in the mountains?"

Zoë gasped, startled. She was damn glad to see the man was Brady Sloane and not the Lone Horseman, as she'd feared. "Jesus," she uttered. "You scared the shit out of me."

He removed his sunglasses and stuck them on his head. "What are you doing out here? Don't tell me you've developed a sudden interest in old mines."

She regarded the crisscrossed boards to the north climbing into the sky, squinted into the sun. "Can't a girl just take a hike?"

He crossed his arms, waited.

She kicked at the dirt, examined the landscape surrounding them for any other signs of movement. "You can't do this, you know—follow me. If they see me with you..." She shook her head. "You're putting me in danger."

"Who's they? Los Salvajes? The Devils? Both?"

She didn't answer.

"The truth is, you're putting yourself in danger," he said. "I'm trying to protect you, Zoë. I don't know what crazy mission you're on or how you play into this motorcycle club rivalry, but I sense you know or have information these clubs want, and apparently they're willing to kill to get it."

She cocked her head. "I wasn't at the casino shooting. I didn't make them turn on each other. What makes you think I'm involved? That I'm—what did you call it—on a mission?"

Sloane grinned. "Because I know you. It's this look you have when a sole purpose is driving you. Like you want to grab hold of it and shake it until the truth comes out."

Her brow furrowed. *Damn.* Maybe he'd paid more attention to her in those days when she'd come to him with ideas about her mother's murder than she'd realized.

"Talk to me," he said. "The biker theory—was I closer than I thought?"

Zoë groaned. She put her hands on her hips and mumbled and grumbled to herself as she turned in a circle. Could she trust him? Should she tell him? He was clearly on to her, and the truth would come out sooner or later, so maybe she should give him something.

She sighed. "Yes."

He took a step back, surprised. "You think, or you know?"

"I know, but I'm afraid if I tell you more, you won't believe me. At least, not yet. Suffice it to say that it seems to be when a certain club has a run to some location once a year, another woman ends up dead."

His eyes widened. "Another? What the hell does that mean?"

"Exactly what I said, and what you're thinking right now."

"Individual or group?"

"Individual."

His features darkened. "How many?"

She studied him. "You won't believe me."

"Try me."

"Fourteen, maybe more."

Sloane's jaw dropped. "Come on. That's not possible."

"Like I said, you wouldn't..." She started to walk away.

He raised his hands. "Okay, okay, you're right. I'm listening."

She turned back toward him. "I can't say for sure, yet, but it's my theory that at least once a year during one of their runs, a woman is raped and murdered. Think that's coincidence?"

"You certainly don't seem to. Which club? Los Salvajes?"

"No."

"Devils?"

She paused, then nodded.

He let out a deep breath. "Your mother?"

"Yes."

"Amber McKinley?"

"Yes."

Now he was paying attention. He rubbed his jaw. "Who else?"

She shook her head. *Not yet.* She'd given him enough.

He tried to stare it out of her. It didn't work.

"And you know this how? A tip from Blade? Or somebody else?"

"I'm not ready to tell you that."

He rubbed and scratched at his jaw and paced. He was growing impatient and frustrated. "Jesus, you're talking about a serial killer, Zoë. You have to tell me what you're thinking. I can't help you otherwise."

She pondered the rich blue sky and blazing yellow sun that promised yet another day of intense heat, not unlike the pressure she was feeling right now.

"What I think, Detective Sloane, is maybe you should find a reason to dig near that bush right there with the flaming-red flowers. But you didn't hear it from me."

CHAPTER 22

Sloane stayed up half the night wondering what kind of story he could come up with that would give him a good reason to convince the Nevada Division of Minerals and the Bureau of Land Management that he needed to dig up a chunk of land on their territory near Big Red. To most people, an anonymous tip of a body buried on the property would be enough to get someone to act, but in Nevada, they received so many such claims that the BLM and local PDs would use up their resources following up on them without additional justification—especially those stories that ended with "somewhere in the desert."

Also, Sloane had no idea whether Zoë suspected there was a body buried there or something else entirely, drugs or guns or evidence of another crime. She hadn't said. Still, this one was specific—beneath or near that fiery red bush—and if he stuck with the body claim, they might be willing to act. So, the next morning, Sloane got on the phone and called the necessary federal and state agencies about digging near the mine, and to his surprise, they agreed. They would send a couple of their people to observe and consult on any safety hazards, and as long as they could be included in any photo op, they would be happy to oblige. And so it was that at ten a.m. two days later, Sloane and Ramirez drove up to Big Red along with one of their best crime scene techs and an excavation specialist from the Nevada Investigation Division and set out to discover what exactly was buried at Big Red.

They parked next to the BLM truck and joined the others gathered near the fenced gate with the giant danger sign warning of the hazards within. "You really think somebody got a dead body over this fence?" the BLM guy said. He was short with yellow-blond hair and a stocky build. "We drove the perimeter. Didn't find a single area where the fencing had been cut or was loose."

"No," Sloane said. "The area in question is outside the mine itself. Down the hill there approximately two hundred yards. Their claim is something was buried near a red bush there."

The guy took off his sunglasses, glanced across the landscape. Sloane knew he had to be thinking the same thing as Rodriquez and the others. "Which one?"

He cleared his throat. "They said it was on a straight path from the fence and tied a shoelace on it." It had been the only thing he could think to do a few days ago to remind himself of the location. Now it would work in his favor.

Again, they all stared in that direction. "Did they say *something* or a *body*? Don't tell me we're doing all this for somebody's buried time capsule," the BLM guy continued.

Sloane realized his mistake. "The implication was a body."

The guy squinted. "They say anything else? No offense, but there are literally thousands of bushes and scrub around. How do they know it's that bush? What the hell would they be doing here in the middle of the night? Sounds suspicious."

"They said they were camping," he lied. Sloane started to elaborate more but thought better of it. All of Quinn's and Zoë's talk of undercovers, confidential informants, and citizens working in cooperation with the outlaw motorcycle clubs made him rethink what he had to say. Those who traded information could be anyone, including this guy or even someone in his own department, and the last thing he wanted was to make Zoë a target by slipping up on a detail that indicated he was lying. Later, he would get the particulars of exactly how she knew, whether it was something she'd witnessed or heard from another source, but he could deal with that later.

"That's all I know. Come on, let's go."

They hiked down to the bush where the shoestring flapped in the wind. The excavation specialist walked the perimeter around the area one hundred feet in every direction, testing the dry, cracked soil for any signs of recent disturbance. With soil this hard and full of clay, it would take a strong man with a substantial shovel to dig beyond the first eight inches or so, yet they didn't see an area that appeared disturbed except directly beneath the bush. Sloane hoped they'd be able to locate the spot on their own without having to call in the team with ground-penetrating radar.

"Looks to me like the spot isn't near the bush; it is the bush," Ramirez suggested.

He and Sloane knelt by the roots, examined them with their gloves and trowels. For a bush that had supposedly been in the desert for years, the soil beneath it was surprisingly loose. At this time of year, when little rain fell, most of the ground was like concrete. "Yes, this is it," Sloane said. "Whatever it is, it's directly beneath the bush."

At just after eleven a.m., beneath the intense desert sun, the team pitched an orange tent for cover and began digging at the direction of the excavation specialist. First, they worked to remove the soil around the roots, then began to snip them away.

To their surprise, the roots were remarkably shallow, possibly indicating the bush had only recently been planted or relocated there. Either way, it told Sloane one thing: they were digging in the right spot.

Once they removed the bush, they each dug, scraped, and brushed at the soil beneath it. It was a tedious process, but the last thing they wanted was to damage any evidence that may lie beneath the surface, especially if they hit skin or bone.

A few inches deeper, a smell they all recognized began to surface, and the flies gathered. Ramirez turned away and tried to catch a few fresh breaths, cursed. "Something down there for sure, partner."

He stuck his trowel in the ground a few feet away, ran back to their truck near the fence line, and retrieved several bandanas. After returning, he handed them out to the team to cover their noses and mouths. As they continued their work, the crime scene tech took photographs of the scene, documenting every part of the process. They didn't want anything going unrecorded.

It wasn't until four hours later that they hit pay dirt. "Think we've got something," Sloane said. He pushed on an area that clearly wasn't earth, felt it give. The excavation specialist took a brush and began sweeping the dirt away until a large splotch of dark-blue fabric began to emerge.

"What is that, denim?" Sloane asked.

"Yes, I think so," she said.

They all picked up brushes, Sloane, Ramirez, even the guys from BLM and the Nevada Division of Minerals, who'd mostly stayed silent the better part of the afternoon, and began to help uncover what was more and more beginning to look—and smell—like a body.

Sloane's nerves jittered worse than the fine dirt blowing across the desert landscape. Who or what the hell was buried out here near the mine? And how in the hell had Zoë Cruse known about it?

After revealing several inches of denim, they finally got to the important stuff—flesh and bone, a bare foot covered in dried blood and mud. The foot, however, was positioned at a wholly unnatural angle to the shin above it, indicating one, or many, bones had been broken—or even severed—to be shoved into the grave.

Ramirez groaned.

Two hours later, they had most of the man's legs—or what used to be his legs—exposed and removed, and in another two, his arms, which lay beneath. By the time they got to the torso, the day was fading into night, and as the sun moved over and painted a fiery reddish-orange landscape across the western Nevada sky, Sloane stood there with the hot wind blowing across his face and saw the dismembered body of a man slowly come out of his grave. And though some decomposition had already taken place, and bullets had done their fair share of damage, the badge resting on his chest left little doubt to his identity. The man was DEA Special Agent Quinn's undercover, the one who'd gone missing after infiltrating the Devils.

"Is that who I think it is?" Ramirez asked.

Sloane nodded. He stood over the body, his heart running a marathon, a thousand thoughts speeding through his head. He looked at the badge, then back to the red bush, began to nod as the intended message became clear: not God speaking to Moses over the burning bush, but the Devils handing down their own set of commandments to the feds—thou shall not mess with us.

CHAPTER 23

Zoë woke early to open the tattoo shop, as Screech had decided to take a mini-vacation to San Diego with the guy he'd met at his church. He'd finally admitted to Zoë that the guy was more than a friend, but continued to insist he would make a great addition to the business. Every day, he would bring it up, and every day, she kept ignoring it. He didn't realize Zoë had far more important things on her mind—things like keeping safe, avoiding exposure, and tracking a murderer of women.

She opened the door and turned off the alarm system when a shadow from the back room made her jump. She wheeled around and gasped when she saw Blade sitting in a chair, thumbing through one of her portfolios. "Nice work," he said, setting the book aside.

"Jesus, how the hell did you get in here?"

He shrugged. "There are ways."

Joining him, she threw her backpack on the counter along with her keys. "Well, a whole lot of good that alarm system is doing me." She smoothed her hair, trying to calm herself.

"Maybe you should answer your phone once in a while so people don't have to go to such extremes to contact you. How long were you planning to ignore me?"

She glanced away, clicked her tongue. "I wasn't ignoring you. I just needed some time and space after what went down at the festival and then the casino. You didn't tell me people were going to get shot and die."

He snorted. "I didn't shoot anybody."

She leered at him. "Hello? I saw you on the news, the footage of when you entered the casino along with four others from your crew."

"Yeah. But did you see us shoot anybody?"

She frowned, thought about how the footage the media repeatedly played was only of the five Los Salvajes members and three Devils going in, but never showed clips of the melee that had occurred inside. "The police are probably keeping that footage for themselves, for evidence."

He chuckled that special Blade laugh. The one that made her skin crawl. "No, sweetheart, trust me, the media loves a bloodbath. It's just that, as it turned out, the camera above the bar wasn't working at the time of the shooting. Computer images are all jacked up. Police can't make out a thing." He took out a jar of chew, scooped a thumbnail of it, and stuck it between his teeth and gums, smiled.

She sat in the chair opposite him. "Gee. I wonder how that happened."

"Tough break for the police."

"They come talk to you?"

Again, that chuckle. "Oh yeah. Me and my old friend, Brady Sloane, we've had a few conversations." He sucked on the tobacco and rapped his fingers against the arm of the chair. "He asked about you. Wanted me to tell you that you should really think about what he said and get out while you can."

His smile vanished. Zoë knew it was trouble.

"Want to tell me why you've been talking to the police? I told you no police."

"I haven't," she said reflexively.

He raised an eyebrow, looked like he could beat the shit out of her.

Zoë fidgeted. "I mean, yes, they came to me, but I didn't tell them anything."

"Them?"

"Sloane and some little weasel named Quinn. DEA."

He emitted a string of curse words, spat in a cup. "How'd they get wind of you?"

She rolled her eyes. "The same way you do, of course. Undercovers, CIs. Sloane said they got intel that I'd been hanging at the clubhouse, then admitted they had officers staked at the festival in Vegas, taking video and notes. He drilled me about what Riot and I were doing there with the Devils."

Blade was not pleased. He muttered to himself, balled his hands into fists. "You telling me I've got a rat?"

"I don't know. I didn't say that." She reached for her backpack, pulled out the new pack of cigarettes she'd bought on the way in. Removed one and lit it. In addition to biting her nails, the stress had her smoking more than normal. "That son-of-a-bitch Quinn had the audacity to ask me if I was delivering meth and guns for you through my shop here, then insinuated I was having an affair and threatened to tell my husband." She exhaled smoke, let it drift across the room. "Piece of shit."

"So what were you going to do?" Blade said. "Just opt out of our arrangement?"

She cocked her head. "I thought about it."

"Hey," he growled, "we're taking heat because of this."

Zoë huffed. "No shit. That's what happens when you kill people."

He rapped those fingers again. Seemed to think about her words, her attitude. She didn't care. She was tired of everyone following her around, telling her what to do.

"Look. We need you in. You don't get a free pass," he said.

"Why? You don't need me anymore. You know what he looks like now."

He rose from the chair, walked over to take a bigger spit into the trash can. "We can't. There's too much heat now. With the incident at the casino, we're going to have to lay low for a time. We can't get close to the Devils, but you and Riot can. You can carry on with the plan."

Zoë laughed. "Are you crazy? There is no way Riot is going to go back in. They beat the crap out of him."

"Riot does whatever I say. Besides"—Blade grinned, gestured toward her with open arms—"he loves spending time with you. Told me that himself."

She rolled her eyes, took a huge inhale of smoke and nicotine. The minute it hit her nervous system, she could feel the charge ignite. "I don't know if it's safe. How do we know that the Devils don't know about us too? All these damn undercovers and confidential informants, no one can keep a secret in this town. I want the Lone Horseman as bad as you do, but I'd prefer not to end up like the last guy he took out."

She recalled the message that Sloane had sent her, notifying her about the body of the missing DEA agent. The media hadn't picked up on it yet, but when it did, shit was going to hit the fan. First the Horseman had lost his secret identity, and now the DEA agent he'd killed had surfaced in the desert. Even if he didn't yet know about her, how long could it be before he put it all together?

Blade's eyes narrowed. A ray of light casting between a gap in the closed blinds highlighted a deep scar on his cheek. "What do you know about it?"

She hesitated, uncertain if she should say anything, but it was clear he already knew something. "The DEA's missing undercover? I know everything about it."

He slammed a fist against the wall, causing her to flinch. "How? I thought you said you weren't working with them. I thought you said you didn't tell them anything. But you must've. You sure as shit didn't tell me. Something you forgot?"

"I didn't forget. I just wasn't sure what it was I saw. When I was with Vero in the RV, the Horseman came in and gave her a picture for her scrapbook. I thought it was strange because it was just a photo of a bush near some old mine. He told me he'd taken care of their latest problem. I didn't put two and two together until Sloane mentioned Quinn's missing UC."

She crushed her cigarette out. "I did some research and realized the photo was taken at an old mine. I went searching for the bush, and that bastard Sloane followed me. He found me out in the desert looking at the landscape."

Blade muttered. "Sneaky little bastards."

"Yeah? They aren't the only ones apparently. How the hell did you know? There's been no news made public yet about who or what they found."

He grunted. Cast a sideways glance. As usual, he didn't care to answer when the questions were directed at him.

"Right," she said. "See why I'm afraid of going back to the Devils? The Horseman knows Los Salvajes are looking for him, and he knows that you can identify him. That makes you a marked man. He connects Riot or me with you, or me with that photo I saw and the body in the desert? We are all dead."

Blade stepped toward her, towering over her like an ogre. "That's why we have to find him first and take him out. Your little trip to the desert will now have the feds initiating a full investigation into the Devils. The Lone Horseman will go underground. We have to go there too."

Zoë gritted her teeth. "I told you I didn't want him dead." She stood and pointed a finger at his chest. "I don't want him buried in the desert. I want him to stand trial. I want him to pay. Dying is not enough."

He moved toward her finger, pressing it deeper, and she could smell his sweat, day-old cologne, and stale beer. "Well, aren't you a sadistic little queen?"

"Call it whatever you want. Dying is easy. I want him to suffer the same way he made my mother, and all those other women, suffer. Got it?"

He shook his head. "It's too late for that. He knows that we know who he is. If we don't take him out first, he'll come for us. And he won't stop. Even if he lands in prison, he'll have others avenge him."

Zoë studied him, the fierce, dark eyes, the long, scraggly hair. Blade was a man who spoke from experience. On one hand, she wanted the Horseman in prison despite the risk. On the other hand, she knew Blade was right. And it seemed an impossible situation to reconcile.

She paced the room. "You're right. His brothers will avenge him."

Blade shook his head. "The Devils? Maybe, but that's where it gets tricky. They may not say so, but if push came to shove, death or prison, my guess is the Devils would choose to have the Horseman disappear permanently rather than risk the feds working him over in prison. Maybe he wouldn't talk, but maybe he would. It's always a crapshoot. They couldn't risk their entire organization being brought down at the hands of one man, and the Lone Horseman—he's got the goods, the worst kind of goods—on the Devils. He goes to prison, they might take him out on their own."

She frowned. "You think they'd kill him?"

"It's a hazard of the job."

Zoë considered it, wasn't sure she believed it. "I don't know. I didn't see that with them. Unless he turned on the club first, I think the Devils would defend him to the end and beyond. That's why I think him going down for the individual murders makes more sense. They aren't club related other than they occurred during runs. The Devils could walk away without incident."

Blade spit into the trash again, wiped his mouth with the back of his hand. She could tell he was growing frustrated with her, just like Sloane had at the mine, but she didn't care. Every step now had to be carefully thought out and the potential results examined before they acted.

His feet shuffled. "You're gambling," he said, "asking the dealer to hit you when I'm telling you it's best to fold. We have to do this my way."

Zoë crossed her arms. "No. Listen, Blade. I get that I brought you into this, but I'm not one of your pass-arounds or old lady. You don't get to tell me what to do. If Riot and I go back in, we're the ones putting our asses on the line. Hear me? If we choose to go back, this gets done my way."

CHAPTER 24

Riot was on board with continuing their friendship with the Devils. Zoë told him she'd reach out to Vero and test the waters first, but, to her surprise, Vero contacted her instead via the generic email Zoë had given her and asked how Riot was doing. Zoë thanked her for her concern and then subtly inquired if she and Riot could visit, citing Riot's wish to apologize to Maverick for his behavior during the festival. It seemed odd to Zoë that somebody who got their face smashed in would need to apologize to the men who'd done it, but there was much about motorcycle clubs she clearly didn't understand—the fights between them for sport included.

Vero mentioned the casino shooting and said the club was planning a memorial and barbeque for Buster the following weekend, and they were welcome to come and join. She stated members would be coming in from all their other charters—including California, Nevada, Washington, Oregon, and Canada—and it would be a good time for Riot to introduce himself if he was still interested in becoming a prospect. They were always seeking new members, but especially interested in growing their ranks now. They were pissed off, and the tensions with Los Salvajes were at an all-time high, but she warned that no guns or drugs of any kind would be allowed at the memorial as the heat was all over their ass. Because of the shooting at the casino, all eyes were upon the Devils.

Zoë thought about the dead undercover agent, wondered what would happen when news of his discovery was released. Heat wouldn't even begin to describe the asteroid that would soon be coming for the Devils.

Zoë just hoped that she and Riot would be able to visit without consequence and wouldn't be riding into a trap. As easy as information flowed between interested parties, and the shooting happened in their own backyard, she couldn't help but fear the Devils might figure out their involvement, especially once the dead DEA agent came to light. Who else besides Vero and those close to the national and chapter presidents would've known about the burning bush?

Sloane had stated he'd informed others on the team that it'd been campers in the area that had called in the tip about seeing men burying something large near the old mine, and planned to tell the media the same. Zoë just had to hope that took the heat off Vero. She would never want to be responsible for the Lone Horseman coming after her.

Once again, Zoë fretted over coming up with a reason to be gone for a weekend, and this time told Max she needed to help a friend move to Sacramento. She would assist in loading the truck, and her friend would drive it while Zoë followed in her car. This way, her friend could get her car there without towing it, and her friend would bring Zoë back Sunday morning. It helped that Zoë really did have a friend moving to the area, but someone else had already volunteered for the job.

The ride to Sacramento was quick and, without the exhaust of fifty bikes in front of them and scenery filled with mountain roads and pine trees instead of dust, far more enjoyable than the ride to Vegas had been. Still, it did nothing to ease the anxiety eating at the pit of her stomach, like an open sore that wouldn't heal. What if they rode up and found a dozen men with guns awaiting their arrival?

She prayed it wasn't a trap. Her life, and Riot's, depended on it.

Just north of Sacramento, they reached the area that Vero had described, a long country road with a smattering of farmhouses surrounded by white picket fences and green pastures. The kind of place the club could play music and raise a little hell without disturbing anybody but the cows. As they neared the property, however, a few things stood out that didn't belong—most notably, a handful of black SUVs parked down side streets and crossroads nearby. That the feds were watching and present was obvious.

It appeared to make little difference to the Devils, however, as they arrived in groups from ten to forty, all proudly wearing their cuts and flying their colors.

Riot and Zoë appeared out of place when they rolled up and parked alone.

Zoë dismounted the bike and nervously removed her helmet, put their gear away. Riot, observant as ever, noticed her distress. "You worried about them knowing?"

"Among other things," she said.

He glanced over his shoulder at the crowd of red and black scattered across the property. The bruises on his face had healed for the most part, but a few stitches remained on his left cheek. "Your family will be fine, and, listen, I know you worry about Max when he finds out about all this, but trust me, he loves you. He's not going anywhere."

She paused a moment, wondered how the hell he knew that she was thinking about Max and Oliver. Maybe she was crazy, but his concern seemed genuine. She nodded. "Thanks. I appreciate that."

"Hey, I care about my fake old lady. Don't want anything coming between us."
She laughed and nudged him.

He got off the bike, engaged the kickstand. "Knock, knock."

"Who's there?"

"Armageddon."

"Armageddon who?"

"Armageddon a little bored. Let's go play in the Devils' sandbox."

At the entrance to the party, which was held behind the farmhouse on an expansive lawn and patio with a built-in outdoor kitchen, two bald, heavily tatted men in cuts frisked Riot while one of their women patted Zoë down. They asked who extended the invitation. "Vero," Zoë said.

They looked across the way at the thin woman in a long braid with a cigarette dangling from her lips. She held up a hand and waved.

"Welcome," one of the men said.

They walked across the lawn to an area where people had gathered in lawn chairs when a fat guy popping the tab on a new beer called out. "Hey, funny man. How's your brains? Got any left?"

Several of the guys turned and started to laugh.

"What the hell do you mean? He didn't have any to begin with. That's why he got his ass kicked," someone else said.

The laughter and teasing continued as Riot falsely stumbled on a bum leg across the lawn, his tongue hanging out and eyeballs rolled upward. They quickly gathered around him, slapped him on the back, and handed him a beer.

Three weeks ago, they'd fought each other, and now they welcomed him as if he was already one of their own. They were like long-lost friends who hadn't seen each other in years.

Zoë breathed a sigh of relief.

Vero, wearing a red-and-black-plaid top and sunglasses, motioned Zoë over, and she joined her. The woman smelled like she'd already consumed a pack of cigarettes for the day, and it was only eleven a.m. "Hey, girl. How was the ride?"

"Nice. Beautiful actually."

"Does the soul good, doesn't it? Come on in. What can we get you to drink?"

Zoë followed Vero to the shade of a large tent where a half dozen kegs and multiple coolers sat open with a variety of beverage offerings. Zoë took one of the red cups and filled it halfway with beer.

From a picnic table nearby, she felt more than saw the women in denim and bandanas there checking her out, lowering their mirrored sunglasses and asking questions of one another. They appeared a little jealous at how easily Zoë had befriended NorCal's matron.

Across the lawn, on another area of green grass surrounded by a white fence, a larger tent was set up with tables beneath it displaying photographs and memorabilia of Buster, their fallen comrade in the casino shooting. Several members stood there talking, while outside others lined up chairs in front of a podium and microphone.

"I'm sorry about Buster. The shooting is all over the news in Reno," Zoë said. "Have they arrested anyone yet?"

Vero pushed herself atop a four-foot rock wall that surrounded the massive porch and outdoor kitchen, sat cross-legged, and lit a smoke. "No, but that's probably for the best. Word is, Los Salvajes got to the camera footage before the police did, so they can't ID any of the shooters. But that's good—for them and us. Nobody's talking, and they won't. It's better that way."

Zoë took a drink of beer, thought about how she could approach the subject of the Lone Horseman. It seemed like since they were talking about recent events, it would be an easy transition.

"What caused this to go down anyway? Rumor said the Salvajes were looking for a Devil they had a beef with. Was that Buster?"

Vero shook her head. "No, and not the other guy that got killed either. He wasn't even affiliated. Just a citizen in the wrong place at the wrong time."

"Damn." Zoë knew that wasn't true, but she couldn't say otherwise. "Riot said LS was asking questions about a guy with a tattoo, a pig all carved up to look like a ham and a devil taking a bite. I said no way, but he said it was true. I guess that got Los Salvajes a little riled up, huh?"

Vero puffed her cigarette, issued a half laugh. "Yeah, I guess it did."

"Sad," Zoë said, "especially if it's bull like they say."

Vero squinted with one eye, cocked her head in a way that told Zoë she knew otherwise—which, of course, she did.

Zoë tried her best to look surprised. "No? It's true? Like legit?" She laughed a little. "I mean, not that it's funny what happened, but the tattoo."

"Yeah," Vero said, "and brazen."

"Damn, you probably know who it is, doing all the ink for the club, huh?" Zoë frowned, turned serious. "Los Salvajes wouldn't come after you, would they? Try to force you to tell?"

Vero waved it off. "Let them try. I wouldn't tell those bastards nothing if they did. Even if I do hate the guy, he's, unfortunately, important to the club. A necessary evil."

So Vero was aware of the Horseman's LS tattoo and history. Which made Zoë question if Vero also knew about the deeds represented on the Horseman's back. She wanted desperately to ask, but she couldn't think of a single way to bring it up without revealing her own knowledge of the man.

After an official service honoring Buster, where many of the guys recounted their memories with him and each of the chapters took a moment in the tent to pay respects privately, the guys fired up the barbeque and grilled burgers, hot dogs, and chicken. Corn, cole slaw, baked beans, chips, and pickles rounded out the fare. Stories were told and laughter abounded.

Zoë sat there sipping a beer and wondered how it was that even though she was surrounded by people she knew had done bad things—dealt drugs, robbed, assaulted, possibly even murdered others—she found herself enjoying their company and sense of humor. She supposed it was the same as those times she empathized with the bad guys on television and in movies, but had to remind herself that they'd have no problem taking her or Riot out if they knew what they were really up to.

Vero's job for the day was to take pictures, as memorials were a big occasion that needed documenting in the club's books. She took a photo of each chapter with all its current members, and others showcasing just the board. After that, she gathered the presidents across all chapters and took a shot, then the vice presidents, and so on. The old ladies also got their time together, with Maverick doing the honors behind the camera. But when it came time for an entire group photo, Zoë stepped up.

She had them gather by chapter then squeeze in, but quickly realized with her standing on equal footing, she couldn't fit them in. Riot suggested she stand on top of the rock wall so she could have the additional height, and promptly picked her ass up and set her up there. A kiss and some additional raunchy moves behind her brought extra cheers and laughs from the crowd in front.

She checked out the image through the lens. "Okay, this one is for Buster," she yelled. "In one, two, three..."

In unison, they raised their glass. "To Buster!"

She clicked off a few images. They turned out perfectly.

After everyone dispersed, Zoë rejoined Vero, who was off to the side with a few of the other women. "We don't get everybody together like this very often. It's great I can get all these photos," Vero said. "But I've got to write down their names now, before I forget."

"Can I help?" Zoë asked.

"Sure," Vero said. "These women can identify their chapter members, so they can document names while we go to the RV and print copies. Some of the ladies want to take memorial books back with them to their chapters."

In the RV, Zoë took printed photographs from the printer tray and pasted them into multiple books as Vero instructed. The women emailed labels from their phones, which Zoë printed, peeled, and placed beneath the matching pictures. Names like Bud "Red Dog" Cooper, Eric "Big Shot" Lansing, Blaine the Music Man, and on and on began to tell their stories. For the next two hours, they did this, while outside, the party raged on.

As evening fell and the women returned to their men, Zoë once again found herself alone with Vero. The woman was focused on the NorCal and national chapters now, and these were also the ones Zoë was most interested in. Every time Vero got up to go to the restroom or get a new drink, Zoë would flip through the pages, seeing if she could find a picture of the Horseman. Finally, she did, standing with Maverick and the national president, a man named A.J. Barber.

A.J. apparently didn't need a nickname, as the man had a reputation of his own. Maverick might've resembled the devil in outward appearance, and the Horseman in his actions, but it was A.J. that bestowed the soul inside—or, better stated, the lack of one. He wasn't a big man, but his solid stance, thin mustache, and empty black eyes made him look like an assassin or the leader of a cartel. Zoë shuddered at the image of the three men standing there together, could only imagine the carnage they'd unleashed in their time together.

The three amigos, as the picture referred to them, were a force to be reckoned with.

Vero returned, caught her glancing at the image. "Anything interesting?"

Zoë didn't flinch. "Yeah, everything. There's so much history here." She pointed at the picture. "Who are these two guys Maverick is standing with? They weren't here today, were they?"

Vero glanced over her shoulder. "No." She grabbed her latest pack of cigarettes and lit one up. Zoë thought, as much as she smoked, she'd probably be dead before she made it to sixty.

"A.J., that's our national president, he couldn't make it today due to some last minute issues that came up, but he'll be down tomorrow. The club has important business to discuss. He and the other presidents, they'll hold church tomorrow all day, maybe the next too."

"And the other guy?" Zoë looked at the initials under the picture, noted the small *LH* in place of any name. "Does he go by LH like the president goes by A.J.?"

Vero blew smoke toward the open window, trying to keep most out of the RV.

She didn't answer.

Zoë took a closer look. "Wait, isn't that the guy who fought Riot? The guy that... knocked him out? Is he coming tomorrow? I'm sure Riot would want to apologize—"

"Hey," Vero interrupted, "no apology needed. Not to that guy. He had no right to step in and do what he did to Riot." She puffed, exhaled. "Piece of shit. I hate that man. I don't know what his mother did to him when he was little, but he's evil. Truly, he has no soul. None. He thinks he can do whatever he wants."

Perturbed, she grabbed a bottle of vodka from the cabinet, poured a few ounces in an aluminum bottle, and mixed it with orange juice and ice. Done with her duties, Vero gave off that air that said she was ready to tie one on. As she mixed the drink, the cigarette dangled, either between two fingers or from her lips. A cigarette was like an extension of her, another appendage, always present.

"The good news is, given recent events, we shouldn't see him for a while. Which is fine by me. Good riddance, I say." She tipped her head back, drank.

Zoë remained quiet for a moment before she dared to ask. "He's the same guy that came in the RV that night at the festival, isn't he? Tried to...whatever...with you."

Vero shot her an angry look.

Zoë blushed. "I started to come out when I saw him, his hands...just briefly." She lowered her head. "I'm sorry I didn't help. I didn't know what to do."

She thought Vero's stare would drill a hole right through her skull.

Finally, Vero flicked her ashes into a used beer can and huffed. "No, you did the right thing, trust me. That fucker has no boundaries."

No, he doesn't. On that, they could agree.

Zoë closed the book, put it aside. It was clear the Horseman unnerved Vero, and she didn't want to talk about him, but this was as close as Zoë had ever come talking about him. She couldn't let it go, not yet.

"Why don't you tell Maverick? Let him put this guy in his place? I see all these other guys—they respect you. They know better than to touch a president's old lady. Why not this guy?"

Vero's chest rose and fell. She smoked the last inch of her cigarette until it burned her fingers. "You don't understand."

Oh, but I do.

Zoë studied her—Vero's fear—knew this was her opportunity. "Jesus, he's the one, isn't he? The guy Los Salvajes are looking for? He's your enforcer, the one who does the deeds others can't or won't. Like you said, a necessary evil."

"What do you know about it?" Vero shot back. Her jaw was set, teeth gritted. She looked like she was ready to pounce from the seat and claw Zoë a new face.

Zoë backed off. "Nothing, just what Riot has explained to me about the clubs."

Vero panted and fumed, then rushed her with a pointed finger. "You can never, ever utter those words around anyone. Understand? Never, not to anyone."

CHAPTER 25

As darkness fell, many of the chapter members departed, but those that remained appeared to be settling in for the night. "Party's not over, boys," Maverick yelled. "Let's head for the clubhouse."

Riot and Zoë prepared to leave as well, as only members could enter the NorCal clubhouse, but Zoë was worried about Vero's ability to drive the RV. She told this to Maverick, who took one look at his vodka-swilling old lady and knew she was right.

Riot stepped up. "Hey, I can do it. No problem. But my bike..."

"We can get it tomorrow. Come on, I'll get you in. Hell, it's my damn club."

"All right, people," he screamed and clapped as the bikes revved and people hopped on. "Let's have a little fun with these nosy fed fucks on the way. Split up and take them for a nice ride in the country before you find your way back to the club."

Maverick stepped up to the motor home's window. "Not you guys," he said. "Vero can tell you how to get to the club. Wait for the feds to all pull out before you go." The Devil gave his wife a kiss.

"Got it," Riot said. "We'll get her home safely."

The three of them waited for everyone to bug out, with an additional fifteen minutes to spare, then pulled the RV out of the drive and onto the long, dark country road. As Riot ambled the big unit around curves and turns, Vero smoked and drank in the passenger seat and slurred directions.

When they ventured east, closer to the mountains, the woods grew thicker and the lanes narrower. Riot slowed the motor home down and strained to see the edge of the road until Vero told him to turn right and follow a second road up a steep hill. Another mile in, and she pointed at a property on the left.

Riot stopped the vehicle in front of the house. The entire place was fenced, with security cameras that outlined the perimeter and a coded entry box out front. Vero ordered Riot to drive past the main entrance, then pull into a drive where an eighteen-foot-high gate greeted them. Vero stumbled out of the RV to unlock a series of padlocks and swung the doors wide. Behind the gate was a metal carport to park and store the RV, complete with utility hook up. Riot drove it in and Vero shut and locked the gate behind them.

The night sounds greeted them as Zoë and Riot got out to follow Vero up the stone path to the residence. At the top, the two of them exchanged a glance. Here they were, inside the enemy's camp. It couldn't have gone any more perfectly if they had planned it out in advance.

She noticed Riot taking it all in, creating a picture in his mind.

Vero started providing details. "The pole barn out back is for hosting church and other meetings. The guys can also garage their bikes and do any needed repairs or maintenance when they meet up." She stumbled on a step, and Riot caught her before she tumbled.

"The addition to the house on the side there serves as the club. It has three offices for the other board members to store stuff and crash if they need and a meeting room. We'll go to the club in a bit. First, I just need to get some things."

She punched in a four-digit code and opened the garage door to the main house. Zoë followed her in, but Riot slowed as he took in the stacks and stacks of crates stored there, which appeared to contain enough guns and ammunition to supply a small army. His eyes went wide.

They went up three steps into a utility room with a washer and dryer and stacks of dirty clothes, then entered the kitchen, which featured white cabinets and stainless-steel appliances. Riot continued to lag behind, and Zoë got nervous. He was obviously taking advantage of this rare opportunity to check things out, but when she tried to urge him to move along, he put a finger to his lips and shook his head. When else would he ever have a chance to infiltrate a Devils' clubhouse—and chapter president's residence—with not a Devil around?

Zoë hurried to catch up to Vero in the living room so she could keep her occupied.

Vero told Zoë to stay put momentarily as she disappeared down a long hall, then motioned for Zoë to rejoin her once she reappeared. She backtracked through the living room to a door on the other side. The clubhouse.

Zoë checked over her shoulder. Riot was nowhere in sight. She silently cursed.

In the clubhouse—which looked every bit a private bar with its pool tables, Devil décor, and neon signs—Vero flipped on the lights and got busy behind the bar, setting out various beers and checking the ice supply in a freezer in back. Zoë helped, wondering how long Riot had before he got caught doing something stupid.

As she heard the engines of the first few motorcycles approach, she held her breath, silently urging him to hurry the hell up whatever he was doing.

Vero suddenly noticed his absence.

"Hey, where's your old man? Riot, get your ass in here and help," she yelled.

He suddenly appeared through the door from the living room, his head popping around the corner like a prairie dog out of its hole. The three others who'd arrived—all prospects—immediately frowned on seeing him in their space.

"Sorry, I got lost trying to find a bathroom. Didn't know where you went."

Vero ordered him to start grabbing cases of beer and packing them in ice. Two of the other prospects concentrated on the liquor, and another laid out shot glasses. For the next half an hour, they prepped and cleaned, until the members began to arrive. Before they began to serve, one of the other prospects, a short, young man with curly brown hair, passed Riot a black vest with the Devils' logo. "You'd better at least put this on so you don't get your ass kicked—again."

They laughed at Riot's expense. He took it. That's what prospects did.

Zoë stuck close to Vero as members packed the clubhouse shoulder to shoulder and told stories of losing the feds through various means. Now that they were free of riding for the night and away from the prying eyes of law enforcement, they could get as drunk as they wanted, and the beer and liquor flowed. A half hour later, the extra women started to arrive.

Riot seemed to be enjoying himself, eyeballs stuck on a wiggling set of tits in his face, until Zoë shot him a look that said he'd better behave, and the guys all razzed him. Zoë could've cared less, of course, but had to play the part.

Vero laughed through bleary eyes. "You two make such a cute couple. Man, I remember being your age. Wild times." She took a shot and threw it back. Offered Zoë one. Zoë took a deep breath, and drank. It burned all the way down. "Next time you come up, you've got to bring me your portfolio," she said. "Maybe we can get you some extra work with the guys."

Zoë looked at the room she was standing in—a paneled bar with long-haired bikers enjoying loud music and a strip show—didn't know how many "next times" there could possibly be. How long could she keep doing this—befriending two outlaw motorcycle clubs and keeping the police at bay before they found out what she was doing? How long could she keep lying to her husband and spending critical time away from her child in pursuit of a killer?

Not long. Not long at all. The truth was, like Riot had done earlier, she needed to make this opportunity count. While all these guys partied and paid little attention, she needed to see what she could discover about the Horseman and the club. Dates and rides, proof that the Devils—and specifically, the Lone Horseman—were in the area at the time each of the women she knew about were killed. If she could get that, then she, or the local police, could seek out new eyewitnesses, or even reexamine the evidence they had. If they had a suspect, it would make connecting the dots easier.

This was where Sloane's experience would be helpful—knowing what it would take to build a case—but she couldn't go to him and ask for his advice until she had solid evidence to give him that backed her theory.

She really needed to find out where Vero kept the history books.

"Hey," Maverick grumbled, breaking her thoughts. Just the sound of his voice made her insides freeze. "You seen my old lady?"

Zoë glanced over her shoulder only to realize that Vero was no longer there. "She must've went in the house. I'll go check on her."

For appearance's sake, she gave Riot a quick kiss on the cheek, then slipped from the darkness and noise of the club into the living room of the main house, where most of the other old ladies now gathered. Many of the locals had even gone home for the evening, needing to tend to their kids. The rest would likely crash here at the house or go to hotels once the party died, likely at sunrise.

"Anybody seen Vero?" she asked. "Maverick's looking for her."

Several of the women gave her a nasty once-over, as they'd done throughout the day, but one nodded to a recliner off in the corner, where Vero had passed out.

Zoë walked over, collected the empty bottle that dangled from her fingertips as well as a shoe that had fallen off her foot. Another prospect's girlfriend joined and helped get Vero down the hall and into the master bedroom.

They moved her onto the bed, propped a pillow beneath her, and removed her other shoe. When Vero roused and mumbled, "No, stay," Zoë told the other girl she'd wait with her until she fell back asleep. The girl shrugged and shut the door on her way out.

Zoë turned on the bathroom light, sat on the edge of the bed, and listened while Vero talked nonsense into the pillow. She glanced around the large room, taking in the pile of Maverick's clothes draped over a corner chair and a dresser covered with loose change, a jewelry box, and a necklace tree. The open closet door revealed more clothes hung at random, as well as a variety of shoes and boots, but nothing that piqued Zoë's interest. What she wanted was to find those books.

The history of the Devils, as told by Vero, wife of the NorCal president.

When Zoë was certain the woman was sleeping peacefully, she slipped from the room and quietly shut the door behind her. Outside in the hallway, she could hear the women talking in the kitchen, and the loud raspy music that came from the clubhouse beyond. As far as Zoë knew, she was out of sight and out of mind.

It was the perfect opportunity.

She turned the knob on the next door, peeked inside to see a guest bedroom with nothing but a table and lamp, a small dresser, and a bed. Farther down was a large linen closet, another bathroom, then, at the other end of the hall, the last room. Zoë tiptoed across the opening to the living room to the other side, then tested the knob. It was open. She poked her head in, then slipped inside.

Jackpot. This was Vero's office; it had to be. The desk was littered with photos and clippings and cut-out fabrics and stickers she used to accent the club's history—or *scrapbooks*, as she'd called them.

Breathing shallowly, Zoë took her cell phone out and cast a spotlight across the room. She was fearful to turn on the overhead light, afraid someone would come down the hall and notice it on. She directed the light across stacks of various books and magazines on the floor to two shelves on the other side. And there they were, all lined up like a reference library. Twenty years of NorCal books, twenty-five of National.

She stepped over the stuff on the floor, cleared a spot on a chair. She grabbed the book tagged with the prior year and flipped to the dates of victim number thirteen. She had them all memorized now: Fox, number thirteen, March 10, California; bucking horse, number twelve, July 5, Idaho; coyote, number eleven, February 13, Arizona.

In March of the prior year, there wasn't a specific run, but a whole layout dedicated to the Devils' twenty-fifth anniversary party. Like today's gathering, it had been held at the farm, and all the clubs had been present. Rather than spend any time looking for specific victims or other connections, she snapped several close-ups of the pages on her cell phone. Flipped the pages, snapped again.

She didn't bother with the rest of the year. Instead, she replaced that book and went directly for the next, this one two years back. Turned to the July Fourth weekend where, sure enough, the annual run was to Boise, Idaho, for the rodeo and fireworks. To Zoë's horror, there were pictures of certain Devils posing with the victim herself, the rodeo queen. There was even one with the Lone Horseman standing in the background, looking at the woman from behind like he couldn't wait to take his prize. Zoë's heart raced and her fingers fumbled nervously as she took the pictures.

The third book showed them in Arizona on a winter hiatus, standing in front of a bar named the Prickly Coyote. The Horseman's tattoo of a coyote full of holes had to be related—how could it not? Maybe the victim had gone to the bar the same night as the club or worked there as a waitress or bartender. Zoë took a dozen pictures, snapped a dozen more from the next year and the next. With every year and every flash, her fingers shook, her heart skipped.

Next door in the clubhouse, as the beer flowed, and the crowd cheered, Zoë continued to grab and snap and seek out dates that matched the Horseman's tattoos until she had ten years of club history. Maybe she didn't know all the victims yet, but at least now she had an idea of the places to look given the dates of the runs. The only one she didn't have a match for was the first victim, and after an extra twenty minutes of searching, Zoë decided she couldn't risk anymore time. She didn't know how long she'd been in the room, but at some point, her luck was going to run out.

She slid the last scrapbook back on the shelf.

It was only then she noticed a few pictures had fallen out and scattered on the floor. They'd apparently come loose as she'd flipped pages, but she didn't know what volume, or volumes, they were from. She scooped them up and muttered. What else could she do but stick them in between the books on the shelves so Vero wouldn't see them? She quickly did so, then shoved her phone back in her pocket.

For the next minute, she listened with her ear to the door until she thought the coast was clear, then slipped back outside into the hallway. Finally, she believed she had what she needed. She'd find Riot and they could get the hell out and hopefully, never return.

CHAPTER 26

Zoë took the information she'd gathered from Vero's office and got to work. She downloaded and enlarged the pictures from the scrapbooks she'd taken and began doing a more thorough analysis of the images upon each page. In the dark room, with only the flash of the camera to light the pages, some of the events were difficult to decipher past the location the club had traveled and the places they'd stopped, but that proved to be enough. The specific locations and dates enabled her to dig through cold cases at local police departments and find probable victims. Once she found a possible victim, she read as much as she could about their case and their lives on social media to determine if anything they said, posted, or liked could represent the corresponding tattooed image on the Horseman's back. Night after night, she went without sleep, sneaking off to the little area next to the living room while Max and Oliver slept.

The first victim she officially documented was the Idaho rodeo queen, as she was the easiest given the photograph of many a Devil posing with her the day before she died with the Lone Horseman standing in the background. The horse and pink saddle were an obvious correlation to the tattoo, and if anyone could make a case against the Horseman, especially if they had any DNA, it could be Idaho.

The coyote ended up being fairly simple, too, once Zoë happened upon an unsolved homicide in Mesa, Arizona, for a woman found raped and shot during the same week as the Devils winter run to the desert. What was most notable about this case was the last place she was seen: the Prickly Coyote, the bar where the Devils had stood outside to take a group photo. The Horseman wasn't included in the shot, but his tattoo of a coyote with a red bandana matched the bar's glowing neon sign to a T.

She was able to gather more details about the woman the Horseman had taken at Sturgis by also digging into a list of the local area's unsolved homicides. As Blade had told her, the woman raped and stabbed there had been married to a member of Los Salvajes' Riverside chapter, and although her husband had remarried, there was no question about his determination to find his former wife's killer—he had an entire page on the web dedicated to her and even offered a reward for information.

She wondered what he would think upon learning that his wife was depicted on her killer's back as a green pig with a sliced throat. If Los Salvajes didn't have enough reasons to kill the Horseman already, this man certainly did.

The three next victims Zoë was able to make headway on included the Horseman's fourth, fifth, and sixth prized ladies. Vero's scrapbook from May the year after Zoë's mother died showed a gathering of the NorCal chapter in Monterey, California, where Zoë quickly learned that a woman who'd worked at the local aquarium had met her fate the same week. The news story detailed how she'd been found in the bay wrapped in netting. The matching tattoo of the dolphin trapped in a blue net on the Horseman's back left no question as to who was responsible.

The Lone Horseman's fifth victim was one of the few he'd taken in the same year. Just two months after Monterey, authorities discovered a local college student in the woods near Bend, Oregon, after she'd taken a summer camping trip there with friends who were all a part of the same Christian ministry. The autopsy indicated that she'd been raped and, oddly, fed a variety of poisonous berries from the wild. As sadistic as it was, this one also left little interpretation compared to the Horseman's tattoo of the green dove. The dove was often symbolized as a messenger, and the Devil had poisoned her. Zoë wondered if the young woman and her fellow students had attempted to preach to him and the Devils during their annual run there that same week.

The sixth victim Zoë was able to document was the woman who represented the eagle with the arrow shot through her heart, which Zoë already knew was the archer found near Olympia, Washington, half a dozen years ago. Still, Zoë researched additional information about the woman and noted the Devils' documented run up the I-5 corridor in the latter part of June of that year.

She discovered number seven was a stripper in Los Angeles notorious for her thigh-high red boots who put on a show involving whips and chains, and number eight, a beautician in Montana who was as tall and lanky as the giraffe that represented her, and died with a broken neck to match. Both of these also lined up with the Devils' travels those corresponding years, the first on a run through SoCal in July, the second on the way back home across Montana from Sturgis.

That left just the first victim, both in Texas—numbers two and nine—and the most recent since Amber McKinley, number thirteen. But the search for the Horseman's victim taken near the twenty-fifth-anniversary party proved elusive. Despite Zoë searching repeatedly through the photographs of the scrapbook pages she'd taken and conducting an exhaustive internet search, nothing popped up that made reference to a fox or a pale-blue trap. Yet one good thing did come from the extra scouring—she discovered a third image of the Lone Horseman, this one taken at the party as he posed with enforcers across all chapters. Once again, there was no name associated with his picture, just that elusive *LH* and the word *National*, but it left no doubt as to who he was—the Lone Horseman was A.J. Berger's right-hand man, the top strongman among the enforcers—the one sent to take care of matters no one else could.

Over the next week, Zoë thought long and hard about what to do with the information she'd collected. Sure, she had dates, locations, and the identity of most of the victims now, but that information would only play well if she let the police know about the pattern at large. Yet, she feared revealing such information to them— especially club photos and images of the tattoos on the Horseman's back—would point to her and Vero if the Horseman found out, which was exactly what Zoë wanted to avoid. So, what could she provide to these individual police departments to strike their interest and set them upon the Lone Horseman's path, without giving away too much?

She sat back in her chair, the blue light of the computer casting a strange glow across the room. A faint hum emitted from the laptop's base, as if it was growing tired of running. She and Max shared this one device, so it got used for everything that wasn't conveniently done from a phone, including her shop advertising and Max's client evaluations when he wasn't in the office. That meant she had to be cautious of clearing the search history every time she was done using it for research, otherwise there would be hell to pay.

She could only imagine the questions Max would have after seeing the word *murder* typed in again and again across various jurisdictions. He'd confront her on the spot, demand to know what conspiracy into her mother's murder she was looking into now.

Not that erasing it would prevent his eventual discovery of her little clandestine operation. She already sensed his growing suspicion, nights when she was certain he slipped from the covers to spy on her, and other things he said or did that made her question what he knew. She'd seen him pick up her phone and try to gain entry on more than one occasion when he didn't think she was looking, and she worried constantly that Oliver had told him about her blocking the doors and windows even before Jason's little surprise visit. Zoë, of course, had dismissed what he did know about the incident to her fear of Max not being around that week, but she knew he didn't totally believe it.

She took a deep breath, fanned herself. With no air-conditioning in the house, the room was stifling, even in the middle of the night. Sweat trickled between her breasts and down the length of her back. She wanted to open one of the windows, but given the current state of things, didn't think it wise. She turned on the small office fan attached to the edge of the desk and let the air stir as she decided what the hell to do.

The more she thought, the more she believed that sending each of the local police departments an anonymous tip, with information solely about their unsolved case and not the tattoos, and suggesting they look at the Lone Horseman, was the best option.

No, it wouldn't give them the overall pattern of the Lone Horseman, but it would present them with a suspect in the Devils' motorcycle club and get them to start asking questions. If she was lucky, a detective in one of the local jurisdictions would start making the same connections Zoë had and unleash an investigation of his own. That would be the best-case scenario, as then the Horseman and the club could never link the discovery of his deeds back to the tattoos, and Zoë, or Vero. The police could work together across all their different jurisdictions and arrest him, maybe link the tattoos once they had them in custody.

Blade and Los Salvajes did not want the Horseman picked up for deeds done; Blade had made that perfectly clear. Neither would the Devils, given what the Horseman did for them and knew about their operations. But Zoë wanted justice for her mom and the many other women he'd murdered. Not to be insensitive, but she didn't really give a rat's ass about what he'd done to his rivals, even less about the drugs and guns the Devils dealt daily. Yes, drugs and guns were terrible, and she didn't care for how the MCs made their living, but the truth was, even if they all got busted and taken off the streets, the criminals and junkies would just get their wares from someone else. That was the problem with stopping any kind of gang, be it street, mafia, or outlaw motorcycle club. No matter how many you arrested and how many chemicals you kept from an addict's arm, there were always more to take their place—more criminals, more guns, more drugs—just waiting to be had.

Which was why she wondered how anybody in their right mind, like the DEA agent who'd been killed, would risk going undercover to bust up such enterprises. It seemed a losing battle.

Over the next several days and nights, Zoë prepared a dossier of each crime, carefully noting information about the victim and related evidence, then added information about the Devils that corresponded to the date that the victim went missing. She made a dozen copies of the two best photographs she had of the Lone Horseman, cropping the pictures to include just what she could of his face and body without anybody else included, then used a paper clip to attach them in the corner.

The only information she included about his tattoos was the image of the pale horse and death as its rider. She figured enough people had to have seen or heard about that image now that it wouldn't trace back to any one person. She decided that if the detectives in the area took interest, but seemed to be struggling in getting results, then she could provide more information—especially about the other images on his back and the link to other victims—when she deemed it safer. She just couldn't risk putting that kind of information out there right now. Unless she knew the Horseman was in custody somewhere, she would be risking Vero's and her own family's safety.

The final night, she addressed the envelopes, then dropped them in the mailbox outside the tattoo shop the next morning. She held her breath, waiting for the mailman to arrive, and when he did, watched him remove the envelopes, place them in the truck, and whisk them away.

Now it would be a waiting game.

CHAPTER 27

Waiting was the hardest part. Every day in between her time working on clients, and every night after Oliver and Max went to bed, she'd get on her phone or the laptop and check the police departments for any updated news. She knew that police work was slow and diligent, but when nothing happened after five days, she damn near wanted to pick up the phone and ask them what was taking so long. After ten, she thought maybe all her work had been in vain.

She sat out on the porch smoking a cigarette wondering what else she could do without straight up going to Sloane and telling him everything. Yet, she knew he had his hands full working with the feds on the investigation into the recently discovered DEA agent—which had become the lead story on the local news the past week—as well as with the casino shooting, so he wouldn't likely have time for her. After the Carson City and Reno casino shootings, and now a dead federal agent in the mix, law enforcement, media, and residents worried they had a full-scale war on their hands.

She heard Max's footsteps approach from inside and pause momentarily before he opened the screen door. His suspicions had continued to grow and things had become tense between them as he'd started to question why Zoë wasn't sleeping and seemed jittery all the time. He hadn't come right out and asked if she'd been lying to him about various matters, but his subtle insinuations indicated he believed it might be true. Several nights the past week, he'd awakened to find her in front of the computer instead of beside him in bed, and now she suspected he often feigned sleep just to see if she'd get up and slink off to the other room.

In addition, he'd popped into the tattoo shop unexpectedly twice in the last week, once for a surprise lunch with Oliver, and another time for coffee. Screech had asked her later if they were doing okay. He told Zoë that he'd noticed how stressed she'd been the past two months, and wanted to know what he could do to help. Zoë told him everything was fine, but she could see he didn't believe it any more than Max did.

Everyone around her sensed she was on edge, including Oliver, who continued to carry around a toy gun and shoot imaginary bad guys.

He didn't know the evil people were real.

Zoë cursed herself. She'd tried her damnedest to be present and engaged whenever others were around, but she couldn't deny where her head had been for the last two months—with the Lone Horseman. Day and night, she'd catch herself thinking about him, wondering where he was and what he was doing. Was he out doing the Devils' business or learning about Zoë and her little investigation? Even now, she couldn't help herself. She pondered whether the man was lying low, like Vero suspected, or was out searching for new prized ladies to murder.

Who was to say he wouldn't get bored and start taking more women than usual?

Zoë shivered, once again feeling that burdensome worry sweep over her like a wave. She wanted to flush the Lone Horseman out of hiding so the authorities could find him before anyone else fell victim.

Max sat down beside her on the porch and rubbed her back, noticing her disturbance. Appreciating his effort, she snuggled closer and tucked herself beneath his arm. It felt good to be protected, if only for a time.

He took the cigarette dangling from her fingers and inhaled once before giving it back. "What's got my lady upset tonight? Don't tell me Screech is demanding more partners."

"No. In fact, he's backed off that lately. He knows I'm..." She stopped short of saying what Max already knew.

"Distracted," he answered and sighed. "Yeah, that seems to be your theme this summer. Zoë Cruse and the terrible, horrible, no good, very bad summer of distraction."

She laughed, thinking about the correlation to one of Oliver's favorite stories. Yet, her heart sank. There was much to be interpreted in those words. "I'm sorry I've been so distant. I don't know what's gotten into me."

"Do you want to talk about it?" he asked, brushing her hair back from her face.

She hesitated, fighting every ounce of her being that wanted to tell but feared his involvement. Maybe he'd no longer think she was crazy, given what evidence she'd gathered, but even if he didn't, she knew he would stop her from going forward and seeing it through to the end. He wasn't stupid; he'd understand the risk involved, to her and their family. Max was the rational one, as well as the survivalist. He'd endured being ostracized by his parents, opioid addiction, and five years on the streets. He knew enough when to leave things alone.

But she wasn't ready to stop. She couldn't.

She shook her head. "Nothing to talk about. Everything is good, really."

His arm slid from the back of her shoulders. He got up to get a cigarette of his own. The light breeze whistled through the top of the trees. Somewhere, a crow cawed.

As he slapped the bottom of the pack against the palm of his hand, she sat on the step alone, sensing his frustration. Max had always been the person she'd confided in and trusted, and now she was keeping things from him. He had to be questioning why.

She thought back to when she'd first met him as just another homeless teen at the shelter, how he'd taken the time to befriend her and teach her how to survive on the streets. It had been he who'd educated her on the perils of the areas where the drug and sex traffickers flourished. It had been he who'd written out a map of all the places to find food or get a free meal. It had even been he who'd stressed to her just how much appearance was important so people wouldn't harass you. He'd told her to get a cheap gym membership, ten bucks a month, so she could shower every day. It didn't matter how much actual working out she did—whether it was just lifting a few weights or riding a stationary bike—the most important part was the shower and having a place to come in from the bitter cold or intense heat.

And he'd been right. Nothing matched how good it felt to come in on a brutal winter day and hang in the sauna or hot tub, or experience a burst of cold air-conditioning in the summer.

He'd never confessed it, but she was also pretty sure it had been Max who'd gotten her the part-time job at the gym. Despite her clean appearance and regular dues payment, the owner had somehow come around to the reality of her situation, and had offered her a job. Max had advised her and the rest of the wolf pack—as they referred to their collection of runaways and throwaways—to work what jobs they could that summer so they could pool their money the following winter and rent an apartment for a few months. And again, that proved to be solid advice. Although one person officially rented the place, they often had ten or fifteen people crashing in the one-bedroom unit.

Zoë waited for Max to return to her. When he didn't, she pouted.

She loved him so much. She hated hurting him this way. She knew he felt like she was shutting him out without reason, and he was right—she was. All she could do is hope he would understand when this was all over and the Lone Horseman was in jail.

He paced the porch, smoked the new cigarette, leaned over the railing. "How's your friend in Sacramento doing? Settling in?"

The way he said *friend* caught her attention, again as if he was implying something. "Good," she said absently. "She likes it there. She says it's pretty, lots of trees."

Max scraped a shoe across the porch, stomped on a spot a couple of times, causing Zoë to look over her shoulder. "Another loose nail. I keep finding them sticking out. I think maybe that's what Jason tripped on that night when he scared you and Oliver."

Zoë turned back around, felt her face flush in the dark. "Could be. Don't know why they're suddenly coming loose like that. I should probably mention it to the landlord."

A pause before he spoke more.

"Thanks again for taking him in," he said. "He really didn't mean to scare you like he did. Hell, I think you might've scared him worse with that gun."

She groaned. "I'm sure I did."

"Speaking of which, I found a couple extra bullets on your side of the bed. Not sure how they rolled all the way over there from the closet, but I put them back in the box. Didn't want Oliver getting ahold of them."

In her later recounting of that night, Zoë had told Max that she'd run to the closet after hearing the noise outside to get his gun and the bullets. But, in truth, she'd already retrieved it and set it in her nightstand earlier in the week. Yet, she feared if she told him that, then he would ask why, and to that, she couldn't answer.

Because I'm afraid of a man, a monster.

She decided not to try and explain. Just hoped he would let it die.

The conversation between them ceased as the night sounds took over. The tension in the air was palpable, as if each was trying to measure the level of deception taking place in between them—and why.

"Maybe we should get away this weekend," he said. "Go camping. Oliver misses you going with us. I can get the SUV prepped over the next few days. With your drive to Vegas I should probably get the oil changed." He inhaled deeply on the cigarette. His eyes squinted at the corners.

Zoë felt every muscle harden, thinking about the odometer in the SUV and how it wouldn't reflect enough miles to have been driven to Vegas and back. *Shit.* She hadn't even considered that. She didn't look at him but could feel his gaze upon her, analyzing. Maybe he'd already checked, and was fishing for an answer.

"Didn't I tell you we drove Kat's car down?" she said.

"What? That piece of shit Honda she drives? It doesn't even have air-conditioning, does it?"

"No, not that one. It was a new one. I think it must've belonged to her new boyfriend."

She studied her feet. The lies just kept piling up, and she feared Max knew it.

He didn't answer, just grunted, then crushed the cigarette beneath his shoe and went inside.

The quiet of the night settled in, and Zoë found it more disturbing than a thousand honking horns. How could she do this to him? How could she risk destroying their marriage? The one relationship in her life that had always been good, honest, and decent was now full of deceit and lies. Max had saved her. Max had taught her to love and trust. Now, they had a roof over their head, food in the fridge, jobs, and most importantly, a son. A son she thanked her guardian angel for every single day.

It had to end. She had to tell him the truth, and soon.

Because all this lying, it was exhausting.

CHAPTER 28

I t was never a good sign when you got a request from the club to meet out in the desert. Even the Lone Horseman, as many times as he'd been out here cleaning up for the Devils, knew he could end up on the other side of club enforcement, and right now, he wondered if recent events hadn't made A.J. and Maverick consider that option. First Los Salvajes had discovered his relation to Modesto, and then the DEA had found their dead UC. Things were not looking good for him.

Taking no chances, he stuck an extra .45 in his waistband, a knife in his belt loop, and a pistol in his boot. In addition, he had a high-powered rifle strapped to the back of his bike. He didn't think his best friend was coming to waste him, but if there was one thing he'd learned working for the Devils, nothing was certain. If A.J. had become nervous after the latest developments, then it was possible the Lone Horseman had been put on the same list that he usually managed.

From a distance, he saw the single headlight of Maverick's motorcycle working its way off the road and through the desert, weaving through an assortment of scrub brush and cactus to get to their designated meeting spot. He rested his hand on the .45 and waited for his arrival.

The Horseman was glad to see he was alone.

Maverick parked the bike and the two greeted each other with the usual enthusiasm, slapping each other on the back. "Brother, good to see you."

"And you," the Horseman said.

They kept the single lights of the bikes shining toward the hill behind them so they could see each other but not have them spread across the length of the open terrain. The dim glare cast an eerie shadow across both their faces.

Maverick checked out the extra hardware on the Horseman's bike. "You expecting to take some long shots?"

The Horseman cocked his head. "First time I've been called to the desert and not the club. Don't have to tell you it made me think twice."

Maverick shook his head. "Don't go there. Short of you taking a meeting with the feds, there's nothing you could ever do that would make me or A.J. turn on you. You have to know that by now."

The Horseman would like to believe that, but knew loyalties only went so far as the risk they presented. And with the undercover agent found, the risk was real. "Why didn't he come out himself, then? The desert is an insult, and he doesn't even give me the courtesy of explanation. That's fucked up."

"He means no disrespect. You know right now, whatever we do, we've got to protect the ranks. No way we could risk meeting at the club. The heat on us, it's real, and it's coming from all sides—federal, state, and local—and not just Nevada."

The Horseman frowned. "What are you talking about?"

Maverick leaned against the seat of his bike. He folded his arms, causing his biceps to inflate like balloons. "We've been getting some strange calls. Inquiries from various law enforcement agencies asking about one of our members and some of our former runs. Idaho, Arizona, California, Washington. One as far back as six years ago."

The Horseman felt confusion arch his brow. "One of us? Who?"

Maverick sighed. "You, brother. They're asking about you. They have two photos. I don't know how they got them, and I don't know how many agencies have them or why they want to talk to you, but what I know is—you're a wanted man. That's why we had to meet out here. The club?" Maverick shook his head. "No good."

The Horseman paced. His gut twisted, confused. "Fucking Salvajes really got it in for me," he said. He cracked his knuckles.

Maverick lit a cigarette, offered the Horseman one. He took it. "Maybe. But you need to know, the agencies that are calling aren't asking about Modesto or the tattoo of that pig. They're asking about the pale horse on your back with death as its rider, and whether you could be responsible for the murder of several women across the west."

The Horseman wheeled. "What? Why the hell would they think that?" But his blood pulsed and his breaths quickened. Who would be asserting such accusations, and calling the club? It could be risky having A.J. suspect him of any such deeds, Maverick too. Especially if...

He sensed his friend studying him.

Maverick spit. "Listen, man. You know how I roll. Don't ask, don't tell. The animal tatts on your back—your prized ladies—I've always considered them your business. I've never asked. But if they are what I'm thinking, and this shit comes back on the club, I don't have to tell you, A.J. won't be happy. With a half-dozen different law enforcement agencies and the feds looking for you, you become a liability. Then that loyalty we have, it gets tested, and the next meeting we have here could be very different."

The Horseman felt a searing heat rise within, causing his skin to burn like fire. His ire at Los Salvajes, at whoever had informed them of the pig tattoo—and now, law enforcement of his pale horse and rider—was greater than any anger he'd previously experienced in his life. Who had done this to him—and why? Worse, how much did they actually know?

He turned to Maverick. "Who the fuck is insinuating this if not Los Salvajes? Someone in the club? Do we have another informant? When I find out…"

A brisk wind blew between them. Maverick's cigarette shed embers into the night sky. "I don't know, but I've got to ask—is it true? These women, are they what the police are implying? Kills made on club runs?" He stared across the expanse of darkness, challenging the Horseman.

The Horseman didn't care for his tone. *Maverick had killed plenty. Who was he to judge?* He stepped up, pointed a finger in Maverick's chest. "Why you asking? You wired? You know I'm not going to answer that."

Maverick huffed. "You just did." He flicked his ashes on the desert floor. The moon glistened off his bald head. "Listen, you got a hard-on for raping and killing women, that's not my call. But you got to clean this mess up, brother. Whoever's got your number, they have to be taken care of before this goes any further."

The Lone Horseman paced, hands on hips, heart ramming in his chest. He couldn't believe this shit was happening. "It will be my pleasure."

Maverick placed a hand on his shoulder, offered a squeeze of support. "If you had to guess how the feds found out about the UC, what's your best guess?" he asked. "The newsies reported campers in the area. You think that's legit?"

"No," the Horseman responded emphatically.

Maverick frowned. "How do you know?"

"They said the campers reported seeing some suspicious men burying something in the desert. There weren't any *men*," he said between gritted teeth. "It was just me. I work alone. You know that. I always work alone. The police don't want to reveal their real source, so they made up a story."

Maverick studied him, nodded. "Yeah. A.J. thinks so too."

"Well, as always, A.J. is right," the Horseman said.

"What about the tatts? Who the hell could've gotten that close to you and possibly understood what your ink represented?" Another flick of ashes. "Again, not prying into your business, but who you been screwing lately?"

The Lone Horseman exhaled a trail of smoke across the night sky. He laughed. "Come on, man, really?"

"Hey, you said it yourself—we could have another undercover. Who's to say the feds are getting clever and putting in a woman? Maybe one of the pass-arounds at the club or a local girl. You got any new regulars that have taken an interest in your ink?"

The Horseman stepped back. "Are you crazy? A federal agent is not going to lay on her back, my friend. And just to satisfy your curiosity, no, I've got no new regulars. You know me, one and done. Besides,"—he crushed his cigarette underfoot—"No bitch could take me down."

Maverick tugged at his beard. "Then who, brother? It has to be someone who knows something about our history and is smart enough to do a little research."

The Horseman glanced out over the desert expanse, took a deep breath. "There's only one person I can think of who can answer that question. That Los Salvajes VP—Blade—he called me out. He's the only one who knows the truth. Whoever told him about the pig has to be the same person who questioned my other ink."

He turned to Maverick. "We find him, we find our informer."

"We get near the Salvajes again, there could be an all-out war."

The Horseman straddled his ride, started the engine. "I'll tell you what. You let me worry about that. You tell A.J. to keep his cool. The VP? That's my job. It's what I do best."

CHAPTER 29

Sloane was sitting at his desk, documenting the day's latest developments on the Reno casino shooting and asking himself if maybe he shouldn't be looking for a career change, when Rodriquez came in, sweating like a man who'd taken a nap in a sauna. He grabbed a towel from his gym bag and mopped his neck and face. "How come I keep getting assigned the dead bodies found outside? Captain has it in for me."

He grabbed an energy drink from the case he kept in a desk drawer. Already, he'd consumed half a dozen for the day, had the empties lined up on the file cabinet next to his desk like spent bullets.

"You know they've discovered traces of cocaine in those things," Sloane said. "Maybe the summer heat isn't the reason you're sweating."

Rodriquez waved him off. "That's just one of those conspiracy theories. It's caffeine. No worse than the coffee you drink. Gets my adrenaline flowing."

He flexed his pecs.

"You know, last night's arrest told me he same thing about the PCP he'd just smoked. Pure adrenaline," he said.

His partner smirked. "You're just pissed off because I have so much more energy than you. You can't keep up because of all the meat you eat. Cholesterol is plugging you up like a bad turd you can't force out."

Sloane quit keying in words and shook his head. What was it with everyone and their stance against meat and the interest in his bowels these days? His pipes and all that? If he heard one more word from his wife or some television doctor talking about his colon and how it needed cleaning out, he thought he might empty his .45 into the television.

He started to respond when he noticed a cache of visitors heading his way. Agent Quinn of the DEA with two other official-looking gentlemen in tow. And by the way they were dressed—Hoover blue suit, polished shoes, and tie—the FBI.

Oh shit. What now?

Quinn made the introductions. "Special Agent Dionne, Special Agent Hall... Detective Brady Sloane." He nodded at the captain's once again empty office. "Can we talk?"

Reluctantly, Sloane got up and followed them inside, catching Rodriquez's raised eyebrow as he passed. They each pulled up a chair, and he shut the door behind them. He leaned against his boss's desk. "To what do I owe the pleasure, gentlemen?"

Dionne, a tall, fit man with shiny black hair, and Hall, his twin minus a few inches in height, looked sternly upon him. "We need to ask you about some letters that have come to our attention."

Sloane was confused. "Letters? You mean, like emails?"

"No. Actual letters sent to law enforcement agencies all across the West."

He made a face. "Okay, what's that got to do with me? Or the FBI, for that matter?"

Dionne snapped his fingers. Hall produced an eight-by-ten manila envelope.

"We were first contacted by a detective working a cold case in Mesa, Arizona. He said two weeks ago he received a letter about a homicide there that detailed the finer points of the crime, then suggested he look at a member of the Devils motorcycle club as the perp, a man known in their circles as the Lone Horseman. Apparently, the man has a tattoo of a large, pale horse on his back. You ever heard of him?"

The fine hairs on the back of Sloane's neck stood at attention. *Here we go again.* A month earlier, he'd never heard of the Lone Horseman, and now, his name seemed to be popping up everywhere: the Reno casino shooting, as a possible suspect in the murder of the undercover DEA. But this was the first he'd heard of the man being related to a killing outside the club.

"I have, yes, but I don't know who he is. If you find him, I'd like to speak with him, though. His name has come up more than once as the possible source of the conflict that led to the casino shooting here last month. In addition to the horse tattoo, rumor is he also has one of a sliced pig with the mark of twelve-twenty-three. As you can imagine, the Devils' rivals, Los Salvajes, don't find that rumor amusing. They believe the Lone Horseman is the man responsible for killing their chapter VP in Modesto a few years back."

Dionne nodded. "Agent Quinn filled us in on those details, as well as his belief that it's possible this same man is responsible for the death of his undercover. If this Horseman is an enforcer for the Devils—as Agent Quinn believes—that makes sense. But, each of the homicides detailed in these letters isn't a club member. They're regular citizens, local women with no apparent ties to the MC. So far, we've heard from detectives in Arizona, Idaho, California, Washington, and Montana. Each of them received a letter explaining how the Devils were in the area at the time of the slaying, and suggesting they should look at the Lone Horseman for the murder. The person stated he or she couldn't bring forth additional details right now, citing a fear for their safety, but attached two photographs of the man in question."

"You got photos?" Sloane grabbed the copies Dionne offered, viewed them. The Lone Horseman was a solid man of average height, with shoulder-length dark hair and equally dark eyes. Both photos were blurry and appeared to have been enlarged from much smaller pictures, but at least it was something. Now he could go back to the casino tapes and see if the Horseman was there. Word in the casino was that he'd been present that night, and possibly even fired the shot that wounded one of the Salvajes. One thing was certain, the guy was busy. Rivals, undercovers, women...

And then it hit him. The Devils, Los Salvajes, Zoë Cruse.

He glanced up, brow furrowed. "You said all the victims were women? How did they die?"

"Raped and murdered, although not always in the same manner. Some were stabbed, some strangled, at least one shot. Yet, this person, whoever it is, believes the killer is the same man. What do you think, Detective Sloane?"

Sloane asked to see the letters, read them, saw the similarities in tone right away. Zoë. It had to be.

"You recently had a woman raped and stabbed right here in Reno, didn't you?" Dionne asked as Sloane became lost in a fog of thought and conflict. Zoë. That's why she'd infiltrated the Devils. That's why she'd reached out to Blade. She was searching for Bella's killer.

He knew it. *Damn.*

"Detective? Your recent case? Did your latest victim happen to cross paths with the Devils motorcycle club? Is there something you learned during your investigation that made you suspicious of this Lone Horseman character?"

He raised an eyebrow. "Maybe it was you who researched these other crimes?"

The image of Amber McKinley—red hair, bleached smile, painted nails—instantly came to him, and suddenly, Sloane saw where this was going.

He glanced up. "Wait. You think maybe *I* sent these letters?"

Dionne pointed to a document that displayed the front of all the mailed letters. "You see the stamp on all the envelopes? Reno. Someone from here mailed those letters."

Sloane sighed. "Yes, I get it, but...no, it wasn't me."

Hall and Dionne frowned. "No? Then who?"

So this is what Zoë Cruse had been up to. No wonder she didn't want to talk to him or Quinn and feared being seen speaking to them. She knew moles were everywhere in this town. How could she risk word of what she suspected about the Lone Horseman getting back to the Devils? Yet, what had made her link this man and the Devils to Bella's murder in the first place, and how had she learned about these other women? He handed the letters back to Agent Dionne. "How did the FBI get involved in this?" Sloane asked him. "Don't tell me each of these local police departments contacted you after receiving a single anonymous letter? That doesn't seem right."

"No. The detective in Mesa added the letter to his case on the national database, and other police agencies began to respond. Then he contacted us. The writer implied that the suspect may have killed as many as fourteen women, so the detective in Mesa was curious to know if we'd heard any such thing. He thought we'd want to be involved. He was right. Since then, we've been coordinating the effort. Caldwell, Monterey, Olympia, Mesa, Bozeman."

Sloane stared at the man, once again stunned by the number Zoë had told him. The man, the Lone Horseman, was a serial killer—and not just of federal agents.

Agent Dionne narrowed his eyes. "I noticed you didn't answer my question. So, I'll ask it again—do you know who could've written these letters?"

"Yes," Sloane said.

"Who?" Quinn demanded, his face turning a deep red. He didn't like being out of the loop, Sloane possibly knowing something he didn't. He twisted and turned, trying to read Sloane's expressions. When Sloane didn't immediately answer, his own mind went to work. "Oh hell. You think it's that girl who's been hanging around with Los Salvajes—Zoë Cruse? That's who you're thinking, isn't it?"

Dionne and Hall immediately wrote her name down.

Sloane stood, hands on hips, and shot Quinn a dirty look. That jackass just couldn't keep his mouth shut. Now, he'd outed her, which defied exactly what she was trying to do with the letters—remain anonymous.

"We should go talk to her." Quinn stood, went for the door.

"No." Sloane blocked his path. "You can't. Don't you get it? If it's her, we need to protect her. I don't know what she knows or what information she's uncovered, but she obviously fears the Lone Horseman's discovery. One misstep and he'll take her out. We could lose this case in an instant, and yours," he said to Quinn.

Quinn danced, agitated. "She's been hiding information from us."

"Maybe for good reason. God knows there are a whole lot of loose lips around here," he said accusingly.

He turned to Dionne and Hall, who seemed more reasonable and open to listening than Quinn. "Please don't release her name—not to anybody. Let me talk to her first and see what she knows. We have a relationship. I think I can get her to talk. Especially now, with these letters."

"How?" Dionne asked.

Sloane told him about Bella's death. Dionne looked disturbed. "Jesus, you think her mother might also be one of the Horseman's victims?"

Sloane sighed. "Well, Zoë certainly seems to believe so. And this time, I think we need to trust her."

CHAPTER 30

Blade found out about the letters Zoë sent. She didn't know how, because not a single one of the law enforcement agencies had posted anything publicly about reopening any of the cases or asking for the public's help on a new development, but apparently Blade had been tipped off.

"How many did you send?" he demanded as she and Riot sat with him in the same corner table in the Treehouse they had before. At another one nearby, a guy with several missing teeth grinned as he laid down a straight to beat his companions. Old seventies rock played through the speakers.

"I don't know. Six, seven."

Riot whistled. Blade growled.

"I didn't make any mention of the individual tattoos, just the horse, the one image that people would notice. I figured once one of the agencies picked him up, then they'd see the smaller tattoos and figure it out for themselves. If not, then I could provide additional information."

Blade slammed his fist down on the table. The glasses jumped and beer slopped over the edge, making a mess. The same toothless man glanced over as he collected his winnings. "I told you, no police," Blade said. "We don't want law enforcement—any LE—picking up the Horseman."

"Why?" Zoë asked, defiant. "Because you want the glory for yourself and your club? What about all those other families out there who need to know what happened to their family members?"

Blade bit his bottom lip, pushed back the scraggly black-and-gray hair that had fallen across his face like a curtain. His breaths, more snorts than air, reminded Zoë of a bull.

"I know you think all this will go down perfectly," Blade said. "In your little world, he'll sit for one trial, then another, and soon, they'll give him the death penalty and all will be well...but I promise you, that will not happen. The minute the Horseman is

THE TATTOO ARTIST

captured, the feds will intervene and trade what information he has about their murdered DEA agent, the Devils, and the other MCs, before they ever charge him with a single one of those women's murders. Even if some local LE gets to him first, it won't matter. The feds will override anything the locals try to do."

He leaned forward, that *LS Bloody One* patch prominent, the one that told everyone he'd killed for the club. "He'll hand over whatever is necessary for us and his brothers to face life in prison, then he'll get some cushy digs and a private cell. There's only one way those women get justice, and that's if we give it to them. Feds tell you anything else, they're blowing smoke up your ass."

Zoë took a long drink of beer, set the bottle down harshly. "I just don't see how we all wouldn't be safer if he was behind bars."

Blade gave a deep chuckle. "Outside or inside, as soon as he learns about the authorities coming for him, he'll search for the responsible party. Someday soon, that will lead to you. But right now?" Blade lit a cigarette. "He'll be coming for me. Your little extracurricular activities have put me and my family in danger, and I don't appreciate it."

Next to her, Riot stiffened. He gripped the beer between his hands.

Zoë's heart pounded against her ribs. Her mouth went dry. "Why would he come for you? Several people must know about the horse tattoo. It could be anybody within the Devils or even a citizen. How's he going to know who outed him?"

"He's not," Blade said, the smoke trailing lazily around his wrinkled eyes. "That's the point. There's only one person he's aware of who might know who that rat is, and that person is me."

A heaviness, like the weight of an anvil, settled upon Zoë's chest. If something happened to Blade or his family because of what she'd sent to the police, she could never forgive herself. There would be no recourse, no apology that could make a difference.

Her eyes widened. "You have to know that's not what I intended. I just wanted other law enforcement to be on the lookout. I don't want him with time on his hands to figure out it was me who tipped the police about the undercover or, worse, get bored and take another victim. I just want him in a cell where he can never hurt anyone again."

Blade inhaled on the cigarette. Smoke exited his nostrils as well as his lips. "Honey, the only place that's going to happen is a grave. Otherwise, even while he sits inside, he can send a few of his brothers to come pay us a visit. I think it's time you understood that."

Zoë lolled her head around her shoulders, gaze casting over the four crusty card players nearby and three women gathered at the bar. She didn't know what to do. She couldn't undo what she'd already done, so what was he hoping to gain from this conversation?

She gripped her beer bottle between both hands and stared at it for what seemed an eternity, hoping the contents inside would grant her some wisdom.

Riot reached over and rubbed her back. "Come on, old lady, it will be okay. Hey, knock, knock."

She smiled wryly. "Who's there?"

"Police."

"Police who?"

"Police don't worry. I've got his back. I'll stay at the house and we'll set up extra surveillance, day and night. We won't rest until this is done."

"*Done*. See, that's what worries me. I don't want to be like the Horseman or..."

She shot a glance across the table, at that *Bloody One* patch.

Blade's face darkened as that deep laugh rumbled. "What? Like me? A killer?"

She started to respond when a disturbance caught her attention. A few of the club members started coughing near the poker table, then the girls near the front. The first sign that something was wrong was the smell—a distinct odor of gasoline. A burly guy with a large beer belly stood up from the poker table and suggested that maybe a bike had tipped over and the gas had spilled out from the tank. Three or four people started for the front door to check, when suddenly a crackling began, smoke began to rise, and the whole place went up in flames.

A blast of heat, intense and suffocating, enveloped the bar, and instantly, everyone understood what was happening. Chairs and tables were tossed aside as men and women started running for the door, and the next thing Zoë knew, her world turned upside down.

Blade slipped from his leather cuts and threw them over Zoë's head. "Get her out of here now!" he shouted.

Riot wrapped his arms around her, forced her head down, and pushed her toward the back room. Yells and screams pierced the air as a large chunk of wood crashed to the floor, then part of the ceiling began to disintegrate. The bar that had seated a half dozen patrons just minutes before caught on fire, and the bartender-owner jumped over the top and ran out, taking one of the women with him beneath his arm.

Riot forged ahead, guiding Zoë between objects like a pinball in a machine. Her shin slammed into something hard, and she felt a searing pain as a protruding nail ripped her shoulder wide open. A second later, she heard Riot and a group of men pounding and kicking on the back door trying to get it open, but it wouldn't budge. That's when Zoë realized the trouble they were in, that the exit had been blocked by something to keep them inside. Smoke roiled thick and black now, burning her eyes and throat. She began to cough.

Riot yanked her away from the door to a spot in the wall where the boards and wood nailed together there had left gaps large enough to see glimmers of the outside.

That the place was haphazardly built, with no insulation or drywall of any kind, could now prove to be their saving grace.

Riot, his mouth shielded with a bandana but no protection otherwise, kicked at the boards until two of them popped free. He launched himself at the small opening with his shoulders and back, causing additional boards to break and daylight to appear. Smoke poured from the hole, informing them of the way out. He grabbed Zoë in a bear hug, then rocked forward and used his momentum to hit the wall again with all his strength, and suddenly, he and Zoë landed hard on the other side in a face full of dirt. He pulled her to her feet, and together, they scrambled away as fast as they could, looking like two people running a three-legged race.

When Zoë was a safe distance away, she flung Blade's leather cut from her head and gasped for air. Riot, however, looked back at the burning structure and let out a voracious roar, then started running back toward it. After stepping back through the hole, he started yelling for people to follow his voice, and began pulling members out and into the light. They stumbled and fell about, coughing and gasping.

Zoë kept waiting to see Blade appear, but after what felt like an eternity watching others come out with no sign of the crusty VP, her anxiety began to spike, fearing for his safety. She got to her feet and began to stumble around the property, calling out his name. Embers fell on her hair, clothes, and skin, biting at her like small insects. She could hear the scream of the fire trucks as they approached the place, which was now fully engulfed in flames.

After they arrived, the water began to flow, and three firemen charged in. But Zoë couldn't see who or what they were able to save before the entire structure began to collapse. Riot, still halfway hanging inside, continued to yell for Blade until two other members who'd already made it out grabbed his arms and pulled him back, kicking and screaming, away from the wreckage.

The terror etched on his face echoed Zoë's fear. He hadn't been able to find his sponsor and get him out before the collapse. As far as they both knew, Blade was still inside.

Zoë shook, breathing heavily, and wondered if the Horseman was responsible for this attack on Los Salvajes. If he was, his response to being outed to local authorities far surpassed any of her expectations. He would never stop, and she would never be safe.

CHAPTER 31

oe was taken to the hospital and, like the others, checked out for a variety of cuts, bruises, and burns. Despite the deep gash that ran from Riot's forehead and down the side of his right eye, and the blood and burns that covered his bare arms and shoulders, he stayed with her, insisting the doctors take care of others before him. Max raced to the ER to be by her side, and wasn't too happy to see another man already there, but he didn't know what Zoë did—that it had been Riot who'd saved her life.

After Max arrived, Zoë pleaded with Riot to let the doctor take care of him, and finally, he obliged. "But let me know if you find Blade," she added.

"Will do."

Max gave him a parting glance as he left—one that said he'd like to finish off what the fire didn't—but thankfully held whatever he was feeling inside. Zoë asked about Oliver, and Max insisted he was fine, that he was with the babysitter at her house.

"What the hell, Zoë?" he asked, his voice cracking. He stroked her arm.

"I know you have a thousand questions, and I promise you I will answer them all, but right now, I just want to go home," she whispered.

Max nodded. After her release, he pulled the truck up and helped her into the cab. Already, her body was growing stiff and sore. She couldn't stop shivering, despite the ninety-degree heat, so Max grabbed a blanket from the back and wrapped it around her shoulders.

They drove home in silence until thoughts of what had happened, along with the void and space between her and Max, became too much and Zoë's emotions overwhelmed her. That reality, that the Lone Horseman may've just tried to kill her and Blade, sank into her core. She burst into tears.

Max, his own eyes rimmed red and fighting a bevy of emotions she couldn't possibly understand, took her inside their house and held her until she cried it out. Later, he prepared a warm baking-soda bath and spoke soothing words as he tended to her, then dried her off and applied aloe to the burns. He said little as she lay next to him that night snuggled beneath his shoulder.

He was such a good husband, her best friend. He hadn't yelled. He hadn't demanded answers. Still, she knew the questions would be forthcoming.

Turned out, Brady Sloane beat him to it, and at ten a.m. the next morning, he was on her doorstep, along with two men in suits and Zoë's least favorite person—Special Agent Quinn of the DEA. They didn't so much ask to come in as demand it, then promptly occupied the living room.

Max offered to go get Oliver and let them talk, but Zoë asked him to stay. He needed to learn the truth. It was entirely possible that her actions would cost her this marriage, but right now, she wanted to ensure her husband's and son's safety. He took a seat beside her on the couch and held her hand.

Sloane made introductions, then asked Zoë how she was doing.

"I'm alive. That's all that matters. And my family." She glanced at Max, squeezed his hand. "But Blade...I haven't heard anything."

"He's alive," Sloane said. "He took in a lot of smoke, and he's got third-degree burns, but firefighters were able to revive him. He's been moved to a burn unit."

Zoë issued a sigh of relief. She felt the tears surface, wiped them away.

"I guess you two were closer than I thought," Sloane said.

"No, it's not like that," Zoë said. "I don't want him or his family to get hurt. I never wanted anyone to get hurt, certainly not to die. That was never my intention."

Quinn, who refused to sit, paced by a window and snorted. "Does that include the Lone Horseman? I mean, if you didn't want him dead, why else go to Los Salvajes?"

Max stiffened. Zoë could sense he wanted to stand and punch the man in the face. Clearly, his initial impression of Quinn hadn't been any different than her own.

Still, Zoë could tell the mention of the outlaw motorcycle club didn't please him. He'd seen all the men in their cuts at the hospital, and was now well aware of who his wife had been spending time with.

"I thought they could help me find him. That's all," she explained to Max as much as the others. "The man with the tattoo I told you about a while back? He's a high-ranking member of the Devils. He's their top enforcer. They call him the Lone Horseman. I couldn't tell you because I didn't want you to worry." She explained how she knew Blade as a kid, how he'd once had a crush on her mom.

Max sat back, turned a slight shade of red. Anger maybe at what she'd been up to, or embarrassment for being kept out of the loop, or both. But, for some reason, he didn't seem overly surprised.

"You could've come to us for that," Sloane said.

Zoë huffed. "You know how I feel about the police. I don't trust you, any of you," she said, looking at the two FBI agents.

"Appears you don't trust your husband much either," Quinn snapped.

Zoë stared daggers at him, fumed. "I love my husband. I didn't want him involved. I was trying to protect him, and my son."

"By getting in between—and even escalating—a war between Los Salvajes and the Devils? By getting a citizen and a member of the Devils killed in a casino shooting? By getting a DEA agent killed?" Quinn shot back.

"Your undercover was already a dead man, and you only found him because of me," Zoë shouted. "Don't you forget that."

Quinn's lips thinned into tight slits. He shoved his hands in his trouser pockets, looked like a little boy of ten who'd just lost a race to a girl.

She turned to Sloane. "What you don't understand is, I didn't have then what I have now. I suspected the Lone Horseman was my mother's killer, yes, but evidence... I knew you wouldn't believe me without more than a story. It was Blade and his club who figured out how I could get in with the Devils, and I did."

"Hence the boyfriend," Quinn mumbled. "Bet your husband didn't know about that arrangement either. Nights spent in the desert and Sacramento with a prospect."

"I did, actually," Max shot back. He turned to Zoë. "When I saw the lack of miles on the car, I pressed Kat for answers. I found out enough to know you'd gone with a man to Vegas. I just didn't know why."

He leered at Quinn. "So you can sit down and start treating my wife with the respect she deserves or you can leave my house."

A small smile crossed Zoë's lips. She didn't know if it was possible to love Max more at that moment. He knew she'd been lying to him, yet he still defended her.

Sloane smirked. Watched Quinn take a seat.

One of the FBI agents finally chimed in. "Why don't we back up a bit? Start from the beginning. When did you first suspect this man of killing your mother? And why? How did that lead you to these other women? We have copies of the letters you sent local authorities in Idaho, Arizona, Washington, California, and Montana. Who else have you sent letters to, and what exactly is the evidence you keep talking about?"

Zoë took a deep breath, held Max's hand, and finally revealed it all. What else could she do? Despite Blade's objections, she wasn't going to let Los Salvajes pursue this alone anymore. That they were up against a formidable opponent who would kill to keep his secret was no longer in question.

She stood to get the notebooks she'd filled with pictures of the Horseman's back, those Screech had taken that first day along with the individual shots she'd later enlarged and cropped. Also included were all the news stories she'd collected from the internet along with cold case files from each of the law enforcement agencies.

They gathered around as she started with number fourteen and worked her way backward. "The tattoo he wanted was macabre but simple really—a tiger with a collar around its neck, pulled tight enough so that its eyes popped out. He wanted a touch of orange on the collar and the numbers inscribed."

She went on to explain their breakdown: state, date, sequence. "He wanted orange because it reflected her personality. Fiery, like she was. Those were his exact words."

Sloane picked up the enlarged photo of the tattoo, felt his heart sink. "Jesus. Amber McKinley."

Zoë nodded. "Only I didn't know that at the time. It was only after I broke down the code that I suspected it was her. That's why I went to her house that day. I was hoping to find something that would confirm my beliefs. And I did. Her mother said she loved animal prints. She had a whole closet full of them. Tigers were her favorite."

She continued, bringing to light the evidence of the Idaho rodeo queen and her horse, Princess; the coyote and the Arizona bar patron; the dolphin and the aquarium employee; and on and on. When she got to her mother, number three, she choked up in telling them about the hummingbirds she used to paint, and how she'd found them spattered with blood upon returning to the house.

Sloane's head lowered with every word.

"And that's it," she said. "That leaves numbers one, two, nine, and thirteen to be found. I've searched, but it could be I'm not entering the right keywords. I'm sure your analysts are far more capable, plus you have all those national databases."

The two FBI agents nodded. "Yes, we do. And we will find them, I promise."

"Good."

Quinn just stared. She'd finally made him speechless.

Like the rest of them, Max sat quietly pondering the spread of photographs laid out before them, but she could tell, the revelation of what she'd been up to overwhelmed him. He sat with his elbows on his knees, hands cupped in front of his face, bottom lip trembling. His wife had lied to him about her pursuit, had spent days and weekends hanging out with outlaw bikers, had put herself and possibly their family in grave danger, but he could not deny that she was right.

Zoë had uncovered a serial killer.

CHAPTER 32

The plan was for Zoë to now take a back seat and let the feds take over the investigation, but as soon as Riot heard the news of their involvement, he came to Zoë and Max and insisted they return to Sacramento to keep their relationship with the Devils going. He explained to Max that if he and Zoë cut a trail now and never showed up again and the Feds suddenly moved in, it would be like pointing an arrow at their heads and telling the Devils that one, or both, of them were informants for the government. That, in turn, would make the Devils come for Riot and Zoë, which, as they all knew, never led to a good outcome. If Zoë really was intent on protecting her family, she needed to continue her friendship with Vero until the feds made a few more appearances, and Riot could say he was no longer interested in becoming a prospect because of the continued heat. Then no one would be the wiser about their involvement. As far as they knew, the Devils didn't know anything about Riot or Zoë—only Blade—and they had already made their intentions toward him clear.

The more Zoë thought about it, and the more she, Max, and Riot discussed it, the more Zoë knew he was right. If they really wanted to be free of the Devils, they needed to make at least one more visit.

The next few weeks were torturous as they waited for their wounds from the fire to heal and little new information came their way. Sloane did call once to let Zoë know the FBI thought they had identified two more of the Horseman's victims, including number nine, a former dog groomer in El Paso, Texas, and number thirteen, a woman in Yuba City who'd disappeared around the time the Devils were hosting their twenty-fifth-anniversary bash the prior year. Come to find out, the woman's last name had been Fox, which showed just how little respect the Horseman held for law enforcement and how he considered himself above the law. He must've been laughing his ass off when he'd had that one inked.

Finally, Zoë reached out to Vero and mentioned that she and Riot were taking a late-summer ride to Oregon and asked if they could stop for the night in Sacramento. Zoë said she wanted to bring her portfolios, as Vero had previously suggested, and show Vero her work. To Zoë's relief, Vero seemed delighted to hear from her and said the guys would enjoy seeing Riot again too. Apparently, things had been beyond tense in the Devils' world and they could all use a little comic relief.

Max wanted to come along but Zoë thought it best if he stayed with Oliver and made everything appear as normal as possible. That it had been a few weeks with no sign of anyone lurking around the tattoo shop or home made them both feel more assured that the Devils didn't know of Zoë's involvement. Max finally agreed, but held Zoë an enormously long time the night before she was due to depart. Since he'd learned the truth, he'd confessed he'd known something was off since Vegas, and that, in addition to pressing Kat, he'd poked into the computer's history enough to know Zoë had been researching motorcycle gangs and missing women. But he hadn't wanted to confront her. He'd wanted her to come to him on her own.

The next day, she and Riot rode up under a sunny sky on a mid-seventies day and wound their way back up the twisty mountain roads to the Devils' NorCal clubhouse. Riot was now positive that the Devils didn't know about their involvement, as in no way would they let them enter the premises again if they suspected them of being informants. Zoë was also stunned that they'd invited them there again—given their rule of members only—yet, Riot oddly wasn't. In fact, he even seemed a little cocky about it, getting a direct invite inside, and she wondered where his arrogance was coming from.

After they parked the bike, Vero came out to greet her and gave her a hug. The guys took Riot into the club. Thankfully, nothing seemed amiss.

The two women enjoyed an afternoon sitting outside in the lone patch of sun they could find among the towering trees, catching up on the latest happenings with the chapter members—a new baby, a couple of birthdays, and a new prospect named Pete. Prospect Pete was always mining for gold in his spare time, which made the name doubly funny. Vero was certain he and Riot would get along famously.

Zoë wondered if Vero would bring up the fire at the Treehouse in Carson City, but when she didn't, Zoë decided against asking about it too. Instead, she inquired if the heat from the feds had died down since the casino shooting.

"No, unfortunately," Vero said. She lit a cigarette. They were always nearby, her favorite accessory. "Things have gotten much worse, in fact. But today is a good day. Listen to them whooping it up in there. They sound happy."

Zoë glanced over her shoulder at the club, where the doors and windows were shut but the voices and laughter broke all barriers. They did sound happy.

Too bad it didn't last.

An hour later, after Vero and Zoë had moved into the RV to get out of a light rain, a crash like Zoë had never heard before came from outside. Chain link rattled, branches and brush crunched, and a loud roar emerged as an armored vehicle plowed through the outdoor fencing near the back perimeter of the Devils' property. Vero rushed to the RV's window and moved the curtains to see what the hell was going on, only to observe a dozen men dressed in black pour from the vehicle, all holding high-powered weapons.

"*What the ?*" she said and let out a string of curse words.

Zoë gasped over her shoulder. The Devils compound was being raided.

She started to run for the door when Vero grabbed her arm. Outside, shouts followed as the men in black infiltrated the clubhouse and they heard the words: "Get down on the ground! ATF!"

Zoë ducked between the seats of the RV, expecting the sounds of automatic weapons to fire and people to die, but, to her surprise, and Vero's too—given the confused look on her face—they didn't. Words were exchanged, then silence unfolded.

Ten minutes later, there was a knock at the door. "Come out, hands where we can see them."

Zoë and Vero did as they commanded. First, Vero trounced down the steps and lay facedown on the ground with her hands above her head, then Zoë. A female agent frisked them, then cuffed their hands behind their backs. She thought if Max could see her right now, he'd probably have a heart attack.

As they propped her to her feet, Zoë's heart pounded with a voracity she'd only felt a couple of times in her life. Once as she lay silent in a tent wondering if the individual outside who'd discovered her camp would enter and hurt her, and another when she ran from police after stealing tampons from a local drug store. She'd never been arrested before, but it appeared that might change.

Vero spit on the ground near the female agent's feet. Snapped her neck right and issued Zoë a look that informed her something was very wrong. The woman was pissed, and not just at the feds. Zoë feared, just like Riot had mentioned, that Vero suspected her and Riot's visit and the subsequent raid was not coincidental.

Talk about crappy timing.

She and Vero were led inside the club, where the guys were lined up against a wall with agents guarding them at gunpoint. As the female agent paraded Zoë down the line, Zoë exchanged a glance with Riot. He appeared no happier than she did, but issued a slow single blink as if sending her a message: *It will be okay. Stay calm. Trust me.*

Sure, right.

It wasn't long before Zoë saw that the raid was a combined affair—both DEA and ATF—and to no surprise, that Agent Quinn was involved. As soon as Zoë saw him, she wanted to join Vero in spitting at his boot. After all the talk and planning between the two agencies and the FBI, the promises of letting the FBI now handle the investigation into the Lone Horseman hadn't gone over well with his ego.

She could hear Blade's words chanting in her head. *There's only one way these women get justice. The feds tell you anything else, they're blowing smoke up your ass.*

Quinn marched with near military precision to the front of the line and, with great fanfare, unfolded a sheet of paper and snapped it in front of Maverick's face. "We have a search warrant. We'll be looking for any guns and drugs in your fine establishment. Hope you don't mind."

He folded it back up, even tinier than it was before, stuffed it in Maverick's pocket just beneath his *President* patch. He tapped on it several times, relished every moment.

Maverick, with his slit eyes and V-shaped beard, had a look on his face that, if it had been directed at Zoë, would've made her run screaming. It wasn't so much a threat as a visual declaration—that Quinn was a dead man.

The DEA and ATF agents fanned out and began to conduct the search.

But not Quinn. He stayed with the Devils to antagonize each member and speak to them in derogatory tones. It was as if he wanted each one to know who he was, and that it was him personally taking each of them down. If he couldn't nab the Lone Horseman, he would find his glory in guns and drugs.

Zoë wondered what stupid-ass move he'd try to pull when he got to Riot. She knew Quinn had seen Zoë riding with him and feared he might out Riot as a member of Los Salvajes. But would he be so vindictive? So callous about their safety?

She didn't put it past him.

Quinn stopped in front of Riot, sniffed in his direction. "Who's this? New prospect?" He looked Riot over. "No, can't be. You've got no cuts and no patch. That must mean you're still one of their grunts, a lowly hang-around."

He stepped forward, got within an inch of Riot's face, puffed out his chest. "Still busy serving them on your knees trying to get a sponsor, huh?"

Riot leered, but the corners of his mouth turned upward. He stomped both feet as if he were lining up in the military. "I'd rather suck their dicks every day and twice on Sunday than kiss your ass, sir."

Quinn turned a violent red. At the end of the row, Maverick chuckled.

"Yeah? We'll see if you feel that way when they do your bidding in prison."

He moved along until he came to Vero. With Zoë standing right next to her, she knew he saw her too, but to his credit, he didn't react.

"You must be the president's old lady. Who's this?" he asked, casting a thumb at Zoë. "Your kid sister?" Quinn issued a wholly inappropriate look at Zoë's body and sniffed. "You don't smell quite as rotten as her, but give it time."

Zoë barely held her tongue.

Quinn abruptly stepped back and shouted orders at two of his subordinates. "Strip each of the men from the waist up and turn their back to face me."

The two looked as if they'd rather eat cow dung, but battled the Devils' grunts and groans to pull back their cuts, and the shirts beneath them, and left them dangling near the cuffs at their wrists. "He must like to look at men's titties while his men conduct the show," one of Devils charged.

Quinn ignored him. He clearly had something else on his mind, and that something was the Lone Horseman. Zoë clenched her fists, wishing she could pound his face. Not only had he raided their clubhouse while she and Riot were there—placing a giant target on their backs—now he was going to bring up the Lone Horseman in their presence.

You stupid, stupid son of a bitch.

While they had their backs turned, Quinn walked the line, examining each man's back. Next to Zoë, Vero visibly stiffened and mumbled. Hot breaths shot from her nose. That she was angry was an understatement.

Quinn issued a circular motion to indicate to his comrades to turn the men around. Afterward, he brought out a photo from his front pocket. "You seem to be missing one of your brothers. Somebody want to tell me where I can find this scumbag? I believe he goes by the name of the Lone Horseman?"

Zoë lowered her head. She wanted to take her cuffed hands and put them around Quinn's neck and squeeze. The photo was one she'd taken from Vero's scrapbooks, and Zoë feared she would recognize it. Quinn was endangering her, and her family, all for the sake of his ego. And she would not forgive him.

None of them moved a muscle.

"I see. Nobody knows him. That would be odd, given the ink on his chest."

He held up new photos in front of Maverick. You recognize your own club logo, don't you? The pitchforks on his shoulders. Colors too. My, my. He must hold a high rank. Maybe even higher than you."

When he received no response from Maverick, he moved back to Vero.

"How about you? You're the club's tattoo artist, aren't you? So maybe you inked a few of these for him?"

Zoë held her breath as he switched to holding up the individual photo to images of the Horseman's back and each of the fourteen tattoos, the very pictures she'd enlarged from Screech's original and given to the FBI. The tiger, the fox, the horse, the coyote...and on and on. Vero stared straight ahead, barely giving each a courtesy glance, until he got to the fifth or sixth image, when something strange came to light. Her brow twitched at the image of the toothless dog from Texas, again at the lion and red whip. And by the time he got to number one, that black cat with a lavender ribbon, Zoë was pretty sure Vero had stopped breathing.

My God, did she recognize the pattern? Zoë wanted to blurt out her question, but had to refrain. Instead, it was Quinn who asked the questions. "Did you do any of these?"

"No," Vero said flatly. "Never seen them before."

Zoë cast her a sideways glance. Was that true? Had she never seen the images upon the Horseman's back before? Vero and the Horseman knew each other well. They'd been to the same clubhouses and events many times. It didn't seem likely unless, because she was an artist and might understand their meaning, he made sure she never got too close.

Another agent in a DEA uniform came in and whispered in Quinn's ear. After a thorough exploration of the house, garage, pole barn, and RV, they'd completed the search. Quinn silently asked him a few questions, to which the man shook his head. Quinn didn't look pleased. Nor did the head ATF guy who joined them, who went on a silent tirade.

Quinn appeared as if he would explode. His face turned purple.

One of the agents brought in two handguns and a small bag of weed and laid them on a table. Maverick and several of the other Devils looked like they were about to bust a gut. Down the row, Zoë noticed Riot smirk.

"Those guns are legal," Vero said. "I have the paperwork. So is the weed, as you know. California law and all that."

Zoë thought of the crates of guns and ammo in the garage she and Riot had seen, and what Vero had once said about the small arsenal in the storage bins of the RV. So how could it be that this—two legal handguns and a small bag of weed—was all they found?

She once again looked down the row of men to see Riot give Maverick a wink.

Maverick spoke. "I'll be expecting a check from the government for the repair to my fence and other property for this unnecessary harassment."

Quinn nearly burned rubber as he wheeled around on a heel and commanded the other agents to let the men go. Then he cussed all the way to his SUV and left the property, tires squealing.

CHAPTER 33

After the DEA and ATF pulled out, the members of the NorCal Devils continued to mill about, wondering why all the security equipment surrounding the property hadn't warned them, and cursing the vile men and women who'd just invaded their property, when Maverick began to chuckle. He clapped his hands, walked over to Riot, and pointed. "This guy," he said. "Two weeks ago, this guy calls me and tells me to clear our site of any guns or drugs. That he heard from a source of his at the ATF that they and the DEA have the hots for us after finding the undercover in the desert, and they might be planning a raid. They're going to do anything and everything to bring us in, even if it means charging us with lesser crimes than what they want." He slapped Riot on the back. "Well, I guess you were right."

Zoë felt her mouth drop. Riot knew this was going to happen? He'd mentioned nothing of the sort to Zoë. "You knew this was going to happen today?" she asked.

Riot shook his head. "No, not today. Not any day. But I heard it was a possibility, and I didn't want these guys to be caught with their pants down. Sure as hell didn't think I'd be here when it happened." He chuckled. "Kind of glad I was, though. The look on that guy's face was priceless."

The guys laughed, but Zoë wasn't amused. To Zoë, this put a target on their back.

Maverick came over and squeezed her shoulder. "No worries, sweetheart. Your man did the right thing. Now, come on, everyone. Let's party."

Maverick might've been okay with how things went down, but Vero was another matter. Her steely, cool manner made Zoë nervous. And rightfully so. While the men went back to playing pool and cards, Vero grabbed Zoë by the arm and led her into her office. When they were inside, she shut the door, wheeled to face Zoë...

And suddenly a gun was in her face.

Zoë gasped.

"What the hell was that?" Vero demanded.

"What? I don't know..."

She held it to Zoë's forehead. "Don't lie to me. Not anymore." Her eyes were dark and menacing. Her top lip trembled.

"I don't understand. What are you talking about?"

"I'm talking about those pictures that man had. Those damn tattoos up close. I'm talking about a photograph he had of the Lone Horseman that came right out of one of my own damn books."

She kicked at the bookcase next to where Zoë stood, let some of the albums fall off the shelf. "Did you think I wouldn't notice that the scrapbooks were in disarray the day after you were here? That pictures had fallen out?"

Zoë glanced at them scattered around her feet, shook. Adrenaline coursed through her body as her mind scrambled for an explanation. "I was just looking through them. Keeping myself busy until Riot was ready to leave the next morning. That's all. You were asleep and—"

"Bullshit. Maybe my husband's buying Riot's little act, but I'm not. You really expect me to believe that you two just happened to be here when the feds raided us?"

She laughed, a wild, demented caw that matched the crazed look in her eyes.

"Who are your working for? Tell me who you are and why you're really here, Zoë of Reno, or I'm going to take you to the middle of that clubhouse, expose you, and you and your funny boyfriend can explain it to the entire crew."

Zoë's blood went cold. This was bad. Quinn had truly fucked them. There was no way she was getting out of here now without some kind of explanation, and Zoë didn't think anything but the truth would suffice. Vero clearly had a nose for bullshit, so if what Zoë gave her didn't pass inspection, then to Maverick she would go.

The gun pressed harder. Vero wanted answers.

"Okay, okay, listen. You're right," Zoë said, keeping her hands in front of her, palms up. She had to get this woman to calm down. "I'm here under false pretenses. I admit it. But I am not working for anyone but me. I promise you that. I came here looking for the Lone Horseman. Riot is here to help me. But we most definitely are not feds."

Vero huffed. "Then why? What do you want with him?"

Zoë took a couple of deep breaths, tried to measure Vero's emotional level. Zoë was certain she'd seen something resonate with Vero when Quinn had flashed those pictures in front of Vero's face—a recognition or understanding of some kind—and right now, she had to trust her instincts. She knew Vero hated the Lone Horseman, had called him a necessary evil. How much more so if she knew what he really did in his spare time?

"Vero, I can tell you recognized something in those images. Those individual tattoos surrounding that pale horse of death? You saw them, didn't you, and the pattern? Animals broken and abused, all inscribed with seven numbers."

Zoë swallowed, tried to keep her voice from wavering. "Well, so did I. When the Lone Horseman came to my tattoo shop two months ago, I saw it too."

Vero's eyes narrowed. It was her turn to feign ignorance. "I don't know what you're talking about."

"The images represent women. The numbers a location and date. The reason I looked through your books was because I needed proof that I wasn't imagining things. All the dates within those numbers, they correspond to club events—runs and gatherings, including your twenty-fifth-anniversary party last year. That tattoo you saw of the trapped fox? I just learned the woman's last name was Fox and she was from Yuba City."

The gun in Vero's hand wavered. Her eyebrows met, parted ways again.

Zoë continued. She had to make certain Vero understood. "The horse with the pink saddle? That was Idaho, the rodeo queen and her horse, Princess, the one you met after a July Fourth holiday run. And the coyote? That was a woman he met at the Prickly Coyote bar in Arizona. You remember being there in February a couple of years ago? You took a photo of the guys outside in the parking lot. And remember Monterey? His victim there was an aquarium employee. Her body washed ashore the day after you left, wrapped in netting more commonly used for dolphins. That's why she's the dolphin. Get it?"

The moment Zoë used the word *victim* instead of the more generic *woman*, the gun in Vero's hand began to shake and the muscles in her face quivered as if they were being short-circuited. Maybe she believed, maybe she didn't. Zoë wasn't sure.

"Did you know he was killing women?" Zoë asked. "Did you, or the club, have any idea? Did you ever see his tattoos before, suspect what he might be doing?"

The gun shook harder. Vero had to stabilize it with her other hand. "What are you saying?" she said through gritted teeth. "You're lying."

Zoë shook her head, pleaded. "Vero, I'm not. He's a rapist and a killer. Fourteen images, fourteen murders. I know he does things for the club—the necessary evils you spoke about—but that's not why I'm here. I'm here because the Horseman is a serial killer. I made it my mission to find him and expose him for who he really is."

Vero shook her head. "Why? Why would you risk it? You said yourself, he's a killer."

Zoë bit her bottom lip, tried to keep tears from welling. "Because the tattoo of the hummingbird with the broken wings represents my mother. She was raped and murdered in Reno when I was fifteen."

Vero took a step back. She blinked once, twice. Looked as if Zoë had just punched her in the face and she might pass out.

The gun lowered. "Jesus."

For the next ten minutes, they simply stood and stared at each other as each tried to come to terms with the emotions they were feeling. While Vero mulled it over, Zoë lowered her hands and slowly began to tell her story—of her mother and the hummingbirds, and how she ran away and exposed her mom to the Horseman's vices. Again, she explained how their lives had intersected.

"He came into my shop in early June. He wanted a tattoo of a choking tiger with its eyes popping out. He gave me a series of numbers to inscribe on the collar. When I saw the hummingbird...I just froze. The three middle numbers, they matched the date my mother died. I didn't know what the other numbers were, so my coworker at the shop took photographs and I did some digging. I soon realized the first two numbers represented the state in which the murder happened, and the last two were the order in which each victim died. He called them his prized ladies."

Finally, Vero put the gun down and, to Zoë's surprise, slumped into the chair behind her desk and sobbed. She shook so badly, Zoë felt compelled to kneel beside her. She stroked Vero's hair. "What? What is it? It's okay. You can tell me. I know you saw something in those images, a glint of recognition. Is it one of the victims?"

Vero nodded. "The cat. That black cat with the lavender ribbon. She was my best friend. She took that cat everywhere she went. And the lavender, she kept soaps in the bath and sachets in all her drawers so every day she smelled like lavender."

She wiped her eyes, applied a tissue to her runny nose. "Jesus. How could Maverick and A.J. not know this? How could the Horseman keep such a secret?" She glanced at Zoë with wide eyes. "If A.J. finds out about this, he'll kill the Horseman himself."

"Why?" Zoë asked.

"Because my friend was A.J.'s first love."

Zoë felt her mouth drop. She knew the Horseman was bold, but damn. The national president's woman? No wonder he couldn't chance having Vero do his ink.

"What about Maverick?" Zoë asked.

Vero shook her head. "I don't know. He and Larry go back a long way. That's the Horseman's real name—Larry Grossman. When he used to play guitar in the Seattle grunge scene, he'd go by Larry Lightning."

Zoë took a deep breath. Finally, she had a name.

Vero opened her desk drawer, took out a two-ounce bottle of flavored vodka, one among dozens. She asked Zoë if she wanted one. Zoë did. It was warm, but it helped calm her nerves. It wasn't every day she had a gun thrust in her face.

She watched Vero drink, could see the range of emotions, thoughts, and conflicts working overtime.

"I have to ask," Vero said. "If you and Riot aren't working with the feds, how did that little shit that came here today get those pictures?"

Zoë sighed, took a seat in a nearby chair. "I said I wasn't a fed and I'm not. But I am working with them, just not in the way you think. That little shit's name is Quinn. He's got a hard-on for the Devils because that undercover discovered in the desert was his, and he knows the Lone Horseman was responsible."

Vero narrowed her eyes. "And how would he know that?"

Zoë closed her eyes. *Shit.*

Vero let out a string of curse words. "Campers in the desert, my ass. You. You are the one that tipped them, aren't you?" She leaned forward, pointed a bony finger. "You were in the RV that night he gave me the picture. You told the authorities about that goddamn bush." She clicked her tongue, anger growing. "Son of a bitch."

"Again, not to bring heat on the club. Only the Horseman," Zoë said.

Vero downed the remainder of the little bottle, got another. Zoë nervously eyed the gun that still rested on the desk. She wanted Vero to stop asking questions now, but she could see that wasn't going to happen.

"And Los Salvajes—was that you too? Their sudden knowledge of and interest in the Horseman?" She unscrewed the cap and tossed it in the trash, huffed. "Of course, it was. Who else besides another tattoo artist could get close enough to that stupid pig tattoo and understand its meaning? Jesus."

Zoë lowered her head. "I don't know what I was thinking, telling them."

Vero grunted. "I'm guessing you were hoping they would do for you what you couldn't for yourself."

"Maybe. Not consciously, but maybe."

The finger was back. "You got Buster killed."

"No," Zoë snapped. "I didn't. The Horseman did. And then he tried to murder a bar full of Los Salvajes members, including their VP, by setting it on fire."

Vero cocked her head, surprised by Zoë's outburst. "Yeah, I heard about that." She mumbled more curses, drank. "Who else has copies of those pictures?"

Zoë cleared her throat, glanced out the window. The woman really wasn't going to like this part. "After I found a few of the other victims, I gave what I had to the FBI. I didn't have a choice. They—and not the DEA or ATF—are the ones that are supposed to be heading up this case now."

Vero's jaw dropped. "The FBI?" She couldn't even say the initials out loud; she had to whisper them. "Tips about a dead UC, pictures to the FBI? How exactly do you not call that working with the feds?"

"I'm not an undercover."

"No, but you are an informant." Vero eyed the gun, stared at Zoë. "If my husband knew what I did right now, you'd never walk out of here, Zoë of Reno."

Zoë's heart leapt to her throat. Maybe she'd said too much. The knowledge of the dead women was one thing, the involvement of the feds another. She suddenly wished Max had come along now and she had a way to text him and tell him to bring back that SWAT team. Because right now, with the gun in Vero's reach, she didn't know what the hell Vero was going to do. Zoë had told her the truth, and now her future was in the woman's hands.

"I want you to know," Zoë said. "I never meant for any of this to turn out like it has. Not for Los Salvajes, not for the Devils, and certainly not for you. I just want the Lone Horseman to pay for what he's done. Everybody else wants him dead. I want him exposed and punished for the crimes he's committed against these women. There are thirteen families out there who have no idea who killed their loved ones, and they deserve to know. I have no ill will against the Devils—except that the Horseman is one."

Vero finished off her two-ounce vodka, set it down.

Zoë continued. "I don't know what you're thinking right now, but I have a husband and a son at home whom I love very much. They don't understand it, but part of what I'm doing is for them. So I can finally be free of the past and move forward. Also, that I consider you a friend is not a lie. I do."

She had pleaded her case. That was all she could do.

"Help me, Vero. Let's bring the Lone Horseman to justice."

CHAPTER 34

Since the fire, the Lone Horseman had remained out of sight, staying in campgrounds and run-down motels. No one had come forth to say that they'd seen anything out of the ordinary at the Treehouse that day, but the authorities knew it was arson and were actively investigating. Still, he wasn't worried. Given the place had no security cameras, and no witnesses had surfaced, he doubted they'd ever be able to pin the responsibility on him or the Devils. Of course, Los Salvajes knew better, but that was the point. The fire hadn't succeeded in eliminating any of them, but he'd made his message clear—keep spreading information about him, and there would be a hefty price to pay.

The Carson City VP was in the hospital with third degree burns, but getting him alone and forcing him to talk no longer mattered. After Maverick had called and told the Lone Horseman about the raid, and the photographs the DEA agent had in his possession, he felt certain that he already knew the source of the shared information and the enemy at hand.

Who else but the queen Devil herself? Vero.

All of this had started right after Vegas, when he'd given her that picture of the red bush in the desert and gotten a little friendly with her in the RV. It must've really pissed her off and she'd decided to get even. That, or she'd learned about his other activities, especially the first victim, and had been waiting for the perfect time to take him down. Either way, it didn't matter. Vero was a dead woman.

All he had to do now was convince Maverick.

He sped along the mostly empty highways, then wound his way up to the NorCal clubhouse. Mav had expressed concern about him coming to the club, but the Horseman assured him that this was a conversation that couldn't wait. He just wondered if Vero would be there, and if Mav would let him question her properly. When it came to Vero, Mav thought she could do no wrong.

He was in for a surprise.

At the back door, Mav greeted him and invited him into the club. There was no sign of Vero, or anyone else. "Old lady asleep?" the Horseman asked.

"Yeah," Mav said. He popped two beers, handed one to the Horseman. "She hasn't been the same since the raid. Spooked her, I think. She's worried about me getting thrown in the can. It's been a long time since she had to operate without me, run this place on her own."

"Well, we're going to make sure that doesn't happen."

They clinked beers, and the Horseman asked Mav to repeat what went down during the raid. Mav told him about the armored vehicle and the agents rushing in, then explained how they rounded everyone up in the club. "The guy in charge made his agents remove our cuts and shirts, and he went down the row one by one looking for you. When he realized you weren't there, he turned his focus to Vero. Asked about the tattoos and whether she'd done the ink. Showed her close-ups of your animals."

The Horseman cursed.

Mav lit a cigarette. "She remained tight-lipped, but I have to tell you, she might've gotten a sense of what those animals represent. Vero is not a stupid woman."

He grunted. "No, she isn't." He leaned on the bar, looked across to the bald-headed beast who was his best friend. He had to be careful about how he brought it up, but it had to be done.

"Listen, I mean no disrespect, but I have to ask...do you think it's a coincidence that agent focused on asking Vero those questions?"

Maverick inhaled on the cigarette, blew out smoke. "What do you mean?"

The Horseman sighed. Looked over his shoulder to make sure that Vero was still absent. "I mean your old lady was the only one outside the board who knew about that bush in the desert. She knew about the pig tattoo as well. And no, she's never applied ink for me, but she's seen me with my shirt off many times. Maybe she paid more attention to the images on by back than I ever gave her credit for. She could've taken pictures of me at some club event."

He lit his own cigarette, squinted as the smoke trailed around his face before he continued. "That picture you told me the agent had of me—that was taken at last year's anniversary party. She took the picture, and as far as I know, she's the only one who had a copy."

The Horseman cocked his head. Let his words sink in.

On the other side of the bar, Maverick underwent a slow metamorphosis, from amusement, to confusion, to ire. His thin-slit eyes narrowed further as he pulled on his beard. "I tell you to figure this shit out and fix it, and this is what you come up with? That my old lady is a rat? That she's selling out the club? And me? Talking to members of Los Salvajes?"

The dim light above the bar flickered.

"Maybe it's not about the club. Maybe she's just got it in for me."

"For what reason?"

The Horseman shrugged. What could he say? Because he liked to tease her and get in her pants? Maverick wouldn't take kindly to his actions if he knew. He might even beat the living shit out of him—if he could. "I don't know. She's never been my biggest fan, you know that. And hell, maybe she figured it out. My ink. You said it yourself, she's smart. Who else could've matched those images up with the club runs? Who else could've tipped Los Salvajes and the feds?"

Maverick pulled out a bottle of tequila, took a shot. When Maverick took to tequila, it was a sign. A notice to all around him that he wasn't happy and was about to unleash. The Lone Horseman understood his anger, but he had a responsibility to present the facts.

"I know you don't want to hear it—let alone believe it—but maybe Vero is working with the feds. Maybe they got to her somehow. Think about it, man, how else did the feds get a list of those guns and ammo they were looking for?" He shook his head. "It has to be someone on the inside. If not Vero, then someone else who has access to that kind of information and those pictures of me. And those choices don't look good either."

Maverick snarled. "Are you pointing the finger at me now?"

He poured another shot, tossed it back, wiped his lips. His eyes bled fire.

The Lone Horseman took a step back. Maybe he just needed to give his friend some space and time. Betrayal was a damn hard thing to swallow, after all.

He sauntered by the pool table, picked up the eleven ball, and rolled it across the green felt into a corner pocket. "Well, if you've got any other ideas, I'm listening. But you have to know, this bullshit didn't come out of nowhere."

Maverick breathed heavily, took another shot, paced behind the bar. He didn't like it, but at least he was thinking about what the Horseman had offered.

"Anybody else new to the club?" the Horseman asked, trying to appear open to possibilities other than Vero. "What about this hang-around you spoke about, the one who gave you the tip on the raid? You don't think it's a little suspicious that he was here when this raid went down?" He took a long pull on the beer.

Maverick huffed. "Of course I did. But why the hell would he tip us off if he's a fed? With the guns we had in this place, it would have been a huge score for him."

The Horseman considered it. "Unless it wasn't the guns they were really interested in, but me. For the little incident in the desert. You said yourself, the lead agent was DEA, not ATF, and he was damn pissed that I wasn't there. Maybe the guns and ammo were just an excuse to get in and this guy isn't ready to give himself up yet."

Maverick's eyes darkened. He grunted.

"What do you know about this guy? Where's he from? Have I ever met him?"

Maverick laughed. "The hang-around? Yeah. You punched him in the face."

"What? You mean that punk from the concert?"

"That's the guy."

The Horseman chuckled, zipped another ball across the table until it clacked against the one ball. He shook his head. "I had my shirt off that night. He could've gotten a look, I guess."

"No fucking way. In the dark, with a bonfire burning?" Maverick said.

The Horseman thought. It had been dark, yet he knew...guys who just appeared out of nowhere and suddenly wanted to be your best friend? They weren't to be trusted. "Los Salvajes were camped next door to us that weekend, sniffing around. How do you know he's not one of them?"

Maverick snuffed out his smoke. "Come on, man. He and his girl were just at the festival, sitting nearby. He engaged with the guys. He's funny, had the guys rolling on the ground talking about porn chicks and cheap producers. And Vero took a liking to the girlfriend. Turns out, she's a tattoo artist too, from Reno."

The Lone Horseman stopped swilling his beer. A silent alarm sounded off in his head. He turned to his friend, feeling his face suddenly go dark and angry. *An ink slinger from Reno?* He recalled the young woman who'd created the tiger. Remembered how she'd tried to take a picture of his back.

He bit his bottom lip.

No, it couldn't be. He'd slapped the camera from her hand and checked her phone, told her straight up, no pictures. Yet, who else had seen his back up close lately? Who else might stare at it long enough to discern the pattern of the images and their message?

A tattoo artist, that's who.

"This girlfriend, you say she was there at the concert with this guy, and later, at the bonfire, where I kicked his ass?"

Maverick nodded.

"Where was she at the time?"

He shrugged. "In the RV with Vero, best I know. Why?"

The Horseman clenched his jaw, glanced at the ceiling, wanted to punch a hole in it. His thoughts raced back to giving Vero the picture of the red bush that night, and how he'd felt like someone else had been in the RV at the time. He'd seen a brief shadow, but had figured it was just one of the other old ladies taking a piss. The girl could've slipped to the back and come out after he left, then saw the picture.

"What other events have these two attended?"

Maverick joined him by the pool table, his brow furrowing at the Horseman's sudden interest. "Buster's funeral. The two of them brought Vero back here in the RV afterward. They stayed for the party."

The Horseman looked at his best friend like he'd lost his mind. "You let a couple of unknowns into the club? Into your house?" The Lone Horseman laughed. "No wonder he knew about the fucking guns."

Maverick bristled. "Vero was wasted. They offered to drive."

The Lone Horseman gave a half-laugh. "Yeah, I bet they did."

He put a hand on his friend's shoulder. "Brother, your old lady got played. I guarantee you, that new ink-slinger friend of Vero's is the woman who tatted my last design in Reno. And I bet you anything, this hang-around, he's got ties to Los Salvajes. She could've seen the pig when she did my other ink, understood its message, and told him. Maybe she got an idea of what the others were about too, or maybe she figured it out later, likely with Vero's help, but I promise you, that's our source."

Maverick curled his upper lip, mumbled words only he could understand. He had the same look as those that departed the casinos late at night, betrayed by the cards or dice, angry, yet deflated.

"You truly think Vero played a part in this?" he asked through clenched teeth.

"Only one way to know, brother. Got to ask the tough questions."

Maverick crushed his cigarette and stormed off. The Lone Horseman could hear him stomp through the house, yelling her name. While he waited, the Lone Horseman cracked his knuckles, preparing to give the bitch what she deserved.

But five minutes later, Maverick came back empty-handed. He shook his head. "I checked everywhere. She's gone."

CHAPTER 35

Max was not happy to hear about the raid at the Devils compound or news of Vero holding his wife at gun point, and was even less thrilled to learn that Zoë had been forced to reveal her true identity. Zoë tried to reassure him that Vero had promised not to reveal the truth, but Max was certain she would eventually slip and the club would come after her and his entire family. Like Zoë, he blamed all of this on Agent Quinn, so when Zoë called Sloane and demanded a meeting, neither of them made an effort to hide their disdain for the slimeball agent. Sloane apologized, stating he knew nothing about the planned raid, but promised he would arrange a sit-down. A few days later, they got the call. He told Max and Zoë to meet them at a diner just outside of town near six p.m. Although the place closed at two p.m., they often used it after hours to meet with confidential informants.

The place was white and yellow, with a giant arrow sign out front that lured passing truckers from the nearby highway. The parking lot was crumbling in several spots and weeds surrounded the perimeter. Zoë thought the police must have a pretty close relationship with the owner to have free entry to the joint after hours. At the back door, Sloane's partner, Rodriquez, greeted them. The place smelled of grease and pine cleaner, but was decorated as a breakfast place should be and painted a sunny yellow, like the eggs they served.

The minute Zoë walked into the restaurant, however, her opinion soured. She saw Quinn sitting there and couldn't help but go for his throat. He quickly retreated as Max grabbed her around the waist and pulled her back. "I'm a dead woman. My family is dead because of you, you arrogant, selfish prick."

Quinn pointed a finger while speaking to Max. "You'd better keep her under control or I'll charge her with assault."

"You'll do no such thing," Agent Dionne of the FBI said, who stood in the middle of the room. "If I could, I'd take a couple of swipes at you myself."

"We had every reason to conduct that raid and look for the Lone Horseman. He killed a federal agent—don't you forget that," Quinn shot back. "That should take precedent over these women."

"We decided what took precedent in our last meeting, Agent Quinn," Dionne said. "You were supposed to maintain a hold on your operations while we conducted a thorough investigation into the murdered women."

But Quinn continued to plead his case. "The Devils were sitting on crates of AR 15s and AK-47s in the garage and in the RV. She said so herself."

Zoë couldn't believe her ears. "I told you that in confidence, explaining how dangerous it was to go back there—not so you could raid their compound. You piece of..."

Max grabbed her arm, gave a slight shake of his head.

"From what I heard, the compound was clean," FBI agent Hall said, smirking.

Quinn snarled. "That's because somebody tipped them off. They had to. And if I had to guess, it was somebody in this room." He paced between parties accusingly.

"Actually," came a voice from behind, "it was me." Zoë turned and felt the air go out of her lungs. In strolled Riot—or what little remained of the guy she knew as Riot—with a fresh haircut and shave. In place of his Los Salvajes cuts, he wore jeans, a plaid shirt, and a badge that said ATF.

"I had to," he said. "It was the only way to try and protect Zoë and me from the Devils. If I'd let you get the guns, with Zoë and I being new to hanging around the club, it would've been game over for us. Sadly, you pulling those photographs out and flashing them in front of the members might've done us in anyway."

Quinn responded with something akin to Riot being a turncoat to his organization, but Zoë was too focused on Riot and his new choice of attire to listen. "Shit," she said. "Are you kidding me? You're ATF?"

He walked over. "Sorry, old lady. For obvious reasons, I couldn't tell you."

She felt betrayed, but Max looked relieved. His wife hadn't been hanging with an outlaw after all. Now things made sense. No wonder Riot had taken such good care of her. No wonder his house had been so sparsely furnished. It existed solely for the operation.

"Blade? Los Salvajes?" she said. "You're investigating them?"

"I was, yes, and I was hoping to stay in, but I got word yesterday they're pulling me out. The powers that be are too worried this will blowback on me and the operation when word gets to the Devils that I'm part of Los Salvajes. Nobody wants another dead agent on their hands. Especially me."

He shot Quinn a nasty look.

Quinn returned the favor.

Zoë shook her head. Blade, Sloane, Quinn, Riot. Was it possible to take anybody at their word? She felt played at every turn.

"So, now what do we do?" Quinn asked.

"You don't do a damn thing," Agent Dionne said. "You sit and let us handle it. We'll conduct our investigation, and when we have enough evidence, we'll pick up the Lone Horseman. If we want the death penalty on the table, we'll need time to work up the two Texas cases, make sure those go first."

Max groaned. "Spend millions of taxpayer dollars keeping him alive. For what? To put a needle in his arm twenty years later? What's the point? You ask me, you should let Los Salvajes take care of him. Eye for an eye."

Sloane rubbed his face. "I'm going to pretend I didn't hear that."

Zoë stared at her husband. "I want him to face those families. They deserve justice. My mother deserves justice."

"I need to protect you from getting further involved. I don't want us spending the rest of our lives looking over our shoulder," he said. "As long as this guy is alive, he's a threat, whether he's in prison or not. We have to make sure the Devils, and the Horseman, they never find out about you."

A commotion erupted in the back and, suddenly, Rodriquez, who'd been monitoring the back door, followed Vero inside. "Sorry, guys. She insisted."

Vero was breathing heavily, as if she'd come from a six-mile run, instead of a walk from the car outside. "Whatever you're planning, it's too late. The Lone Horseman knows about you."

They all turned to stare at the thin woman wearing faded jeans and a flimsy top, with her hair pulled back in a single braid.

Late last night, the Horseman arrived at the clubhouse and I heard him and my husband talking. At first, he blamed everything on me, until Maverick brought up you and Riot, and the Horseman figured it out."

Zoë stepped forward. "Wait. How did you find us? Did they follow you?" She glanced at the back door, outside the curtained windows, fearing an ambush.

"No. I left last night. I couldn't take the chance of staying." She stared at Quinn. "That stunt you pulled? You put a mark on my head as well as Zoë's. The Lone Horseman will never let me live knowing I'm the one who got careless and let Zoë in. To him, it's my fault that he was exposed, and always will be."

"Wait. Answer Zoë's question. How did you find us?" Riot asked.

She did a double take at his appearance, lingered on the badge, issued him a look better reserved for dog turds. "I knew it. ATF. Fuck." She shook her head, turned to Zoë. "I found your tattoo shop and waited outside, then followed when you left. I was worried the Lone Horsemen would show up, and I wanted to warn you. Little did I know this is where you'd end up, but it's just as well."

She finally turned her focus to the rest of the men in the room—the two FBI agents and Sloane. "You should know I hate law enforcement. The only reason I'm here is to save Zoë, and myself. So don't take what I'm about to say as any kind of change of heart. It isn't."

She smoothed her shirt as if she didn't know what else to do with her hands. Without a cigarette, she was lost. "I have a proposition. I will give you the Lone Horseman, but only if you try him for the murders of the women, and nothing else. No guns, no drugs, no charges against the Devils. I don't think he'd talk anyway, but if you even try to start negotiating, all bets are off. The club has ways of making things happen, inside or outside prison walls."

Riot stepped forward. "What are you suggesting?"

"I tell the Horseman I found the source of the leak and bring you both in. Maverick and I will take you to a pre-designated place to hand you over to him. Then the FBI comes in."

"My wife is not going back in there," Max said before Zoë could chime in, and she knew better than to argue. After the raid, he was done with Zoë playing detective.

Agent Dionne paced, thought. "We can put in an agent. It might work."

"How?" Zoë asked. "Maverick would know it wasn't me the minute he saw me. So would the Horseman."

"We can disguise the agent, cover her face and arms," Agent Hall said.

"And my husband will know what's happening. He'll be on board," Vero said.

Sloane and the FBI were listening, but Riot appeared uncertain. "No offense, Vero, but I've never known a MC to voluntarily turn in one of their own to the feds, especially one with the knowledge the Lone Horseman has of the Devils. How can you be so sure Maverick, and the national president, will be on board with this?"

She flipped her braid over her shoulder. Her stance was resolute. "Because they don't yet know what I do about the Horseman. Specifically, his first kill. But when they do, trust me, they'll get on board. You let me worry about my husband and A.J. Berger"

Riot shook his head, paced. Zoë had never seen him this unsettled. His nervousness made her jittery as well. She really wanted to believe in Vero's plan.

Quinn wasn't happy with the arrangement either. "Come on. This guy killed an undercover DEA agent. You really expect me not to pursue that?"

"Yes," Vero said.

"Why?"

"Because this is what Zoë and all those other families need. We do this, it has to go down my way." She walked over to him, stood toe to toe. "And I don't want you involved. If I sense your interference or see your ugly face there, I may just shoot you myself."

CHAPTER 36

The next week, Vero called to say that her husband was on board. It had taken him some convincing, but once Vero told him of the Horseman's first kill and the FBI's promise to only pursue the Horseman for the murders of the fourteen women, Maverick had come around. Like Vero, he knew the Horseman well enough to understand he would blame Vero no matter what occurred. She let the enemy infiltrate the camp, and she would pay a price.

The plan was for Maverick and Vero to convince the Lone Horseman to meet them at a string of warehouses near Vacaville where Vero would deliver Zoë to him so he could do the unthinkable, while Maverick took care of Riot. It was dubbed Operation Pale Rider, and all the players had a part to play, including the FBI, who would move in and take the Horseman into custody before anybody got hurt. The Horseman originally wanted to meet in the desert, but Maverick convinced him they needed to take care of this near one of their facilities so they could control the aftermath, code words for cleaning up the mess. "No chance witnesses this time," Maverick said.

Riot agreed to play his part, but Zoë was to be replaced by an undercover FBI agent, a woman about the same size as her with matching eye and hair color. She'd be blindfolded and dressed in long sleeves so it wouldn't be immediately apparent that she wasn't Zoë, and placed in the trunk of Vero's car. When it came time to make the trade, Riot and Maverick would stage a fight as a distraction, and the undercover agent would assist in taking custody of the Horseman along with the rest of her FBI comrades. Zoë questioned whether the fight that would occur between Maverick and Riot would be anything but real, however, as it was clear Maverick was beyond pissed to learn of Riot's real occupation—and he didn't even know about Riot's relationship with Los Salvajes yet.

Zoë understood that she couldn't be a part of the action, but asked Sloane if she could be nearby, where she could witness the operation as it unfolded and see the Horseman taken into custody. Max also requested a ride along, skeptical to let his wife out of his sight. Sloane was at first reluctant, but eventually agreed to take them in his SUV. He wouldn't be a part of the operation, and the three of them could watch from the sidelines, out of harm's way.

The day Operation Pale Rider was to occur, the three of them drove to California and met the team at a popped-up command center a few miles outside the Vacaville warehouses that would be the scene of the takedown. All the law enforcement agents buzzed, excited to be part of the big event. Zoë imagined that this was what they lived for, when the hard work paid off and they could go in and make a big arrest.

As the sun set low in the sky and cast a thin red line on the horizon, Zoë began to pace the camp, a nervous energy taking over. She turned away offers of food and drink, and barely listened as others tried to speak to her. Max wrapped his arms around her and spoke softly in her ear to calm her down, but even he started to look unnerved when the female undercover put on Zoë's clothes and copied her hair and makeup. Seeing how much she resembled Zoë from a distance was unsettling.

The undercover spent the next thirty minutes running in place to get sweaty and applying dirt and motor oil on various parts of her body and clothes to make it appear she'd spent hours inside a trunk. Riot, too, jumped around and shadowboxed, earning a layer of sweat while expelling some adrenaline.

When Vero and Maverick showed up near nine p.m., things moved quickly. The female undercover agent was bound, blindfolded, and positioned in Vero's trunk. A razor blade was tucked in a makeshift pocket accessible to her wriggling fingers, and her gun disguised within the trunk's felt lining. An agent applied some makeup to roughen up Riot a bit and make it look like he'd put up a fight, but Maverick decided he needed the real thing and took a cheap shot to his jaw. The agents came to Riot's defense and reprimanded Maverick, but he—wearing his cuts and looking every bit of the Devil he was—just spit on the ground and laughed. They attached a small camera and microphone to Riot's shirt, just as they had done the UC, then bound and blindfolded him in the same manner and placed him in the back seat of Vero's car. Final instructions were given, the door was shut and the trunk lowered, and off they went.

Maverick led the mission. The plan was for he and Vero to ride around and come in to the warehouses off I-80, just as if they'd made the long ride straight from Reno.

Sloane found a place to park that sat high on a hill overlooking the area where the exchange was to occur. A line of trees partially blocked the path, but Zoë found a space between the leaves and planted her face in binoculars to watch everything as it went down. Max huddled in the back seat, preferring to listen to the audio version as it came through Sloane's radio.

The first words came over the static near ten p.m. "Subjects approaching."

The headlights from Maverick's Harley and Vero's car exited the highway. For a moment, they disappeared on a couple of side streets, then reappeared again once they entered the slew of mostly abandoned structures. They parked near a unit labeled D–1 and stopped.

The lights from the vehicles shut down, and they waited in darkness.

Ten minutes later, a single headlight appeared a dozen units away and began making its way through the square blocks. The bike stopped at the end of the drive before Vero flicked the headlights of the car, and he proceeded.

Zoë caught her breath. It was the Lone Horseman. After he rolled forward, he and Maverick exchanged a few words, then the Horseman took off his helmet and dismounted. Together, they approached Vero's car.

"Targets approaching subject number one."

Subject number one was Riot, sitting in the back seat of Vero's car. Zoë's stomach rolled. She prayed Riot would be able to handle whatever came his way. Despite the fact that he hadn't been truthful to her about being an ATF agent, he was one of the rare good guys. He'd put himself out there for her and saved her life.

From inside the car, a small voice said, "Knock, knock."

A faint, "Who's there?" emitted over the channel. It was Vero from the front seat.

"Veteran."

"Veteran who?"

"Veteran because we're coming to get you."

Zoë turned to Max, couldn't help but smile. Leave it to Riot to still be making jokes as the Lone Horseman stood outside his door. Even Vero gave a light chuckle.

The door opened, and Maverick pulled Riot out by the arm. Once free of the car, he pushed him in the back and let him stumble before he lined him up in the alleyway. Now that Riot was with the men, all of those involved in the operation could hear the conversation.

Maverick ripped the blindfold from his face. "He wants to see you," he said.

Zoë's heart pounded, trying to imagine what Riot was feeling.

The Horseman grabbed Riot's chin and turned his face left and right. "I hear you weren't happy with the modifications I made during our last meeting. Let me fix that for you." He reared back and popped him square in the nose.

The crack emanated through the microphone. Zoë grimaced.

Riot bent over and blood poured. But a minute later, he just smiled though red teeth and spit at the Horseman. Maverick stepped in before the Horseman could get in another swing—or in Riot's case, a headbutt. "Enough. Not here. Not now. Let's get the girl."

He motioned to Vero to open the trunk. She flipped the lever from inside and the lid went up. Maverick walked over and scooped the agent up in his arms as she mumbled and moaned beneath her taped mouth. Vero was quick to round the car and rummage around the trunk in search of the shoe that had fallen off the woman's foot, all while slipping the Glock from its private hiding space and sticking it in the back of her pants.

When Maverick set the agent on her feet, Vero said, "Here, let me, she's mine." She took hold of the agent's arms and directed her, blindfolded, to stand near Riot. Those observing from afar couldn't see much of what Vero was doing behind the agent, but knew her next step was to hand the shoe to the Horseman to distract him enough while she transferred the Glock from her own waistband to the agent's.

Vero handed the shoe over. "Don't forget this. No trace."

The Horseman took it, grunted.

Zoë held her breath as she noticed a tug at the agent's back. *Good girl, Vero.*

Riot begged for Maverick and the Horseman not to hurt Zoë. "She's done nothing wrong. It was all me." These were his go-to code words to use to let the FBI know that everyone was in position. Now, while they waited for them to arrive, the agent playing Zoë would work to cut through the tethers binding her wrists with the razor blade, and Riot would continue his pleas until things between him and Maverick heated up and a fight ensued. The Horseman would watch and laugh as the fake Zoë cried for her boyfriend, then all hell would break loose.

Except the Lone Horseman apparently had other plans. The minute the four of them settled, he pulled his gun, held it to the undercover's head, and demanded Vero release the blindfold. "Hurry up. I want her to see me before I blow her fucking head off."

"Whoa!" Maverick said. "Not here. I told you."

"I'm tired of taking your directions, brother. You said she was mine. I'll do what I want with her. Now take it off."

Zoë gasped. She lowered the binoculars and shot a glance at Sloane. "Now what? He'll know it's not me the minute that blindfold comes off." Max slid to the front of the back seat, anticipating the next move.

"Leave her alone," Riot shouted and lurched for the Horseman, but again, Maverick intervened, this time pushing Riot against the side of the warehouse and giving him two brutal punches to the gut. This was how they'd staged the beginning of the brawl, and now, the fight was on. Despite the presence of the Horseman's gun, it was clear they both knew they had to go forward with the plan to distract the Horseman and give the agent a chance to work her hands free.

It worked, but only long enough for the Horseman to grow angry and fire a warning shot in the air, prompting Vero to scream, afraid the Horseman had already shot the undercover agent, and Maverick to pull a weapon of his own.

Now the two—Maverick and the Lone Horseman—had their weapons trained on each other, and everyone went tense, sensing things were about to go drastically wrong.

Through the binoculars, Zoë could see Riot wriggling backward, knew he was frantically cutting his tethers so he could grab his gun. They wanted to take the Lone Horseman alive by any means necessary, but if push came to shove, they'd have no choice but to shoot him.

"Put the gun down," Maverick commanded.

"What're you going to do? Shoot me? Fuck you. This bitch ratted. I'm going to take her out the way I want."

"This isn't the place. We can't have any more mistakes."

Vero stood by, shaking and appearing confused.

"Where is the FBI?" Zoë asked Sloane. "Please tell me they're coming. They need to get in there. Otherwise, he's going to find out the truth."

Then, just as if he'd heard Zoë's words, the Lone Horseman reached over and ripped off the tape from the agent's mouth and the blindfold from her eyes.

Gasping, the agent instantly lowered her head so her hair would fall into her face, but the Horseman brushed it back. He yanked her chin up to force her to look at him.

"What the hell?" he said. He ripped the shirt she was wearing from her shoulder, looking for the tattoos that lined Zoë's arm. "That's not her." He wheeled to Maverick. "That's not the right bitch."

He started to raise his gun again, but a shot from behind made him—and all the rest of them—duck and run. The roar of motorcycles racing down multiple lanes of the warehouse complex buzzed like a swarm of insects.

Several shots were exchanged between the Lone Horseman and his pursuers—who turned out to be Los Salvajes—before three black SUVs started barreling toward the scene. Riot and the undercover, both now free of restraints, managed to get to safety, but couldn't make any moves toward restraining the Horseman without getting in the line of fire.

From the car, Zoë watched Maverick take cover behind Vero's car while the exchange between rivals occurred, but the minute Los Salvajes began to bug out, saw Maverick move quickly toward the Horseman with his gun drawn. "Shit!" Zoë said. "What is he doing? Maverick is going to kill him. He's going to kill the Horseman."

Riot and the undercover, seeing the same, rushed out from behind a building and shouted at Maverick to drop the gun, but he apparently had no intent of complying. Whatever deal he'd agreed to, it appeared he was about to renege on it. Vero wheeled to see her husband coming fast, as did the Lone Horseman, who must've understood his new status with his friend, and grabbed Vero as his hostage.

Zoë imagined it was difficult to discern what was going on in the streets below. It was even harder from the passenger seat of a car parked high on a hill a block away. But what ensued next could only be described as total chaos.

As the black SUVs swooped in and agents poured out behind open doors, the Horseman fired several rounds to hold them, and Maverick, off, then shoved Vero in the car and took off with her in it. Those left behind, confused by Maverick's intent, weren't sure whether to stay and secure him, or pursue the Horseman, and stood around shouting at one another until Maverick dropped his weapon and laid upon the ground. Riot yelled for the others to head out as he stayed behind with the lead Devil, who was now pleading for them to save his wife. Agents scrambled like ants at a picnic, running for their vehicles to follow suit.

Zoë slapped the dash of Sloane's car. "Don't just sit here. Follow him!" Although they were two streets and several stoplights away, she thought they might be able to cut him off. But the Lone Horseman clearly knew the warehouse district well, and outsmarted the few vehicles in pursuit until his lights simply disappeared. Sloane swerved in and out of traffic and managed to catch up to him within a few city blocks, but a red light suddenly stopped him cold. Cars lined up in the lanes three and four deep, and he had nothing but a horn to urge others to let him through. They didn't.

The faint taillights of Vero's car disappeared.

Zoë screamed her frustration. She couldn't let it end there. The Lone Horseman had Vero, and he was a killer. To her husband's and Sloane's surprise, she bolted from the car and ran up next to a motorcycle stopped at the front of a lane. The rider had no idea what was happening as Zoë yanked him from the bike, then hopped on herself and took off in pursuit.

Vero had saved her from the wrath of the Devils once, now Zoë had to do the same.

CHAPTER 37

Shocked at what had just occurred, Sloane yelled into traffic, urging drivers to get out of his way. When he finally had a path, he proceeded through the light that was now green, then accelerated on the other side of the intersection. Beside him—sitting in the passenger seat now after failing to run and catch his wife—Max yelled directions and kept his eyes glued to the bike's taillight. Sloane weaved in and out of traffic as best he could, but couldn't keep up as Zoë glided the motorcycle in between cars with little effort. By the time they got out of the city streets, Zoë was but a memory, having hit the country road and opened the throttle. Max was beside himself, a panicked, sweaty mess.

"What the hell is she thinking? She doesn't have a gun. She's not wearing a bulletproof vest or even a helmet. If the Horseman gets ahold of her, he'll kill her without a second thought."

He made the kind of sound Sloane imagined he'd also make at the thought of his wife or daughter in the hands of the Horseman. "Listen, we're going to find her. Take a deep breath."

Sloane got on the frequency Operation Pale Rider shared and explained what happened, then sent out the coordinates of where they'd lost Zoë on the motorcycle following Vero and the Horseman. "Last seen heading north on Gibson Canyon past Farrell Road. We need someone up here who knows the area and can post blockades."

The FBI was already on it. They'd put out an all-points bulletin for Vero's car with the license plate, informed law enforcement that the subject was armed and dangerous and had a hostage. They used reverse 911 to issue a shelter in place order for all residents off the canyon road, and they ordered checkpoints set up at every crossroad with more than residential access.

With every word, Sloane could see Max shrink in the seat next to him, imagining the unthinkable. "We're going to continue north," Sloane announced. "Will update as needed."

They wound up the road and slowed at every intersection to look down the side roads but, just as the FBI had stated, most appeared to end with a large house or two at the end of the street. They started and stopped, checking for any sign of Vero's car or the motorcycle Zoë had confiscated. At one point, they saw taillights turn in a driveway and go dark, but it wasn't Vero's car.

Finally, they rounded a hill and came upon an intersection where a vehicle had pulled over and had its hazard lights flashing, warning of an unseen danger. In the car's headlights, a young man in a red shirt and a petite brunette stood staring at something while shaking their heads. The man had a phone to his ear, speaking to an unknown party on the other end.

Sloane pulled up. As soon as Max saw the motorcycle laying on its side in the middle of the road, he sprang from the car. "It's hers. It's the bike," he shouted.

Sloane introduced himself. "The police are on their way," the woman said.

He walked over to the accident scene and suddenly realized why the couple looked perplexed. Despite a pool of blood on the pavement, Zoë was nowhere to be seen. Max ran up and down the side of the road, calling for his wife, but it was dark, with nothing but a crescent moon to guide his path.

Sloane scrambled back to the car, retrieved two industrial flashlights from his trunk, and handed one to Max. Together, they walked through the ditches and scoured the brush, but found nothing. "Where the hell is she?" Max screamed.

Sloane turned to the couple. In the distance, sirens erupted. "Did you see a young woman about your age when you arrived?"

"No," they said together.

"That's what we found puzzling," the guy continued. "I mean, someone was clearly hurt, but there was no sign of anyone. No blood trail, even."

Max wrapped his head in his arms, screamed Zoë's name again and again.

The girl standing nearby shivered.

"His wife was on the bike," Sloane explained. He got on the radio, issued an update to the team. "We found the motorcycle, but the girl isn't here. We need everyone available to search by foot and helicopters above looking for that Toyota."

Alternating flashes of red and blue illuminated the night as the local police and an ambulance arrived, only to find they had no one to care for. One of the paramedics knelt by the motorcycle to examine the pool of blood. "Looks like a head wound. Seriously, she's just...gone?" He cast the beam of his own flashlight to the edges of the road and beyond.

The police asked the same dozen questions of the couple that Sloane had, then turned back to him to ask what had happened earlier. "This have to do with that APB that went out?" they asked.

"Yes." He filled them in on the operation and the fugitive they were on the hunt for. "He's killed at least fourteen women, and now he's got another one as a hostage." The officer let out a whistle. The other said, "Damn."

Just then, the roar of a motorcycle rattled the night. It was Maverick, with Riot riding bitch, which would've been funny to Sloane if not for the seriousness of the situation. They both slid off, raced to Sloane's side. "Any sign of my wife or the car?" Maverick asked. Like Max, he appeared in a panic, like he'd never forgive himself if something happened to his old lady.

"No, I'm sorry," Sloane said. He started to ask what the hell had gone wrong at the warehouse, but decided that could wait for later as Riot took off toward the bike in the road, set it upright, and hopped on.

"Wait, this is an accident scene. You can't just..." the paramedic said.

He didn't listen. "The Horseman may've gotten to her. Maverick, you take the side roads west and I'll go east. Look for anything suspicious. Hopefully, she just took off walking, maybe to a house to get help."

They revved the bikes and headed out.

The next to arrive were five members of Los Salvajes, including Blade. He looked sympathetically at Max as Sloane derided him for trying to take out the Lone Horseman and ruin their operation. "You've got a lot of balls showing up here."

"We got a tip that the Devils were going to kill Riot and Zoë. I was trying to save them. I didn't know there was an operation underway. Clearly, it was a set up."

Sloane shook his head. "Tell it to the judge. For now, maybe you guys could head north on up the canyon, look for anything suspicious between here and the roadblock set up at Cantelow Road. We're hoping Zoë may just be staggering up the street in a concussive state, and the Horseman doesn't have her."

Blade's face darkened. "And if he does?"

Sloane shook his head. Swallowed dry spit. "Just find her."

Blade nodded and commanded his troops to move ahead.

A black SUV occupied by Agents Dionne and Hall and three other agents, including the undercover, arrived. "Helicopter just left and should be here shortly," Dionne said. "Roadblocks are up on routes between here and Bucktown. He couldn't have gotten far."

A moment later, Riot and Maverick returned to the scene. Maverick looked ill.

"The Camry is ditched off a side road up the hill. It's empty. I think he jacked a different vehicle. And"—the NorCal president took a moment—"there was blood in the back seat and two cell phones. My guess is, he's got my wife and Zoë now."

CHAPTER 38

Zoë woke in the dark, blood sticky and drying to the side of her face. Her hair hung around her cheeks clumped in masses, and her head spiked with pain, as if someone were trying to drive nails into her skull. The intensity left her vision blurry and caused the room to spin. Off to her left, she could make out a trough of some kind, and in front of her, something hanging, although she couldn't tell what it was. It swayed a little, casting a moving shadow on the wall behind the only light source in the room, a single naked bulb with a pull chain that was shining several feet away.

Where in the hell am I? In a basement or a barn? The odors of wet earth and manure seemed to indicate a barn, but another smell—like varnish or paint—didn't fit. She glanced around, fighting the pain of every eyelid movement. The floor was dirt, but the walls appeared to be made of cement blocks.

She wondered how long she'd been unconscious, and how she'd gotten here. The last thing she remembered was the operation going horribly wrong and Sloane driving. She'd jumped out to steal a motorcycle and had fled up the canyon road, then...a sudden swerve and darkness.

She stuck out her tongue, tasted dirt and blood. Her lip was busted and her teeth ached, as if several might be loose. Had she wrecked the bike and hit her head on the pavement? Is that why there was so much blood and pain coming from her head? Or had the Lone Horseman hit her?

Yes. She thought the answer to both questions was yes. She recalled seeing him approach as she'd laid on the ground, moaning. Could see Vero's anxious face in the passenger seat, tied up and mouth sealed. Had he picked Zoë up and put her in the car? Yes, he must've. She remembered nothing about the ride afterward.

She wriggled her fingers, realized her hands were tied behind her back to something that felt like the spindles of the chair she sat in. Her feet were also bound, secured to the legs. It was a simple wooden chair—the kind purchased with a cheap kitchen table—and her first thought was it couldn't be that sturdy. The wood wasn't even real but made of laminate, easy to splinter and break. Could she hit it against something and get free?

A groan came from inside the room and Zoë realized she wasn't alone. *Vero?*

She glanced out of her one good eye and tried to focus. Listened intently, waiting for it again. When the moan emerged, it sent a cold wave down Zoë's spine. It sounded more animal than human—and hurt.

Vero, where is she? When the object hanging from the ceiling swayed, and the sound occurred again, Zoë realized with a revulsion reserved for horror movies that it was Vero. The Lone Horseman had tied her wrists above her head and hung her from a hook in the ceiling, leaving her body to dangle limply. Zoë thought she might throw up. Had the Lone Horseman hurt her? He must've. Yet, she was alive. That was something.

She wondered if Sloane and Max were out there looking for her and Vero, prayed it was so. But how would they ever find them in this dungeon? She needed to get free from this chair and get her and Vero out of there. But how? And where was the Lone Horseman?

She got her answer as something cracked up above and off to her left, and cool, fresh air poured in. No light followed, however, which meant it was still night. A creaking sound and a thump ensued, then she saw him, the Horseman, backing down on a wooden ladder. Now Zoë understood they were in a crawlspace of some kind, one where the door opened to the outside.

She closed her eyes and pretended to still be knocked out. She didn't want him to know that she was awake, not yet. She needed to formulate a plan.

The Horseman walked over to check on her, tilted her chin up, opened her eye. She stared vacantly, let her head loll from side to side. He grunted, disappointed, then walked over to Vero. Vero stirred and moaned, unhappy by whatever was happening to her. Zoë opened her eyes just enough to see the Horseman kiss the back of her neck and run his hands down the length of her body.

"Finally, we have some alone time together. I can hardly wait to get between those legs of yours." He pressed himself against her as he trailed his hands down her abdomen to the waist of her jeans. "I'm finally going to take what you've been unwilling to give me, and no husband of yours will be able to stop it. In fact, you know what I'm going to do? I'm going to let him watch. Just as soon as he shows up here to rescue you—and if I know him, he will—I'm going to knock his ass out, and when he comes to, the three of us can have a little fun."

Zoë closed her eyes. *Sick bastard.* She had to figure out a way out of this.

Vero groaned as the Horseman put his hands in places they didn't belong.

Zoë held her breath and fought the urge to cry out or try to fight the Lone Horseman while bound to a chair. She had to remind herself that although Vero was suffering, she was still alive, and Zoë had to make sure she stayed that way.

When the Horseman was done playing, he planted a long kiss on Vero's lips then walked back to Zoë and did the same thing. It took every fiber in her being not to flinch or resist, but the images in her head—of what she wanted to do to this man—grew ever more violent. Still, for now, she had to let things unfold and wait for him to leave again.

He whispered a warning. "You're next, sweetheart. And then...you die."

His footsteps clambered up the ladder and he pulled the door shut. That was followed by a scrape of metal on metal, like a latch or a lock outside.

As soon as he was gone, Zoë spit, spit again. She despised the taste of him.

"Vero, it's me, Zoë. Are you okay? Can you hear me?" she asked.

A faint moan followed.

"I know. I know you're hurting. Hold on. I'm going to get us out of here."

Easier said than done, especially in her current condition, but what else could she say? She glanced around the room between the sticky strands of hair, the dull roar in her head continuing. She needed to find something that would help her get out of this chair, but what?

Behind her was a metal storage shelf filled with various items that she couldn't see. Maybe something there? She hopped on all four legs and twisted at the same time until she had the chair turned around. Now she could see a toolbox, bags of Fertilizer— hence the manure smell—and boxes containing who knew what. There was also an old mirror propped up against a side wall, and that caught her attention. She hopped over to study it. A reflection stared back at her, but it looked nothing like the woman she remembered being.

I need to break that mirror. But how? She tried to stretch her foot out to see if she could reach it, but the tethers were too tight. She needed her foot to do the job, which meant she needed to break the leg on the chair.

This was becoming a domino effect.

She slid as far as she could to the right corner of the chair and put all her weight there while her right leg pressed the leg of the chair inward. She started to rock it back and forth while keeping the pressure, just begging it to buckle. When it did, she went down face-first, looking like a three-legged dog.

But that was okay, because she had what she needed now. She stretched out her leg, the broken leg of the chair dangling from the tethers near her ankle, and scooted across the floor toward the mirror with the remaining chair still attached to her body. She kicked at the mirror once, then twice, until large chunks of glass fell to the floor. Vero gasped at the sound, but Zoë didn't wait to see if the Horseman heard. She scooted around on her side and backed up until her hands reached the glass. She found a sharp piece still partially intact in the mirror, and began to rub the leather tethers against it. She sensed Vero watching, willing her to break free.

Finally, she felt one snap, and then a second. She brought her hands out front, which were reddish purple and stiff from being bound, and wriggled her fingers and rubbed her palms together to get the circulation flowing. Then she went to work on her feet.

In five more minutes, she was free. She selected a piece of glass from the floor, went to Vero and cut her down. Vero tried to hug her, but her arms were useless. God knew how many hours she'd been hanging there. Zoë rubbed them to get the circulation going, then told her to sit and regain her strength. While she did, Zoë went back to the chair and broke the remaining legs. She used the glass to whittle down the stubs to sharp wooden stakes, handed one to Vero and kept one for herself. She slipped a shard of glass in her pocket just for good measure.

"Give me one too," Vero whispered. Zoë selected one from the floor and handed it to her. Vero held it for a moment before she put the sliver of glass in her pocket. "Wish I'd had this an hour ago." She glanced at Zoë, looked ashamed.

Zoë asked if she was okay. "I'm so sorry. There was..."

"I know. It's not your fault." She looked at the chair leg in her hand. "So, what now? We going to take him out with these? No match for a gun if he brings one."

"No, but it's all we've got. We could try breaking through those doors, but when I heard him shut it, I heard a large scrape afterward, like it had an outside lock. So if we try to open it, we're going to make one hell of a lot of noise. Better we wait for him to come back, then overtake him. The question is—do we wait for him to come down and attack him here, or blindside him at the top?"

Vero, broken and bruised, one side of her face swollen and her eye near shut from a beating the Horseman must've administered, glanced up at the ladder and door. It was only about five steps up. "Blindside. We have to get out of this hole or we'll have no chance."

Zoë nodded. "Agreed."

She grabbed a flashlight from the shelf. Turned it on and was happy to see light. "This. We can literally blind him with this the minute he opens the doors. Then we each plant a stake in his gut and push him back."

"And if he has a gun?"

Zoë swallowed the dry spit and blood in her mouth. "Best to run like hell in opposite directions so at least one of us has a chance."

She sighed, feeling for her cell phone where she normally kept it. "I wish we had a way to contact Max and Maverick. Do you know where we are?"

Vero nodded. "We're at an old associate's house. Gus Tinkerton. He used to be a patched member but left the club after a particularly nasty beating he received at the hands of the Angels left him disabled. Still, he and many of the brothers remained close." She touched the side of her face. Zoë imagined it must hurt like hell, like her own wounds.

"After Larry caused you to wreck by swerving out in front of you, he put you in the backseat of my car and drove us up here. We aren't far from the canyon road we were on, but I don't know if Maverick will think about this place or even remember that the old guy lives..." She paused. "Lived here." She looked at Zoë. "Larry slit his throat soon after he let us in."

Zoë sighed. *Shit. Another dead body.* "How many hours do you think we've been down here?" she asked.

"I'd say four or five. It'll be sunrise soon."

"They won't stop looking for us," Zoë said. "Not Maverick, not Max."

Zoë thought about her husband and what she'd done to end up here. Breaking from Sloane's car to steal a motorcycle and pursue a killer, with no protection and no help, while leaving Max behind. What the hell had she been thinking?

As if Vero knew what she was pondering, she grabbed Zoë's hand and squeezed. "I know you did this for me. Thank you. Also, I think you should know. You're certifiably crazy."

Zoë grinned, her teeth hurting. "Takes one to know one."

They chuckled in the space they shared until they both heard a rattling above. Zoë quickly turned out the light and climbed the right side of the ladder while Vero hung to the left, weapon at the ready. Zoë repeated her safe words in her head, those phrases Max had taught her to use when her anxiety felt out of control. To say this was one of those times was an understatement. They waited in the silence, listening only to the sounds of their breaths until the door flew open.

Zoë flashed the light, bright and white on the Lone Horseman's face. Bounding from the top step, she charged forward with the stake in her right hand until it met flesh, and Vero rushed from the left until she met with the same resistance. Together, they pushed the stakes in deeper until the Horseman left his feet and he landed on the ground with a thud.

"Go!" Zoë commanded. She flipped the light off, and together, they took off, running into terrain and territory they didn't know. After ducking under several trees, and crossing a brief expanse of grass, they found a long dirt road and continued down it until they hit pavement.

Through the early-morning fog, the air wet with dew, they escaped, running on adrenaline and hope until, far in the distance, they saw the first sign of headlights.

CHAPTER 39

A month later, Zoë sat at the kitchen table, enjoying a cup of coffee and a chocolate croissant when she saw the police cruiser roll up in the driveway. She licked a bit of sweetness from her fingers and watched as Sloane got out of the car and walked up the steps.

She opened the door before he could knock. "What brings you out this morning?"

"Wanted to check in, and talk."

Something in his voice made her feel uneasy. She invited him in anyway.

His footsteps sauntered across the kitchen floor. Zoë offered him a seat but he chose to lean against the counter instead. "How have you been?"

She wrapped what remained of her croissant in a napkin and set it aside. "Had one hell of a concussion, but all the stitches are out, so I'm healing, at least physically. Vero is doing well too. And the Lone Horseman, I hear, unfortunately." She wrinkled her nose. "I should've aimed a little higher with that stake, huh?"

Sloane cocked his head. "You did say you wanted him alive so he could face trial."

She sighed. "I know." She warmed her coffee, asked him if he wanted a cup. He shook his head. "At least it's over. We can all move on now."

Sloane subtly shifted his feet, looked at the ground. His silence made her wary.

She put a hand on her hip. "It is over, right?"

"I mean, yes, for the most part, until trial. The FBI has been busy. They have identified all the victims, and DNA testing is underway in five of the cases. Everyone is standing true to the agreement. So far, it's proceeding just as we all wished."

Zoë stared at him, knew there was something he was leaving out. "I sense a *but* coming on here."

Sloane sighed. "I do worry," he said.

"About what?"

"About the Lone Horseman."

"About him giving up the Devils? Trading what he knows for a lesser sentence? The feds aren't pursuing that, are they? The FBI assured me..."

"No, they've kept their promise. No one has asked, and he hasn't volunteered. Even with Maverick's apparent change of heart at the last minute, he has proven to be loyal to the Devils, much to Quinn's chagrin. No, I worry, Zoë, because he's making fast friends within the prison ranks, especially among the leaders of the Aryan Brotherhood. There are rumors he's already asking for favors. Like...if others would be interested in finishing what he didn't get to for a price."

The air left Zoë's lungs as quickly if somebody had popped them. "You mean come after us? Me and my family? Vero? Possibly Los Salvajes?"

Sloane slowly nodded.

Zoë pulled out a kitchen chair and slumped into it. She buried her face in her hands. "Won't this ever end?"

"I'd like to think so, but..."

She stared out the glass doors to the little backyard. "This is exactly what Blade warned me about. He told me that my plan would never work as long as the Horseman was alive, because he would never stop pursuing his revenge. Los Salvajes, and even Vero, have some protection. I don't."

Sloane nodded. "I know."

Zoë got up and paced the kitchen. She was glad Max was at work and Oliver at school so they wouldn't have to see the worried expression on her face. "What do you think I should do?"

He shifted uncomfortably and crossed his arms. Zoë knew then that this was what Sloane had truly come to talk about, and she was suddenly sorry that she'd asked for his opinion.

"Just, before you make any snap judgments, hear me out, okay?"

Oh Lord. This couldn't be good.

"Right now, as a suspected serial killer, the Lone Horseman is damn near a hero to the men within those prison walls. The publicity he'll receive as each trial approaches will only increase that adoration. He'll be revered and feared, and will quickly move up the ranks of the Brotherhood. So you have to ask yourself—is forcing him to go on trial for these murders and getting justice in the courts really worth your family's safety?"

Zoë squeezed her eyes shut, feeling all her former frustration and anger surface. She wanted to cry, but she wouldn't. "What's the alternative? Kill him now?"

"Yes, but there is one other way. The only way to be free of the Horseman, other than death, is to make him out as a bad guy. And in prison terms, that means one thing—a rat. I know you dislike Agent Quinn..."

"You think?" she blurted.

He raised a hand. "I know, but, again, if you think about the alternative—the possible harm that could come to you and your family—maybe it would be best to get the Lone Horseman to turn traitor and give up his outlaw brothers. The man has information. Murder, guns, drugs, the whole lot. We're not talking about just one or two members of the Devils here. We can shut them down, along with taking out several chapters of Los Salvajes, Angels, and more. We give him plea deals in exchange for his confessions about each of the women and information on the clubs, the families will get closure, and we'll take one hell of a lot of bad guys off the streets. Plus, you'll be in the clear because everyone inside will be aware that he's a rat and can't be trusted."

Sloane glanced at her, eyes pleading.

He continued. "They'll have to move him to a single cell, somewhere his own brothers or rivals can't get to him. You'll be safe, Zoë, and your family too. Isn't that most important? I know you don't want to hear it, but maybe Quinn was right. This case is bigger than you."

Zoë punched a fist into her opposite hand, blinked away tears, shook her head. "That wasn't the deal. The Devils, they went along. Vero convinced them to give the Lone Horseman up, and they didn't have to. Neither they or Los Salvajes wanted him inside because they knew the feds would try to screw them. And now, here you are, trying to do exactly that. You make him a traitor, and you become one too."

Sloane took a deep breath. "It's not the same."

"It is the same. If you turn on them, your word is no good."

"We lie all the time. So do they."

She shook her head, disgusted. Just when she was starting to like Sloane, and even trust him. She planted her feet. "They could've taken him out. Hell, they still could, especially if they hear the feds are cutting a deal."

It was his turn to look wary. "Is that a threat?"

She remained staunch. "I won't let them go down. They helped me."

"They're thugs, Zoë. Gun runners and drug dealers."

"That psychopath murdered my mother. He killed countless other women. He's a serial killer. And you...what? You want to put some bikers away for weapons charges and drugs that some other club will just take over the minute you get their rivals off the streets? It never ends. You of all people should know that."

Sloane slid his hands in his pockets. He huffed.

She knew that he knew that she was right.

He brushed a hand through his thinning blond hair. "I'm just worried about you, like I've always been," he said.

"If that's true, then you'll help me."

"I'm trying," he said, his own frustration clear. "What else can I do?"

Zoë resumed pacing, chewed a nail. A thought popped in her mind, but it was crazy. She tried to push it away, but it returned. Finally, she gave it consideration. She had an idea, but could it really work?

She turned to Sloane. "All we have to do is show that the Horseman is a rat, right? You said yourself, once the guys inside know that, he's done climbing the ranks or asking for favors."

"Yeah, so?"

"So, let's make sure he's labeled a rat. Or rather...inked as one."

Sloane tilted his head, unsure of what she was proposing, until the reality caught up with him. "Wait, you want to...?"

And then Brady Sloane did something completely unexpected. He bent at the waist and started laughing like a crazy man.

CHAPTER 40

G etting Zoë inside the Northern Nevada facility where the Horseman was being detained meant Sloane getting Zoë a work ID and arranging for the Horseman to be taken to the prison's infirmary at a dedicated hour. Sloane provided a nursing uniform for her to wear, and gave her instructions to follow when she got there. He even managed to smuggle a legitimate tattoo machine inside instead of one of the prison-made varieties, those often created from things like ball point pens, toothbrushes, and batteries. Sloane couldn't believe he was undertaking such actions, but had taken as many precautions as possible, including making the arrangements through confidential channels to lessen the chance that anything could blow back on him. Which meant, if she got caught, she was on her own. It would be up to her to formulate a story.

After all that had happened, Max would in no way be on board with what she was about to do, so the night Zoë was to go, she told him she had a wealthy client who wanted a personal house visit, then drove north to the prison. She parked at a lot used by the other prison employees, then hopped the bus with them and rode in the rest of the way. Shift change was at three p.m., so the bus was full.

The guard at the secured employee entrance paid little attention to her ID as she laid her purse on the belt to send it through the X-ray, and even less to her as she glided through the metal detector. Once inside, she did as Sloane instructed and looked for a guard wearing a small shamrock pin. She was supposed to tell him that she was new, and ask him to point her in the way of the infirmary. Whether she would be led to the real infirmary or just a room they planned to take the Horseman to, she had no idea, so she couldn't very well just follow the signs inside. He would give her a series of directions that she needed to pay precise attention to and follow. After that, the second person she was to search for was a janitorial inmate with *EWMN* tattooed across his knuckles—the moniker for *evil, wicked, mean, and nasty*—and ask him where she could find the ladies' room. Sloane told her he'd be mopping the floor, as he always did.

It all sounded easy, but who knew what unexpected surprises lay in wait.

On the other side of security, she saw a guard with strawberry-blond hair standing alone at a corner, a small green shamrock pin attached to his right shirt pocket. Upon closer inspection, she noticed there was a small *Kiss me, I'm Irish* tag above it. After taking a deep breath, she walked up to him and explained she was new and asked about the infirmary. He rattled off a series of hallways, two rights, a left, another right, then simply walked away. Zoë turned and began her journey.

Walking inside the dull gray prison walls, even in this minimum-security area, made Zoë feel vulnerable on multiple levels. First, it felt like she was breaking and entering, coming in under false pretenses, and second, she felt like a terrorist, the enemy within. She didn't know why, but she was certain every person who passed her issued a sideways leer, as if they knew she was plotting bad things and deserved to be behind bars. She wasn't a prisoner, but the hostile environment made her feel as if she were.

Soon after making the fourth turn next to a water fountain the guard had mentioned, she saw a janitor in light-beige coveralls mopping the floor. He had a patch over one eye, a mess of thick black hair, and furry, dark eyebrows to match. She observed him mop the floor, left, right, left, right, checked his left knuckles. Sure enough, the letters were there—*EWMN*. As she approached, she slipped on the wet floor, and he grabbed her arm to stabilize her.

"Careful there, señora. *Lo siento.* I meant to put the sign there," he said in broken Spanish. He walked over and moved it to the spot where she'd slipped. *Caution. Wet floor.*

Now you tell me. She could've ended up in the infirmary for real.

She asked if he knew where the nearest ladies' room was.

"*Si,*" he said. Pointed up the hall. "To the right there. Nobody uses it. You may take your time." He gave her a subtle wink, then went back to mopping, whistling while he worked.

A brief shiver rolled across Zoë's shoulders and down her back.

She took a few more steps down the hall that smelled of bleach and stopped at the door. It was a handicapped bathroom, unisex, according to the sign that hung on it. Inside, the room was exactly as advertised, equipped not only with an oversized commode and sink but grab bars and rails situated around the room at chair level. That proved to be useful, especially when it came to restraining the prisoner who lay facedown on the gurney there, immobile and unresponsive. The only thing that was surprising was the door on the other side, which appeared to lead directly into the infirmary. Zoë tiptoed around the gurney to open it a hair and peek in. There were three other patients in the beds, but all seemed to be sleeping or sedated, and no nurses or doctors were present. All was quiet on the western front.

Zoë shut the door and relocked it from both sides. Her heart pounded. She'd asked Sloane for an hour alone with the Lone Horseman and the needed tattoo machine, and it appeared he'd given her exactly what she'd wanted.

She reached under the sink, felt for the taped brown bag there, found the tattoo machine and a few vials of ink. She pulled it free and removed the tape. It was small but fit solidly in her hand and, best of all, ran on battery power. She turned it on, couldn't believe how quiet it was, no louder than a man's electric shaver.

As the machine started to run, the Lone Horseman sensed somebody else was in the room and began to move. Zoë had told Sloane to inform those who would be bringing him to give him no sedatives or other drugs that could make the blood thin, yet the Horseman clearly wasn't quite himself. She imagined that they'd had no choice but to give him a little something to calm him down.

He craned his neck sideways to try and get a look at her, but she stayed behind him. The guards had stripped him from the waist up and, with the bright fluorescent lighting, that pale horse and all his prized ladies stared up at her, begging for justice.

Up until today, the Horseman had wisely kept his hands and neck free of tattoos— as those were the two easiest areas for witnesses to identify suspects—but that would change now. She would place her design at the base of his neck.

She removed the stencil and disinfectant from her bag.

Restrained facedown in a private room, the Horseman probably thought he was about to be sexually assaulted, so the minute Zoë began to wipe down his neck and apply the stencil, he raised his head and started mumbling beneath the duct tape secured over his mouth. She wished she could see the expression on his face; knowing that odor and wondering what the hell was happening.

The minute the machine started and she forced down his head, he began screaming into the pillow. She even thought she could make out some of the words. "What...hell... drawing..."

The tattoo was simple enough. The rat itself was an obvious analogy, but it was the puppet strings that rose above it, the government logo imprinted on its side, and the Devil the rat gnawed on, that made it even more telling. Below the image, she wrote: *No Trust, No Honor, No Respect.*

The last thing she did was for Vero and the club, as requested. As part of the deal, they wanted the Horseman's colors stripped. The pitchforks were on his front shoulders, and there was enough play in the restraints that Zoë could get to them; the problem was, in order to do so, she would have to kneel directly in front of the Lone Horseman's face and slightly raise each shoulder to color them black. Yet, this was her moment. She wanted him to see her face and know who had done this to him. She didn't want him to hold power over her ever again.

By now, he had to know by the weight of her grip and the touch of her hands that his artist was a woman, but it was clear he never imagined just who that artist was until she slowly lowered herself down and met him face-to-face.

The whites of his eyes widened and he pushed against the restraints, grunting. She wondered if he would soon choke on the duct tape.

"The club wanted me to send you a message." She pushed up his right shoulder, colored in the ink on each of the prongs. Every time he resisted, she dug the needle in harder. She repeated the process on the left. Afterward, she turned off the machine and remained in front of him, watching all his sweat, snot, and blood drip to the floor.

"You asked about my eyes. Remember? I told you I was adopted. Well, I lied. They're my mom's. You probably recognized them because my mother was the woman represented by the hummingbird on your back, and her eyes were the last thing you saw as she took her last breath. You took her life, and now I'm going to make sure I return the favor. But not by death. That would be too easy. No, I left you a gift that will just keep on giving, make you a marked man no matter where you go or what prison they throw you into. It's going to make your life a living hell, just like you always wanted."

As he screamed into the duct tape and banged his wrists against the padded restraints, she applied a layer of petroleum jelly and a bandage to the tattoo on his neck. Later, the guards would remove it and ask where he got the ink—as, typically, it would cost an inmate time in solitary—but once they saw the image, they would understand and ask no more questions.

When she was done, she knocked twice on the infirmary door as Sloane had instructed, and slipped back into the hallway on the opposite side.

Sitting on the bus with the intense Nevada sun beating down through the windows, and waiting to return to the parking lot was the longest twenty minutes of Zoë Cruse's life. Finally, at the top of the hour, when the bus began to rattle and rumble down the long road leading out of the facility, she wiped the sweat from her brow and the tears from her cheeks. Giving the Lone Horseman that tattoo felt like payback for the permanent scars he'd given her. The ones across her wrists, and the one that wasn't as visible, etched across her broken heart. Now, at least, she hoped to be able to find some peace.

CHAPTER 41

Zoë watched a silver Chevy roll up in the driveway, a guy of about fifty wearing cowboy boots and hat approach. He extended his hand and introduced himself as Chester. "I'm here to pick up the furniture?"

Zoë finished wrapping the baking dish in her hand and placed it into the box of miscellaneous goods left over from her weekend sale, then led him up the porch stairs into the house. "This is it," she said. "All that's left. They're used, but they've still got life."

He took a look around the living room, walked over to test the couch cushions and examine the coffee and end tables for nicks and scratches. "Looks good to me. My granddaughter don't need nothing fancy, just something to set up house quick. Got a baby on the way and a no-good husband. How much you want for the lot of it?"

"You can have the entire house for five hundred. Got a twin and queen bed, the couch, recliner, coffee and two end tables. Oh, and a kid's and adult dresser."

"I'll take it," he said.

Max's footsteps echoed across the mostly empty hardwood. He shook the man's hand. "I can help you load it."

"Me too," Oliver said, bounding down the hall.

Zoë stood back as the men loaded the furniture in the truck, first the beds so the box springs and mattresses could protect the side of the truck, followed by the remaining items tucked in between. She didn't know how, but they managed to creatively stack it to get it all in a single load. They covered the haul with a few blankets and secured it with bungee cords.

Before they put up the gate, Zoë grabbed a nearby box. It rattled and clinked as she carried it from the porch and handed it to the man. "Here," she said. "This is a set of matching dishes that didn't sell. Set of eight plates, cups, and bowls. Some silverware in there too. Tell your granddaughter I said good luck."

The man nodded and slid the box on the passenger seat. "Thank you. She'll be much obliged. And good luck to you as well."

She, Max, and Oliver waved as the man drove away.

Zoë turned to look back at the house, and the few items she still had to pack up so she could drop them off at the Salvation Army before they headed out. "Just about done," she said.

She sighed and pushed a wayward strand of hair from her face. Her hair was pulled back in a bandana, her clothes were filthy, and every finger and nail was chipped, cut, and bruised, but she didn't care. Tomorrow, they were headed out to a new life and a new adventure. She'd sold the business to Screech and his friend, and she and Max had just enough money to start over.

"What's the weather like in Austin?" Oliver asked. "Will I still be able to ride my bike like I do now?"

"Of course, buddy," Max said. "Texas is a big open place."

"Can I get a dog?"

Zoë glanced at Max. "I told you," she whispered. She turned to Oliver. "I think a dog—or dogs—would be a good addition. Maybe even some chickens and a cow or two."

Oliver jumped up each step two feet at a time. "Really? Cool."

Max laughed. "Yes, really."

They'd chosen Texas after weighing several factors, climate and cost of living among them, and settled on Austin. Like the University of Nevada was to Reno, the University of Texas was a city unto itself in Austin, with fifty thousand students, and tattoo artists flourished. Unfortunately, so did homeless youth, so Max's skills would be in high demand as well. Their long-term goal was to buy some land outside the city where they could build a shelter, have some therapy animals, and give kids a new beginning.

Max ruffled his hair. "Let's go finish up inside."

Zoë stayed outside and finished boxing up what remained of the yard sale. The only things they were taking with them was the personal stuff: clothes and memorabilia, things like her mother's Bible, baby book, and family photographs. And, of course, her glass hummingbird collection. That, Zoë would always cherish, even more so now, given what it represented.

As for the Lone Horseman, the FBI had linked his DNA to eight murders and counting, and although he was trying to make plea deals, state after state was itching to get their shot at him, especially Texas. Apparently, his new negotiations with the feds weren't going exactly as planned either, as they didn't seem interested in trading for other information, and his time rising in the ranks of the prison gangs had ceased as well. Now, according to Sloane, he was getting passed around as much as the girls at the clubhouses he used to frequent. He often fought and begged for a solo cell, but the guards told him they couldn't accommodate him due to their overcrowded facility. Just last week, he'd taken a few swings at a prison guard so he could get thrown into solitary and have a moment's rest.

And that's what Zoë wanted. Maybe it sounded awful—vengeful, even—but she didn't want death for him, not right away. Instead of confessions and plea deals, she wanted him to have to face the families of his victims and be sentenced accordingly. She wanted him to continue to rot in there, slowly, day after day, suffering a deliberate, endless hell. Death was too easy for the devil.

Quinn complained, but Sloane and the FBI continued to point out that MC activities were exempt from charges as part of the arrangement. They advised Quinn to stick in his lane, and be thankful he'd found his undercover's killer.

After finding out Riot was an UC himself, Blade, of course, had no more use for Riot, but didn't wish him harm either. In fact, he seemed sad he would no longer have the loyal funny man by his side. Zoë texted him to ask how he was doing, but had never received an answer. She understood that she was probably not high on his favorite-person list, but strange as it might seem, hoped they could remain friends when this was over. Despite what he and Los Salvajes did for a living, she still liked Blade on a personal level. He'd listened and helped her, and that was a whole lot more than she could say for anyone else in her life, other than Max.

Zoë had wanted to reach out to Vero before she left, but decided it was best not to. She'd escaped from near death at the hands of a sadistic killer and was back to life with her old man and the club. She could at least rest knowing she'd played a critical part in getting justice for her club sister and friend.

Zoë stacked the remaining boxes in her SUV and shut the hatch. Max and Oliver did the same with the few final items they dragged from the house and added to the small trailer they would be hauling behind Max's truck. After Max slid the gate shut and locked it, the three stood with their arms around one another and took one last look at the house.

"Hey," Zoë said. "Knock, knock."

Max giggled. "Who's there?"

"Juno."

"Juno who?" Oliver and Max said in tandem.

"Juno I love you both right? Let's hit the road."

ACKNOWLEDGEMENTS

Many thanks to Michelle Hope for editing and Nick Zelinger for a fantastic cover design. Thanks to Melissa Yahr, proofreader extraordinaire, and to my entire Advanced Reading Team for early reads and reviews. You are the best!

The Motorcycle Clubs represented in this book are fictional and not intended to reflect on any actual clubs or persons therein. But thank you to those who enlightened me about their general operations and procedures. Also fictional are the many tattoos and colors mentioned, although in concept, tattoos and their meanings are very real. Thanks to the many who post videos on YouTube informing us novices of how to do things we're not familiar with, such as creating a tattoo and riding a motorcycle. What did we ever do without you or the internet?

About the Author

LORI LACEFIELD writes suspense thrillers that keep you turning the pages late into the night. Her Women of Redemption series features heroines who may not be perfect, but who perfectly kick-ass when given a second chance. Titles include *The Advocate*, *The Fifth Juror*, and *The Tattoo Artist*. Lori also writes the Frankie Johnson, FBI Local Profiler series. Titles include *99 Truths* and *The Art of Obsession*. (Available Spring 2021) You can read more about Lori at www.lorilacefield.com. Sign up to receive news, enter her latest giveaway, and receive a FREE novella at https://www.lorilacefield.com/news-and-giveaways.html.